The Citadel

By

John Delahunty

Published 2007 by arima publishing

www.arimapublishing.com

ISBN: 978 1 84549 185 7

© John Delahunty 2007

Printed and bound in the United Kingdom

Typeset in Garamond 12/16

Swirl is an imprint of arima publishing.

arima publishing
ASK House, Northgate Avenue
Bury St Edmunds, Suffolk IP32 6BB
t: (+44) 01284 700321

www.arimapublishing.com

To my wife Irene & sons Johnnie & Lloyd.

Chapter One

Day One - Thursday

The time was 5.45 am on a cold and frosty February morning. But this was nothing to how Jack Deer felt inside. He'd spent the past twenty five years, a lifetime, building a construction empire, which stretched the globe. And today it finally dawned on him, that he stood to lose it all through an innocent misjudgement of faith and trust. Conniving Board Members had all conspired against him to steal what wasn't theirs. But Jack wasn't the type to sit back and let it happen. He was a fighter, street wise and academically clever to boot. Trouble was, if he didn't do something in the next two weeks, he would lose it all, so he had to move fast. He knew it and so did the Board. The race was on.

It had all seemed like a dream as Jack lifted his weary head from his pillow, a very bad dream.....a nightmare. But then this was no nightmare, this was reality....a living nightmare. It dawned on Jack, only moments after rubbing the sleep from his eyes, that today was the day that would spell out the fate of his Empire. Built from everything he held dear, his marriage, children, home and comfortable lifestyle, all put on the line as a sacrificial gamble. Against all the odds he had pulled it off and made it work.

Jack wasn't one of those obnoxious self-made men, who liked the sound of their own nauseating voices with clichés of ; -

"And I started with nothing."

He had also started with nothing but unlike many of his contemporaries he was not the type to push his success in your face. Instead he just moved from one venture to the next, never satisfied that he'd achieved his goal, always pushing back the boundaries to better and further himself. The stakes were always high but no matter how high they were, Jack was never fazed and continued on as though possessed.

He'd pushed back the boundaries alright but had he finally pushed them back too far? .... Today was his day of reckoning....'Had he blown it?'

He sat at the side of his bed with his head slumped in his hands. After a minute or so, he resigned himself to the fact that his world, as he'd tried to create it, was to end. Sluggishly, he made his way to the bathroom, splashed some lukewarm water onto his face and looked at himself in the mirror.

"You stupid bastard," he said to himself, staring at his reflection,

"You stupid, stupid, stupid bastard," he said aloud.

He turned around. His wife, Sammy, was standing in the doorway, clad in a long satin dressing gown, embroidered with fine golden thread. It pictured a peacock, displaying all of it's fine majestic feathers.

"If only I felt that proud." Jack said in a low demoralised monotone voice, as he stared at the peacock.

She walked up to him, cradled his face in her hands and said,

"Jack, we've been down before and we've come back. Don't worry love, you've still got us, no matter what happens."

Jack patted her on the shoulder as he walked passed her on his way to the bed. She followed behind, arms folded, an ever faithful and loving wife, always there to support him when the chips were down. And boy, were they down.

Jack sat on the end of the bed. Sammy sat next to him. Jack started,

"You do realise that it means we've lost everything."

"Look, we'll bounce back, we always do."

"No, I don't think you understand...."

"Oh it'll be alright," Sammy interrupted.

"NO, SAMMY, IT WON'T BE ALRIGHT."

Jack shouted. He stood up from the bed. Stretching and taking a deep breath he tried to explain rationally, using his hands as he always did.

"It means we've lost the business, houses, cars. You'll have to give up the good life. Extravagant things like your women's luncheons, and those bloody charities of yours will all be a thing of the past."

She interrupted, "Jack, calm down. I don't think it's as bad as all that."

"CHRIST ALMIGHTY WOMAN, GET YOUR HEAD OUT OF THE SAND. WE'RE NOW A BLEEDIN' CHARITY. CAN'T YOU SEE THAT ? WHY DON'T YOU EVER BLOODY LISTEN TO ME ?.....WATCH MY LIPS........WE HAVE LOST IT ALL............AM I GETTING THROUGH TO YOU IN THERE ?.......CHRIST ALMIGHTY."

Sammy knew in her heart that it was all true but couldn't bring herself to admit, or accept what was to happen. They were once the pride of their family, mentors of their children and envy of their friends. Now, in one day, they could lose it all.

How were they to face failure ?

How were they, or how could they, look family and friends in the eye ever again ?

These thoughts kept flashing through her mind and tears began to swell in her eyes. As they trickled down her cheeks, Jack walked over to her, sat beside her and put his arm around her. "I'm sorry babe. I didn't mean to shout at you. I'm just so angry at those bastards for what they've done."

Sammy, buried her head into his chest, sobbing,

"Oh Jack, what are we going to do ?"

Jack squinted his eyes and nodded his head knowingly and said,

"I'll think of something."

There was a pause as the two of them looked at each other.

"Come on," said Jack as he twitched his head toward the door.

"I'll make you some coffee."

He kissed her forehead, stood up, put on his silk dressing gown and made his way downstairs. She followed closely behind him, her head bowed, rubbing her nose in her perfumed tissue, taken from a solid silver tissue box on her dressing table.

In the kitchen, Jack made Sammy a cup of black coffee and himself a mug of tea.

Sammy sat at the breakfast table with her head hung low and her dark lank hair exposing the tops of her ears. She looked as though she had been condemned and was awaiting execution.

She raised her head to face Jack,

"Where did it all go wrong?... I just don't understand it. Maybe we've got it wrong and its not as bad as we think it is."

Jack was having a hard time containing himself.

"No, we haven't got it wrong, and it's probably worse than we expect," Jack said in a commanding voice.

Sammy blew into her tissue.

"But how's it all gone so horribly wrong?" she said, staring down at the breakfast table, shaking her head with a look of unabated disbelief.

Jack passed Sammy her cup of coffee as he drank his tea.

"Well!" Jack said in an uncannily cheerful voice, with his eyebrows raised. Putting his mug gently down onto the breakfast table, he continued.......

"It's those bastards on the Board of Directors of...... 'my' company.....who have obviously been plotting my downfall for sometime. Let's face it, no-one has anything to gain from this, except them. With me gone, they'll be able to vote themselves any salary they see fit and award themselves shares in the company, once they've taken the knife to it. They'll be richer than in their wildest dreams. They'll be in positions of power in the international business markets and have a great deal of influence in many world governments. I'll give it six months before they all retire and award themselves pensions well in excess of what they 'earn', now.

"But mark my words, I'll have each and everyone of them ten times over for what they've done. Those bastards will regret the day they ever turned against me......by God they will."

Just then, a key could be heard turning in the kitchen door. It was their housekeeper, Mrs. Briggs.

She was the stereotypical 'mother-figure.' A large woman in her late fifties, with grey silvering hair worn in a bun. She was never without her apron ; her second skin. She always had it on ready for any womanly domestic household chore. Sympathetically spoken, nothing was too much trouble. The greatest compliment you could pay her, to make her day, was to tell her that her cottage pie was delicious. She was the type of woman to become euphoric if you asked her for seconds. That, *'in a nutshell,'* was the housekeeper, Mrs. Mary Briggs.

"Good morning," said Mary rubbing her hands together.
"Terribly cold out there this morning, cold enough to make an Eskimo shiver."
Only Jack acknowledged Mary's presence with the sound of 'UMM' from tightly closed lips. It seemed as though Sammy had gone into a trance.
"We'd better get showered and dressed," Jack said, staring at Sammy. Lethargically she shuffled off her chair. Her head hung low, she made her way slowly and silently out of the kitchen and up the stairs. With her head sunk into her chest

and her lank hair, she looked a shadow of her former self, and to Mary she looked like a zombie.

Mary's usual sprightly energy had been brought to a standstill as she stared with a disapproving frown at Jack, who was following close behind Sammy. Jack turned to look behind him. Mary was looking up at him. She raised her eyebrows, cocked her head to one side and half pointed to Sammy.

Jack said nothing. It was neither the time nor the place and he continued following Sammy slowly upstairs to their room.

Sammy went straight back to bed clutching a handful of tissues.

Jack made a call on the intercom instructing Tel, his chauffeur, to have the car ready. He then went into the bathroom, shaved, took a shower, splashed on his favourite aftershave and put on one of his Armani suits. He made his way downstairs, through the reception hall and down the marble steps at the front of the house to his car. He left without saying goodbye to either Sammy or Mrs. Briggs. He was deep in thought not just planning his next move, but his next ten moves. Just how exactly was he to regain his company? A company that he had built from nothing, putting everything he had to lose on the line, risking it all. And how was he going to make those deceiving bastards pay the price for their treachery?

In front of him was a brand new Bentley – a car he renewed twice a year, every year. Tel ceremoniously opened the back door. Jack, saying nothing, climbed in and sat down. Knowing something was seriously wrong Tel didn't greet Jack with "good morning," but just quietly closed the car door. Tel took his seat, and started the engine. A quiet 'purr' could be heard from the car as it pulled away. Only the frosty gravel made any real sound as it was ground and crunched under the tyres as the car made its way effortlessly down the driveway toward the manor gates. When the car was approximately thirty meters from them, a signal was sent from a transmitter built into the grill of the car and they opened silently and gracefully. They closed just as elegantly once the car was clear of the gate pillars.

Jack was oblivious to anything about the journey as they moved quietly through the idyllic country surroundings of his estate and then through the contrasting busy streets of London, on the way to the office. Everything seemed as though it was all happening in slow motion, as though it wasn't real.....but it was very real, and Jack knew it more than anyone.

As the car pulled up into the reserved car space marked 'PRESIDENT' Tel got out of the car and opened the door for Jack. Jack remained seated. Tel bent down to look at him and said, "We're 'ere Guv."

Jack didn't say anything or even look at him.

"Are you OK boss ?" said Tel in a concerned manner.

Jack still didn't acknowledge him. He got out of the car and made his way to the main entrance of the building. The doors automatically opened, as he walked through into the lavishly decorated foyer.

Marbled mosaic floors beneath his feet, crystal chandeliers crowning the ceiling, oak wood adorning every conceivable piece of furniture, desk, wall panelling, tables and chairs. As he walked through the reception area passing the chesterfield suites, he was greeted by just about everybody. He answered no-one as he made his way purposely to the glass pod lift. He could see the lift descending, but made no effort to look at it directly.

There were a number of executives hovering around the doors of the lift's entrance.

All the men were dressed in either black or charcoal grey three piece suits, black brogue shoes and pristine white shirts. Each wore either a red or blue company tie with the emblem of the consortium embroidered on it. The emblem was of a Stag standing proud with a lion either side of it. As expected, each tie was crowned with a neat and tidy Windsor knot. The women all wore official, yet stylish, pastel coloured suits. Each one of them wore a bow of either red or blue and a company brooch in the style of the consortium emblem on their right lapel.

But the atmosphere was cold. Nobody spoke and Jack didn't take his eyes from the seam of the stainless steel guard doors in front of him.

The lift rang when it stopped and the guarding doors slid open.

The operator was dressed in all the formal company regalia. Black patent shoes in which you could see your face. Light grey trousers with a burgundy stripe down each side, a matching coat with gold braid on each shoulder and two columns of brass buttons running up the front of what appeared to be a never ending tunic. The uniform was finished off with a peaked hat that had the emblem of the consortium at the front. Yet another reminder to Jack of what he had created.

Jack had a hand in everything. The uniforms, the building décor, the design of the company emblem, even the company letterhead. Nothing, but nothing, about Jack was ever cheap or tacky. He was a perfectionist. Everything, down to the smallest detail was just sheer unadulterated excellence. Anything of the company, '*his company*', that had a face to present to the public, clients or the media was going to be one of 'class'. It was very expensive on the scale that Jack had instigated but as he had always insisted,

"First impressions always count. If you want class, you have to pay for it. If we spend a penny to look good, we will get a pound back in revenue."

Jack had proved this to be the case time and time again, on different deals and contracts gained throughout the world. The consortium was valued beyond all the greatest expectations and wildest dreams of everyone who became associated with Jack's dream.

The only thing that lacked lustre was the two second smile on the operator's face. When Jack was not happy, no-one else was either. Jack walked into the lift and turned around to face the doors. Not surprisingly no-one else got in and the doors closed. The steel guard doors closed and the operator automatically, pressed the button to the twenty-fifth floor.

Jack stood motionless, his eyes fixed directly ahead, almost as though he were mesmerized.

"Nice morning for it, Sir !" the operator said politely. There was no reply, not even a nod. His face dropped and he turned back to face the lift doors. The operator said nothing more and there was silence until the doors opened. Jack made his way down the long corridor to the boardroom. He opened the highly polished ebony doors. Facing him was an expanse of glass. The view over London was spectacular and breathtaking. From this viewpoint all the historic landmarks and more, could be seen in all their splendour. Standing in front of the windows, many of the architectural marvels built by the consortium and Jack's own hands could be gazed upon and admired. This room was the nerve centre, where it all happened. This is where all the decisions were made, this is where the 'big boys', the 'guardians' of the consortium met. This was the Citadel they knew and ran.

Seated in front of him were all the members of the Board. Senior and junior members all regimentally lined up along either side of the long rectangular ebony table that matched the doors. The junior members sat at the lower end towards the entrance. The higher the rank, the closer you sat to the top of the table.

The room fell silent. All faces were upon Jack. And what an imposing figure he was. He stood tall and straight, six feet two, broad shouldered, with a tidy middle-aged frame. A strikingly handsome man. Blonde hair, which was starting to grey at the sides, piercing blue eyes, high cheek bones with a chiselled chin and jaw line. His skin was weather beaten and ruddy. His laughter lines were prominent, which only added to his good looks. His hands were like shovels and his fingers were like sausages....*they'd seen many calluses in their time.*
He had presence. He walked tall and proud. A confident man who knew what he was about and where he was going in life.

He looked at each and everyone of the Board members. It seemed like an eternity. Jack had no intention of speaking until they did. He made his way forward. He was a man with a mission and he intended to carry it out. Passing the juniors to his right, some rightfully looked down in shame, other hard-nosed ones, the ones trying to impress....either that or they just didn't have a conscience, looked straight at him as though they had nothing to fear. How wrong, stupid and naive they were. They wouldn't have been where they were today if it wasn't for Jack. Little did they appreciate that if he could pull them up, then he could also put them straight back down again. Reaching the middle section of the table he came face to face with some of the senior executives, who all looked him in the eye. Some inflated their chests and poised themselves as though it was a psychological stand-off between stags in a forest ready to fight for the mating rights to the does. But this wasn't as trivial as that and all parties knew it. In no time, the executives backed down and looked to the others for support.

It wasn't forthcoming from any of them.

He walked to the top half of the table.

Now he was among the seven senior executives whom he knew were behind it all. These were the governing guardians of the consortium. These were the people in whom Jack had misplaced his trust. These were the men who had betrayed him.

He stood by the side of Lord Andrew Barron, who'd half-turned around in his chair to look at him. Jack looked down at him. Barron sat proud and defiant. Jack never relented from his piercing gaze. Barron deflated and looked to the others feeling very uncomfortable. With the burden of an overpowering glare upon him from the man he had betrayed, he felt helpless and wished for rescue from the others. It never came.

He was a Lord in name only. He was living proof that it was wrong to bestow such a prestigious title onto generation after generation just because in centuries past an ancestor of his may have done a 'great and wonderful' deed for his country. The only thing 'great' about Barron was that he was a 'great' disappointment to his family. He had failed in just about everything he'd ever done or attempted to do. He believed himself to be better and greater than other men because of his background, his privileged upbringing, and title, unearned as it was. Every time Barron failed he was bailed out by his family. They were forever doing it. Seeing how others did well and succeeded he grew more and more envious of people and life in general. He grew so envious of those that succeeded, especially, *as he saw it*, those of a lower class, such as Jack Deer, that he would wallow in their eventual failure or downfall. Taking great joy in somebody else's misfortune he would do anything to bring them down to his level. To bestow such a noble title as this onto such a sorry man was a crime. Relishing in the fact that he was a Lord, he made a point of letting people such as the family gardener and housemaids know who was in charge. They would all have to call him 'My Lord,' the women having to curtsy and the men having to tug their forelocks to him as a sign of respect. He wasn't worthy of tugging his forelock to a mule let alone have people do it to him. His position and title had clearly gone to his head. He believed himself to be in the eighteenth century.

Sitting beside him was Simon Rothchild, a smarmy little bastard of whom Jack had always said, *'he's got one of those faces that you'd love to punch, but once you'd started, you knew you wouldn't be able to stop.'* He was renowned and infamous for opening his big mouth and putting his foot in it. He always spoke before his brain was in gear. He was the first to speak, unable to resist breaking the silence.

"Didn't expect you so early Jack." Rothchild said in a nauseating tone.

Still Jack said nothing.

"No. I didn't expect you to be in so early either," came a patronising voice from the seat next to him.

It was Sir Henry Warlton. An obese city gent who spoke so far back that at an instant you had him summed up as being from a 'well to do' and privileged background. And the assumption would be correct. He was born into the right family and had been surrounded by the right people all his life. He'd had the best education. Private and public schools and private tutors. But as Jack had said so many times, it made no difference, he was,

'As thick as shit, a piss ant had more brains than him. If he had two more brain cells he might be able to talk to plants.'

Anyone who ever spent more than ten minutes with him knew all there was to know, and it wasn't much.

Warlton had obviously only ever been able to attend distinguished establishments of learning through the connections of his family. The strings that must have been pulled.......one can only imagine.

But none of that mattered. He was where he was because of who he was and who he knew. The first lesson of life.

The only reason he was on the 'Board of Directors' was quite simply because of this and his title. Even his title was gained under false pretences, as Warlton was the most slovenly swine you could ever have the misfortune to meet.

He had 'worked' in the city purely in 'non-functional roles' with no creativity or initiative coming from any company or government department to which he was assigned. Instead, other departments doing fabulous work and being constructive in everything that they handled, came under the jurisdiction of Warlton........at least on paper anyway.

When the Honours List was compiled after the end of the war, Warlton was 'working' in the Defence Ministry. The Ministry was praised in Whitehall for the gallant role it had played in the service of its country, so Warlton had to be given credit for the work that others had done. Warlton was in the right place, at the right time. Through nepotism, he knew those who were to compile the list. There was only one way in which credibility could be seen to be awarded and this was in the form of a knighthood.

His title had brought a tremendous amount of custom to the different firms and companies that he'd been associated with over the years. That and his Masonic links were the only two reasons Jack had seen fit to put up with this cantankerous old twit who,

"Didn't know his arse from his elbow."

Jack was seething but didn't show it. He said nothing. He was waiting until he could look the mastermind behind the conspiracy in the eye. Sitting opposite Barron, Rothchild and

Warlton were Lord Arthur Cavendish, William Peterbough and Joseph Fairfax.

Sitting in Jack's seat at the head of the table was Charles Moore, the mastermind behind it all, poised as though he were a King from the Middle Ages. He was the sly, underhanded snake's poison, who had plotted, connived and manipulated the others into betraying Jack. A tall, thin man with black hair and a grey complexion which made him look more gaunt than he already was. He looked ill and had an eerie and hypnotic presence. He was always immaculately dressed. He was quietly spoken and never displayed any emotion. His background was the same as most of the Board, that of a highly educated man, but he was sinisterly devious in thought. His was a waste of intelligence because of the way he used it. He was on the Board because, at times, Jack required someone of his *'qualities'* when dealing with the nearly, but not quite, corrupt world of International Business. Jack reasoned that so long as his opposition had people like Moore, then Moore had a place within the company.

This was the man Jack wanted to avenge most of all.

He had always coveted what Jack had strived to build. Never admiring him for the fantastic achievements and brilliant work done, but instead always plotting a way to take it from him, and to have it for himself. Knowing that once he had it, he would dismember it piece by piece. This was the kind of man who took genuine pleasure in the misfortune of others. He was a bad one and as the saying goes,

'If you never saw him again it would be too soon.'

To Moore's left sat Joseph Fairfax. Fairfax could be summed up in three words, tall, dark and handsome. He had black greying hair that was always combed and tidy. His brown eyes were complemented by a slightly tanned and healthy looking complexion. A thin face with a strong pronounced jaw line, as though he gritting his teeth with lips closed. He was the same height as Jack, six foot two inches. Clothes hung on him perfectly, they should have, they were all tailor made. But he was more than that. Family background, schooling, and most of all he had connections in highest of places.

Fairfax was Jack's most trusted companion and confidant. He had helped Jack get the company off the ground and into the mighty league of world business. Jack, although successful, could never have gone as far as he had without the recruited help of Fairfax.

"What are you doing here Jack ? You know you're finished," he said coldly, looking towards Moore.

Jack said nothing.

Fairfax stood up and turning to Jack continued,

"Due to the incompetent way in which the company has been run…..for which you are responsible,"

with a sly smirk on his face, Fairfax continued,

"….the Board has exercised its right to remove you as President by a unanimous vote. You neither have the right to question it, nor oppose it. If you remember, you did sign the declaration of company policy, pledging obedience to it yourself. Giving the Board the right to remove any Board member, including yourself, should confidence be diminished in any way. *"Putting your balls on the line"*……as you so eloquently put it. This obviously impressed an awful lot of our clients, and so the work orders came pouring in. However, we never saw as many of the benefits of your bravado as 'we' would have liked and we decided that we wanted a bigger slice of the cake than you were prepared to give. So, should you refute the decision to remove you from the company, then not only will our shareholders be informed of what has happened……..as it is our duty ……..but so will our clients, and should any action be taken on your behalf to refute 'Our Decision'…….. "

Fairfax looked around the conniving entourage, with arms apart showing the palms of his hands as though he was addressing his brethren,

"…..then I'm sure that you would be taken to court and sued personally for breaching contracts made with different companies and governments, gaining money under false pretences. Oh, and a whole number of other charges brought against you. None of them true or valid of course, but it can and will be arranged to look that way. Should you oppose us in any way, we will create such a scandal, it will completely destroy this consortium. You'll end up in prison and we'll be left to pick up the pieces. The consortium will be dissected and sold off piece by piece, and you'll be the only one seen to be dirty over the whole thing.

"How do you think it would look in the headlines that you're living a luxurious lifestyle with majestic houses, private jet, lavish cars…..kids that went to the best schools, all on the shareholders' money, whilst the value of their share holding has plummeted ? You wouldn't last five minutes. Money would be pulled out of this consortium so fast, in one blink of an eye it would all be gone. There would be a government investigation and you would face criminal charges for seemingly non-payment of taxes of the 'companies' owned by the consortium. So it's quite simple…..'JACK'…….you either adhere to our decision gracefully, keep your mouth shut and accept our nominal pay off after all things must look good on paper…..or…. we…."

Fairfax looked around the room emphasising the fact that the boardroom members present were the 'beating heart of the empire'.

"We will see to it that any, 'investigative committee' has all the help needed to ensure you go away for a very long time."

Jack stood rigidly, glaring at Fairfax, without saying a word. The room's temperature had dropped to what felt like absolute zero, the intensity of suspense was almost too much to bear.

Fairfax, never looking away from Jack, added one last gut-wrenching comment, which felt to Jack as a mental kick in the teeth.

"Oh and by the way, your Hampshire home and Bentley are company assets, you have until the end of the month to return them."

Jack stood motionless, glaring at Moore. The room was deadly silent. Fairfax looked at Moore and then Jack, "Well!"

Jack walked to the head of the table and turned to face this pack of wolves. He stood beside Moore who had half turned around in his chair to face him.

Jack could feel a rage in his chest as he clenched his fists ready to punch any of these disloyal bastards in front of him. He wanted to so much. But Jack knew that their consciences could walk under the belly of a snake wearing stilts and a top hat. If Jack lost his cool now, they would surely prosecute for assault and Jack Deer would never be able to make anything of the pieces left behind. Addressing them in a low and authoritative voice and keeping his arms uncharacteristically by his side, he announced,

"You will regret the day that you ever met me, each and everyone of you, because 'By Christ', I will make you all crawl on your bellies for what you've done to me."

Jack looked coldly at each of the seven directors in front of him. The room was stunned into silence. The atmosphere was so intense it could have been cut with a knife. Jack pointed at Fairfax calling him 'Judas.'

"You sided with this vermin just because I wouldn't go into the arms market."

Jack screwed his face up, squinted, and shaking his head slowly from side to side said with an acrid tongue,

"You must have been harbouring that resentment of me for years. You slimy bastard."

Fairfax retorted,

"You knew how much moving into the arms market would have meant to me. I introduced you to all the right people. I helped you to get where you are. I helped recruit all the right people. I helped you make this consortium what it is today and I asked for one thing. The one thing that you knew meant everything to me. If we'd gone into the arms market for sure we'd be supplying to the states rather than the other way round. It would have made us billions not millions. And how am I rewarded ?... You get all pious and holier than thou. I became nothing more than your side kick."

Jack curled his top lip,

"No...that's not it. You wanted to use me to make amends for your failings, for not following in your father's footsteps into the military. You couldn't cut it so you thought you could coerce me into appeasing your family with the next best thing." Fairfax said no more. He took a deep breath through his flared nostrils and stared at Jack.

The Board members sat looking at Jack expressionless and motionless, some like William Peterbough and Lord Barron swallowed nervously.

Jack, always maintaining his upright posture made his way to the door, opened it and passed quietly out of the room.

Fairfax had mixed feelings. He was in awe of Jack's short, sharp and vindictive delivery letting all the Board members know he wasn't going down without a fight. But he also felt hurt and embarrassed at the way Jack had personally assaulted him. One of the juniors tried to crack a funny but immediately Fairfax shouted,

"SHUT UP YOU FOOL."

Fairfax leaned forward and with his fingertips touching the end of the table in front of him, dismissed the rest of the junior members. After they had all hurriedly made their way out of the room, he addressed the senior Board members. His delivery was as clear and concise as ever, but had an uncharacteristically cold tone.

"Now you listen to me, I know Jack Deer better than anyone in this room. Twenty years in fact. So mark my words very carefully, he's the type of man who has the potential to come back and get at each and everyone of us here just as he said he would. Unless we all stick together and follow through with this takeover, then there is every chance that Jack Deer could, and if given the slightest chance, will, have his revenge on all of us. So don't underestimate him by any means because believe me, he's the most determined man I've ever met in my life."

There was an attentive pause by all in the room, a pin could have been heard to drop on a fleeced carpet.

"Gentlemen, you have been warned."

He stood upright from the desk. The room remained silent.

A wheezing chuckle broke the silence. It was Sir Henry Warlton. Fairfax stared at him but Warlton didn't take the hint that this was no laughing matter. Dismissing what Fairfax had just said and still laughing conceitedly he said,

"The man is nothing but a half-educated, working-class peasant."

"That's rich coming from you, Sir Henry." Fairfax said in a sarcastically cynical voice.

"What do you mean?" Warlton said indignantly. He stopped laughing immediately.

"You....'Sir'....have been privileged by your birth and fed with a silver spoon all your life. He built all this by himself against all the odds......that........Sir Henry, is the mark of a truly clever man."

"If he's so bloody clever then why is it that we've been able to takeover this consortium, because as we all know, its been like taking candy from a baby." Warlton said with a cocky smirk on his face.

Sighing in sheer contempt of Warlton, Fairfax replied,

"Seven against one! Nothing clever about that Warlton. The way in which we advised, managed and accounted for everything, there was no way in a million years that Jack would have been able to keep track of everything. Slyly....or.......'Masterfully'....whichever way you wish to think of it, we've connived together to bring him down. It's been successful, but only because we've stuck together. But should we falter now, then Jack Deer is not going to be a bad penny who is just going to go away. Let me assure you gentlemen, he will still be a force to be reckoned with, if we don't stick together."

Warlton, so self-righteous in his own being and thoughts, sat there with a smug grin on his face, proving all of what people thought of him, and what he was.......very stupid. He was dismissive of Fairfax's warning.

"Well, I don't think we have anything to fear from Jack Deer. He's just a one hit wonder who was, to his kind, some sort of.....'working class hero,' I've seen this sort of thing before. What is it the commoner's say ? 'The boy did good!'. Pathetic, bloody pathetic! We run the show here, we always have and we always will."

Warlton sat back with the same smug grin on his face, whilst everyone looked to Fairfax. The exchange of words had intensified an already heavy atmosphere.

"You are a very ignorant man." Fairfax said impassively.

All but Rothchild agreed with Fairfax, and knew he was right, but nobody came to his aid in backing him up. Instead they just sat silently and waited for Warlton's response. It was a tennis match of harshly, exchanged words.

Fairfax stood confidently, looking at Warlton knowing that he was right, and that the others knew he was too. Warlton remained slouched back in his chair, still with the same ugly grin on his face.

"Well, I agree with Sir Henry," said Simon Rothchild, sitting beside him.

"I don't think we have anything to worry about, and what's more, it's true, Jack Deer is no more than an uncouth, foul-mouthed peasant, who had delusions of grandeur. He is, and will always be, a jumped-up little shit."

Both Rothchild and Warlton laughed together, then the others joined in with forced chuckles. Each one of them wanting to be seen as part of the crowd .....as part of the baying pack. The exception was Moore. He sat stone-faced.

Rothchild stared at Fairfax awaiting his response. Fairfax lazily moved his gaze from Warlton and looked to the other Board members.

"I will warn you all once again. If you carry on with this notion that Jack Deer is no more than a subservient working-class baboon, then you will all be on your bellies sooner than you think."

Fairfax tried unconvincingly to persuade them of the potential threat of Jack Deer, but they were unrelenting in their self-righteous thinking. They were too full of themselves to listen to anyone, but themselves. He sat down with his head lowered, slowly shaking his head from side to side and sighed.

Charles Moore, the mastermind behind the scheme, spoke for the first time.

He was of the same schooling and background as Fairfax. He was his senior by only one year. They both went to Cambridge studying the same courses, playing in the same rugby team and were even members of the same amateur dramatics group. After completing and majoring in their studies they attended Sandhurst, as both came from military families. Their histories were almost carbon copies of each other. He spoke directly to Fairfax, knowing that he was correct in what he had said. But he had to make it look to Warlton and the others that he too, was behind them, purely because Warlton still had a tremendous amount of clout throughout the city and government with his connections.

"Look, just who do you think you are? Telling us who to watch out for. You were only invited into 'our' plan when everything had already been set up. Even that was debated by all of us here at great length, because of your long association with that 'lower class scum.'"

Warlton shouted, "YES," expressing his agreement with Moore. Moore paused, looked to Warlton, stared at him, then looked back at Fairfax.

"We were still unsure of you. Whether or not you were going to spill the beans. In fact, thank your lucky stars you were invited to join us, otherwise you'd have ended up in the same boat as Jack. If it wasn't for us getting rid of him, our plan couldn't have been put into motion. You're a very good spokesman Fairfax, as you've just proved. You did a brilliant job convincing Deer that if he kicks up a 'hoo-ha' about the whole thing he would go to prison. Your magnificent performance was worthy of an 'Oscar.' But that's the only role you've played in this scheme.... up to now. Remember it was us who momentarily brought the share prices down to deceive Deer into thinking that his empire was crumbling. We will make consensual decisions in which direction we shall go next and it's not up to you to take it upon yourself to run this show. You may have helped Deer build this consortium but we're in control now. We didn't do all this for you to take his place."

Staring at Moore, Fairfax swallowed, cleared his throat and said,

"Gentlemen, I suggest that we close this meeting and carry on with our plan as we have a long hard journey ahead of us if we're to achieve our goal."

It was apparent to everyone that Fairfax had been corrected and was going to adhere to the guidelines of Moore. As everyone knew a confrontation now, by Fairfax, would put him in an impossible position. His back would be up against the wall. With the influence that Moore had, he would be in the same boat as Jack Deer. Moore was renowned throughout the business world as being the coldest, most black-hearted, cut-throat bastard anyone had ever known. There was only one side to be on with Moore and that was his.

There was a brief pause. Peterbough stood up and announced,

"We've done what we had to do and I'm going to the Marlborough club for a drink and a.......'*good time'*. I'm off and anyone who wishes to join me is welcome. Good day gentlemen."

With the exception of Moore and Fairfax, they all stood up from the table and left for the Marlborough Country Club of which they were all members.

Fairfax sat straight-faced, shaking his head at them as they gathered at the boardroom doors like a marauding murder of crows, a black mass of stereotyped, black pin-striped suits.

Once they had left he stood up, pushed his seat neatly up against the table and made his way out of the boardroom to his office, never giving Moore a second look as he walked to the door.

"You're a well-respected man Joseph and I like you, we all do, but don't ruin it by getting any ideas that you have powers above your station."

Moore leaned back in his black leather chair. Fairfax stopped at the doors, turned to Moore smiled, and looking at the floor said,

"I haven't, I only want what's best for us."

He looked at Moore. There was a second of silence that seemed to last forever. Moore replied,

"Good...........Good. I know you'll do well by us."

As Fairfax passed through the boardroom doors, Moore called to him, Fairfax walked back into the room.

Moore stood smiling at him,

"You really did do well with your delivery to Deer. You even had me in awe of your monologue. It was very powerful and so believable that even I was convinced of your determination to have Deer put away should he create a fuss. It was a good show Joseph, a damn good show. In fact it reminded me for the first time of our acting days together at Cambridge. Do you remember?"

Joseph began to grin,

"Yes, very much so. They were happy times. We had no worries. Only thoughts of aspiring to the stages of the 'West End' or 'Broadway'.....how good and innocent those days were."

"You were the best then Joseph, and as you've just demonstrated to us all, you still have the talent. Why did you never pursue the career?" Moore asked Joseph affectionately. He, too, was remembering the good old times of their University days.

Almost sarcastically, Joseph answered,

"What and have my immediate family and relatives frowning, showing their disgust and sheer distaste at one of their own, reduced to acting on the stage. It's bad enough I followed a commercial career, rather than one in the military. But, one in the acting profession..........never. If I had become a member of equity, the joke in my family would have been,

"You know who I mean 'Joey' the one suffering from equity." I would have been treated as some sort of leper. It would have been the worst thing I could have done. But as you've noticed acting is still a love of mine."

Moore, in an instant turned back to the cold, hard, uncompassionate man he was. To be affectionate wasn't in his nature. It went totally against the grain for him, it was only a show. He was the master of showing crocodile tears because this is what he was all about. Looking directly at Fairfax, he said,

"Just remember to keep in line and you'll do just fine by us Joseph.... just fine. You'll be my right-hand man. You know how to pull this off better than anyone."

Joseph nodded, opened the boardroom doors and walked into the corridor. Rothchild was talking to Warlton. Fairfax caught his eye.

"Are you not coming Joseph ?" said Rothchild inquisitively with raised eyebrows.

Fairfax stopped, looked at him and for the first time realised what Jack had said about him all along. He really did have one of those faces that if you were to start hitting you couldn't stop.

The way in which the question was asked was so blatantly obvious, it ruined the whole exercise of asking in the first place. Rothchild was forever trying to embarrass Fairfax. If he went with them, then he wasn't above them after all, if he didn't, then he was an unsociable ass. Either way, Fairfax couldn't win. The personality clash between the two was like rubbing sandpaper on sandpaper.

Fairfax simply replied,

"Someone has to mastermind the operation from here on in. I have work to do. I simply couldn't spare you any of my precious time. But thanks all the same."

The raised eyebrows of Rothchild dropped to a frown, his lip curled as it did so. As always, Rothchild had just been made to look the ass. Rothchild grumbled,

"Your loss."

"I think not." Fairfax muttered to himself as he walked to his office.

He sat at his desk, picked up the telephone and started dialling. Unusual in the respect that 95% of all his phone calls always went through his secretary. He didn't trust anyone and wanted the plan to be a success.

Moore came into the office and he replaced the phone handset.

"I've just come in to ask you down to the club. I think we all deserve a drink after this morning's escapade. You more than anyone. I can't get over that speech, it was magnificent."

Moore really did mean what he said, because it was a speech which he thought brought Jack Deer down. This was something he liked to see happen to anyone, but especially him. In admiration of Fairfax's delivery he saw it as being one step nearer to coveting the consortium.

"Thanks, but no thanks. There are a few things I'd like to tidy up and finish off."

Moore, nodding his head, said "OK," and then made his way to the door. Joseph sat waiting for him to leave. Moore opened the door, and turned back to him,

"By the way, no hard feelings I hope, about what I said to you before. I had to make it look good. If I'd sided with you and gone against Warlton, he may have ruined it for all of us. You know what a cantankerous swine he can be sometimes, behaving like a small child throwing a wild tantrum. I knew that you'd be man enough to take it, after all, it was only show on my part."

Truth was, Moore couldn't care less how Fairfax felt, playing sly politics, of which he was a master, was what he was all about.

"No hard feelings on my behalf. I'm made of sturdier stuff than that Charles. You of all people, should know that."

"Good, I knew you'd understand. Well, if you change your mind you know where we'll be."

"OK, I'll think about it."

"Maybe see you there then ?"

"Maybe."

Moore left and the doors swung closed behind him. Fairfax picked up the phone and continued where he'd left off.

Chapter Two

Day One – Thursday Afternoon

After leaving the office, Jack made his way quietly and calmly to the car not speaking to anyone. He got into the car and told Tel to take him home. He telephoned Sammy to tell her he was on his way and about the outcome of the morning's events. There was a horrible silence.

"Hello !...Sammy, Sammy are you there ?...Hello"

"Yes, I'm here," Sammy said in a trembling voice.

The penny had finally dropped with Sammy. It had hit home, and hit home hard, what dire straits they were in. Jack told her not to worry and that he wasn't going to take it lying down. He told her he would be home soon, to which she simply replied 'Ok' and put the phone down.

Jack was about half way home and still thinking about what had happened when he rolled his head back and said aloud,

"Those fucking bastards."

Concentrating on the road ahead, Tel, on hearing Jack, but not quite catching what he had said, turned, looked over his shoulder and asked,

"What was that Guv ?"

"Oh, nothing Tel, I was just thinking aloud."

"If you don't mind me sayin', you don't seem yourself Guv. In fact, you haven't been yourself for some time actually. Is everything alright Guv ?"

He spoke sympathetically, knowing something was amiss.

"Que sera sera, Tel, Que sera sera." Jack replied in a surprisingly nonchalant way, which was quite strange considering what had just happened that morning.

"What ?" said Tel with a screwed up, perplexed look upon his face.

"Oh, nothing Tel," Jack sighed, "Nothing."

Just then the telephone rang. This was the last thing he wanted, to be disturbed by phone calls. Jack snatched at the phone, tutting under his breath,

"Hello," he said quickly.

He was cut off. Already in a bad mood, he banged the hand-set back down onto its holder, muttering obscenities under his breath. All quiet, Jack again had time to think, when his silence was again broken by the telephone.

Upon hearing the voice on the other end of the line he told them to 'hold on' and instructed Tel to put up the soundproof glass screen. Only once it was fully up did Jack continue the conversation.

Tel looked in his rear-view mirror and could see Jack talking intensively into the phone waving his hands flamboyantly as he always did. "Boy, it must be serious,"

Tel muttered to himself. He shook his head from side to side. He knew that Jack was in deep trouble but had no idea how much trouble.

Just as before the silence was deafening with everything passing-by in slow motion. It was only Jack's mind that was racing.

The car turned off the main roads and drove through a small wooded area. They came to a clearing, and moved gently up an incline towards a majestic looking house which could be admired from a distance.

They approached the gates of 'Deer Manor'. The land, the road, the house, all owned by Jack. In reality, they were all assets of the consortium. All this would be lost were the vultures to move in at the end of the month.

The gates opened and the car quietly passed under the black wrought-iron archway which bore the crest of the Deer family. Jack had designed and made the archway himself. This was yet another reminder of what he'd achieved and stood to lose, or rather, have stolen from him. The sound of gravel grinding beneath the wheels of the car broke the otherwise still countryside air, as it made its way up the spruce-lined driveway to the house.

To call it a house did not do it justice at all. It was neither a house, mansion nor manor but a building of such majesty it was more than worthy of being a stately home. It was such a magnificent piece of architecture, it was a palace, a Citadel even.

Although modern, it was built of stone, white marble and granite. It was modelled on the Greek temple of Parthenon on the Acropolis. Magnificent in every detail, designed by, and built by, Jack. This was his most prized personal achievement. Again, yet another masterpiece from his many wonderful and gifted talents.

The car pulled up behind a Range Rover parked in front of the steps, leading up to the front of the house. He knew he'd seen it somewhere before but couldn't place it. His mind was on one thing only. How he was going to gain back the consortium and bring down those who'd conspired to steal it all from him.

Jack didn't wait for Tel to open his door. He stepped out of the car and looked up at the pediment supported on the Greek style marble pillars. Within the pediment was a hand-carved tympanum, depicting hunters in a forest pursuing a deer, with a lion either side of it.

Jack thought to himself,

"If those bastards think that's an analogy to me, then they'd better think again. They've bitten off more than they can chew and I'm going to see to it that those fuckers choke on it all."

Tel just looked at Jack, bemused.

Jack made his way up the steps to the massive oak-panelled doors which had brass door handles in the shape of a lion's head, each the size of a man's fist. One of them was opened by Mary, the housekeeper, looking quite disturbed, panting for breath after running downstairs to greet him at the door.

"Come quick Mr. Deer," she said, flapping her hands toward herself, gesturing to him to move quickly.

"What is it Mary ?"

"It's Mrs. Deer, she's collapsed and the doctor's here."

"Oh, my God," said Jack, breathing out a sigh of anxiety. "Where is she ?"

"She's in her room with the doctor."

Jack ran across the hallway and up the stairs. Levering himself on the white banister to gain more speed he almost flew onto the landing. As he ran frantically across it, he barged through the doorway straight into their bedroom.

The doctor was standing by the dressing table, putting miscellaneous items back into his brown leather bag. Sammy was so pale, she looked grey. Jack knelt by her side and held her hand. He kissed first her forehead and then her hand and told her that he loved her. He then quickly turned to the doctor and asked,

"What's wrong ?.... What's the matter with her ?.... Is she going to be alright ?"

The doctor clicked the clasp closed on his bag, picked it up and turned around. Looking at Jack he pointed to the bedroom doors and started walking toward them without saying a word. Sammy, although coherent, didn't stir. She just lay there with dulled eyes, affixed to the photographic portrait of her, Jack and their two children, John and Laura, taken on their first trip to Disneyland.

Jack stood up from the bed and followed the doctor out of the room, glancing back for a brief moment at Sammy. The doctor closed the doors softly behind Jack and put his finger to his lips. Jack, panic-stricken and his heart racing, asked the doctor once again the questions he'd just asked a couple of seconds before.

"Please, Mr. Deer, calm down," the doctor said in a very low voice to try and appease him and not disturb Sammy at the same time. "Your wife has had a shock.....a mental shock."

Jack brushed his fingers through his hair. The doctor continued,

"Now she's alright for the time being, but she mustn't in any way be disturbed or alarmed."

Jack was now in a state of shock himself.

"Do you understand Mr. Deer ?"

Jack didn't reply.

"Mr. Deer," the doctor said, in a formal, slightly raised voice to get his attention.

"Yes." snapped Jack.

He continued,

"Now I've given her some sleeping pills to make her rest for a while, and I'm prescribing Citalopram, an anti-depressant from the SSRI group of drugs. This will help her present condition but if there's no improvement over the next five days she will have to be admitted for further treatment." The doctor looked to Jack who had a look-less stare.

"Mr. Deer....Do you understand..... Mr. Deer ?"

Jack looked at the doctor but didn't answer him.

"Mr. Deer, do you understand ?" the doctor repeated.

"Yes doc ...yes, I understand," he said softly, nodding his head.

The doctor touched his shoulder, as if to reassure him.

Jack just looked at him and asked what had caused her to go into such a severe state of shock, all the time knowing in his heart what the reason was, but until he heard it from the doctor he was in denial.

Seeing the anxiety in Jack's face, the doctor was careful not to cause greater distress.

"In cases similar to this, it's usually psychological. In such cases, whatever a person holds dear, such as children, their spouse or parents, news that they have had something traumatic or fatal happen to them, is the most common cause. However, I've spoken to Mary and I know that's not the case in this particular instance. The patient usually gets over the worst of the initial shock after two or three days. In some cases, even the death of a pet could cause such a condition......or even financial loss."

Jack stared at him.

"So, please, Mr. Deer don't be too alarmed. After your wife has had a good rest, she will be able to tell you what's upset her and the best medicine of all is going to be a listening ear from you. Hopefully, after a few days, she will start to come round, so don't be too alarmed at this stage."

Jack knew instantly that the phone call he'd made to her earlier from the car after the meeting was the cause. He felt rotten to the core. He'd confirmed Sammy's worst fears, as it was evidently clear that she had never truly believed that the worst scenario could ever happen. Thinking back to when they first got up that morning, he remembered what she had said,

"Maybe we've got it wrong somewhere and it's not as bad as we've made it out to be."

Only through that phone call did it finally hit home, that everything they'd worked for all their lives was to disappear. In the space of one month it was going to seem as though all they had achieved and accomplished had all been a marvellous dream. Now they were to wake up from a beautiful sleep only to have to face the cold hard callous truth of reality, in which all that they had left were their memories of better times with few material reminders.

Jack thanked the doctor for coming to the house and tending to his wife. He would have asked him to stay for a cup of tea, but he simply was in neither the mood nor frame of mind to show him any hospitality. Jack was so obsessed with what had happened, he couldn't think of anything else. With his wife now taken ill, he had to focus his thoughts constructively on what he was to do next. He showed the doctor to the door and thanked him once again. Not waiting for a reply, he shut it and walked to the lounge. Closing the lounge doors gently behind him, he sat down to think. Both Mary and Tel knew that when he retired to the lounge with the doors closed it meant that he wasn't to be disturbed. Over the past month or so, Jack had been doing this more than usual. He would make and answer telephone calls in private, instead of casually speaking, not caring who could hear. Sitting down, he began to think of his years of struggle to get where he was today. How it was all going to be taken from him and how he was going to have to outwit the Board to keep from losing it all..... If he could keep from losing it all.

Jack was a multimillionaire. He owned properties in many countries throughout the world, that were registered in his name, and were not assets of the consortium. He had many different investment interests in different companies and was a major shareholder of government backed blue-chip companies. He was never going to be poor. However, to lose the empire he had built from nothing, sacrificing everything and to have possessed the power that it wielded, was almost too much to bear for any man who could appreciate such a prestigious position.

Not once throughout all the years, had Jack ever abused the position of being a high-powered and wealthy businessman. Nor, as so many other men before him, had he ever thought of himself as untouchable by the law or morality.

At sixteen, he left school and went immediately to work, all the time studying at night school, paid for by himself. Even from a young age, he had always worked tirelessly to better himself. He passed his 'A' levels at eighteen and gained a place at Durham University. But he never went. Just when he was to have started, his mother was taken seriously ill. With his father on invalidity pay from an accident that had happened a year earlier, (permanently putting him out of work), there was no money coming in. So Jack took it upon himself to be the bread-winner. He went to work on local building sites to provide for the family. Jack was the eldest followed by his twin brothers, Thomas and David, younger by four years, and his eleven year old sister, Megan.

University was his best chance ever of escaping from the brainwashed, inverted snobbery of his surroundings. The negativity only ever came from one quarter...his father, who truly believed that such places were not for the 'working classes.' Even if his son were to have graduated, he believed that he could never and would never be accepted by those of the 'upper classes.' His father had the unreasoned notion that these places of higher learning were only there for the rich and privileged. As he saw it, it wasn't his son's place to be gallivanting in circles of....'the elite'. His father feared that Jack would only be making a fool of himself. He was so ignorant, words fail. To be fair, his beliefs may have had credibility over a hundred and fifty years ago, but not in this day and age.

More to Jack's credit he never thought ill of his father, as he understood that he was only a product of 'his' surroundings.

They came from a poor county mining town, where few had ever had the chance to go to university, everyone left school at sixteen. Higher education was thought of as being for the 'posh people.' None of the town's brightest kids had ever been in the privileged position of having a supportive family who could send money for books, food, clothing and the like, even if they did go to 'Uni'. All young men and women of the age were expected to go out and earn a living. For some, to know that their kids were living off a grant and therefore off the state would have been quite simply, shameful. The people of that era all suffered from 'Pride'.

So Jack's fate had been decided for him. He worked locally on building sites, as this was the highest paying employment available to him.

During his two years at night school, he had met Sammy. After his final exams, he married her. She was pregnant with their first child, John. One year later when their second child Laura was born, he started his own contracting business. Staying away from Sammy and the two babes in arms for months on end, putting their house up as collateral to finance the whole thing and all the time still helping to support his mother, father and sister. His brothers by this time had left home and were setting up lives of their own.

Though all this put considerable strain on his own marriage and family he persevered, convincing Sammy that it would all be worth it in the end.....and how right he had been.

The work orders of his new contracting business just kept on flooding in and it just grew and grew. Through success after success he expanded his concerns. He built his own warehouses, shipped his own processed materials, (made at his own processing plants) and constructed offices and building yards worldwide. Before long, he was managing construction projects and maintenance contracts for the British and foreign governments, building dams, power stations, roads, schools, hospitals and the like. Jack had gone from strength to strength, enlarging his empire in all directions without over stretching any of his financial resources or personnel. He employed almost fifty thousand people worldwide and gave each of them a fair day's pay for a fair day's work.

The only thing he ever insisted on, or demanded, was loyalty. If he was given this, then he'd be more than gracious in return. But if he was cheated or crossed in any way, then he would personally go out of his way to redress the situation. To mess with him, was to mess with the wrong person.

He once paid for all medical bills for a peasant employee working as a cleaning lady at his Hong Kong offices.

Her daughter had been seriously injured in a road accident with a truck which belonged to a subsidiary company.

It was brought to his attention purely by chance when he happened to notice a picture of a similar truck on the cover of a local newspaper. He asked his interpreter what it was all about and once he had all the facts, he moved into action.

A terrible accident, as she had run straight out into the path of the oncoming truck, giving the driver no chance of stopping. The girl suffered a fractured skull and a broken arm and leg. After coming out of a coma five days later, she was kept under observation in hospital for six weeks to recuperate. The physical harm done was exceptionally light, considering that by the doctors decree, she shouldn't have survived.

If it hadn't have been for the intervention of Jack, the little girl most certainly would have died, as the mother could never have afforded the hospital bills.

She'd worked for the company for ten years and had no record of illness or lateness. Jack paid the bills anonymously so as not to start a cascade of begging letters from other undeserving cases. Jack also had a counsellor sent to the driver, so that no long-term guilt would be carried by him.

This was what Jack Deer was all about. A man of true moral fibre. A man who had a sense of right and wrong, a sense of truth and justice. He was no pushover though, and he certainly wasn't soft. He could be just as ruthlessly punishing as he was generous. This was the case in India, where one of his cement processing works was based. He was informed of a court case in which a number of local workers at the plant had been stealing building materials from the stores and selling them on the black market. He personally flew to India and recruited the best lawyers to ensure a conviction against them. Although the men cried poverty in the courtroom and that they had only done what they did to get more money to feed their families, it was proved to be a downright lie. As Jack saw it, these men deserved to be prosecuted and lose their jobs which had paid twice the average local wage.

Whenever something like this happened Jack made it his personal business to find out everything possible about the people and circumstances. As in the case of the cleaning lady and that of the thieving Indian workers he would get to the bottom of things, finding out the truth and the circumstances around situations before making any decisions.

He showed every compassion to those who showed him loyalty, and was merciless to those who in anyway tried to deceive or cheat him.

Instead of wallowing in self-pity, Jack sat there thinking hard about what he was going to do and all the permutations of any action he might take. Already a couple of hours had passed which seemed like seconds. What had taken him almost a lifetime to build wasn't, if he could help it, going to be snatched away from him in only a couple of weeks. He was tired and decided to get some rest. Opening the lounge doors he called to Mary as she was dusting the paintings on the landing. He walked up the stairs to meet her.

He told her not to inform either John or Laura about what had happened. He didn't want, or have time, for a full scale family panic on his hands. Mary, protesting and disagreeing with him, had no choice but to obey his instruction. Putting his hand up to his forehead and rubbing it, he told her that he knew she meant well but that keeping them ignorant was the best thing. After all, Sammy would probably recover in a day or so. Mary, still not convinced, reluctantly agreed. Jack then went to lie down in one of the guest rooms.

Whilst all this turmoil was happening the 'Board Members,' with the exception of Fairfax, had all made their way to the Marlborough Club. Fairfax had taken it upon himself to now spearhead the takeover scheme, despite the warning by Charles Moore to be careful.

This was an exclusive club, primarily for entrepreneurs, company directors and lawyers, stockbrokers, bankers and even high ranking government officials. The concoction had the stench of money, power and position. But as with all other clubs of this ilk it had its fair share of shysters, chancers and call girls.

Although Jack was a member of this club and others like it, he rarely frequented them. He only ever attended dinners and special functions, to be introduced to prospective clientele, where deals could be made and a tremendous amount of custom acquired. For as much as Jack didn't like the club, it did have its benefits.

The entourage arrived at the club and one by one they were greeted by the manager. He was as pompous and stiff upper-lipped as they were. They all shook hands with him, made pathetic small talk and made their way to the half doors of the cloakroom, all of them so idle, that their overcoats had to be peeled off their backs by the cloakroom attendants. It was as though they were snakes needing assistance to shed their scaly skins. They entered the lounge. Loud and boisterous, they shouted greetings to friends and associates. Just like an oil slick sprayed with dispersant they broke up and went to all corners of the room to mingle.

The club was conspicuous by the absence of women but they could be *arranged and bought* if so desired.

Charles Moore, neither acknowledging nor speaking to anyone, sat down in a Chesterfield armchair in the corner of the room.

He was shortly joined by Warlton, Peterbough and Rothchild. Peterbough called one of the waiters over and ordered drinks for them all, without so much as a please or thank you.

Still trying to reaffirm his stance on what he had said about Jack earlier in the meeting to Fairfax, Warlton said,

"Well, what a bloody good show that was this morning. With Deer out of the way and us now fully in control we really can go places and make the consortium reach its true potential.....before we dissect it."

All but Moore looked at him, smiling.

Rothchild joined in,

"Yes, it was a perfect .....no, 'masterful' takeover. All that precise planning has paid off and without a hitch. Deer and his pathetic threats of making us 'crawl on our bellies.' Just who the hell does he think he is ? I ask you ! Gentlemen, we have nothing to fear from him and Fairfax is wrong. We can forget Jack Deer. We've seen the last of him."

"Hear, hear," said Warlton in support of Rothchild.

The drinks arrived and one-by-one, the waiter placed them on the round oak table they sat around. No-one spoke or even said thank you to him as he returned to the bar.

Once again the same familiar self-conceited grins returned to their faces. Re-establishing their thoughts about how clever they had been and how they had toppled the headman so that they could take what wasn't really theirs. All but Moore had this attitude.

"Fairfax is right." Moore said, in his usual quiet, charismatic voice. They all looked at him. The aura was stifled and the smirks were beginning to disappear from their faces.

"Oh yes...how exactly ?" Peterbough said with disdain.

Both Warlton and Rothchild were silenced.

"Deer is a clever man and if given the slightest chance to regain what we've taken from him, he will. Make no mistake gentlemen, Jack Deer isn't a man that you can as easily dismiss as you all evidently believe."

"Oh, come now Charles, we've been through all this. I think you may be taking what Fairfax said this morning too seriously and too much to heart," Warlton said dismissively.

Peterbough just had to say something,

"It was your decision to finally have Joseph on our side. What did you say to him to get him to join us ? It must have been something extraordinary because after all it was you Charles, who constantly warned us about letting Fairfax in on the scheme in the first place and how we weren't to put our trust in him lightly."

"Gentlemen, as you know, I had reservations, more than anyone, about Joseph, because of his years of association and friendship with Deer. I was always doubtful of him joining us to get rid of Deer but he's surpassed even my best hopes. That speech he made convincing Deer that it was all over, was a magnificent performance. Deer took it all, 'hook, line and sinker.' I couldn't believe how powerful it all was."

"Yes, we know all that, so what did you say exactly ?" Rothchild asked in excited anticipation, again proving that he had never heard of the 'golden silence' or if he had, he certainly never practised it, always opening his big trap wanting all to hear him. He was living proof that *'empty vessels really do make the loudest noise'*.

"I really am intrigued as to how you actually convinced him to join us," Peterbough added.

Moore continued, with all of them mesmerised, Rothchild more so than anyone.

"I convinced him that he was never going to be anything more than Jack's personal assistant. That the notion he had in his head that Jack had built up and made the consortium, was a myth in his mind, and his mind only. In reality, it was he that had pulled it off and pieced it all together. I reminded him that he was academically brighter and smarter than Jack and it was Jack who relied on him, not the other way round. I asked him that if it hadn't been for his management and administration skills, and the contacts he introduced to Jack, in clubs such as these, then where would Deer have been today? I simply convinced Joseph of his importance and of what he had personally done for Jack in getting him this far, and finally I asked him in what way he'd benefited from it all? Position wise, I made him see that as others saw it, Deer was grinding the organ and that he was the monkey dancing the tune. With this seed planted for him to think on, knowing it would leave a bad taste in his mouth, I then struck the final and clinching blow."

Moore pausing, leaned forward to drink from his gin and tonic poised on the table with bubbles slowly rising from its depths. Rothchild leaned forward in his seat, and with a mixture of enthralment, impatience and anticipation of what Moore was to say next, anxiously enquired,

"Yes, yes and what was that exactly?"

Moore took a gulp from his glass to lubricate his throat, and glanced at Rothchild out of the corner of his eye as if to say, 'Give me a chance'.

Putting his glass down, Moore slowly sat back into his chair. Crossing his legs and putting his hands and fingers together to form a pyramid with his elbows resting on the arms of the chair, he continued, "What would his family think, especially his father, if he was head of his own arms manufacturing factory for the government? Coming from a military background, this would meet with his father's sheer delight, to know that his son hadn't fully turned his back on his ancestral military background. Having come from one of the most prestigious and prolific military families, this would be the closest thing that he personally would ever get to being remotely connected with the army and finally gaining some sort of respect from his father."

"But we don't have any arms factories........anywhere." Peterbough said frowning, screwing up his face.

"True, but with his slice of the cake I sold him the idea that he would be able to start one."

"Well I never....you sly old fox." Rothchild said, grinning as he slowly sat back into the soft leather sofa.

Warlton and Peterbough couldn't see what Rothchild had seen so clever in Moore's convincing persuasion of Fairfax.

"Brilliant! You're a genius. You played on the old fatherly approval strings. You sly, dirty trickster, Moore.....you cold-hearted wizard." Rothchild said in elation. Turning to face Warlton and Peterbough, he explained,

"He's always been some sort of a failure to his father for not serving in the forces and his father has always let him know it. Coming from a Sandhurst military family and all that. For him to be M.D. of his own arms factory would certainly have redeemed his father's approval of him."

He turned to Charles.

"You clever bastard Moore, you clever, clever bastard."

"Did you know his father is dying?" Rothchild asked tentatively.

"Of course, what better time to talk to Fairfax of his father and push him into joining us."

Rothchild and the others looked cold and hard at Moore in sheer adulation of what they now all saw as Moore's brilliance. Even they were surprised at just how low Moore was prepared to stoop.

All the members of the Board stayed until early evening before returning home, or as was so often the case with several of them a quick trip to the 'Pelican' for a bit of *'bought love.'*

From the outside, the club was a very respectable and typically English......'Gentleman's Club.' But from the inside, its dealings were a little more shady. For those that were inclined, it was a place where arrangements could be made to meet up with a 'vice girl' or 'rent boy'. Whatever your fancy.

The 'Pelican' was an hotel, built, owned and run by the consortium. It was of such splendour and luxury that only the world's most famous and wealthy stayed there. One of the tallest hotel buildings in London, it was a mighty landmark for the whole city to be praised and admired.

A helipad crowned the structure for high-flying VIPs who were just too important to travel on public roads. It had nine restaurants complete with their own chefs. Each specialising in serving food from their country of origin ; France, India, Japan, Mexico and a host of other countries. It had an Olympic sized swimming pool, two fully fitted-out gyms, complete with trainers and nutritionists. It even had its own private cinema and theatre in which films that hadn't even been released could be seen. This was sheer Utopia. With its fifty rooms, all no less than king size, all with the modern trimmings, there had never been complaints from any of the guests other than that the stay had been too short.

Jack had spent millions on its design, construction and internal decoration. In his farsightedness he knew that if his prospective clients were to be sent to such a place as a sweetener with everything on the house, then any deal he was negotiating was 99% in the bag.

Day Two - Friday

The members of the Board assembled at the conference room to be informed of the next step and how the news of Jack's departure would best be announced to the company's minions and the media.

Sitting at the head of the table was Moore, immaculate in every detail as he always was. Flanking him on his left side was Fairfax, with documents on the table in front of him. Sitting to his left were William Peterbough and Lord Arthur Cavendish. Opposite were Lord Andrew Barron, Simon Rothchild, and Sir Henry Warlton. They had now all assumed their new seating positions as the norm. Sitting further down the table on both sides, were all the other members.

Moore asked for everyone's attention.

"The final details of the plan have been drawn up and to explain them to you all is Joseph."

He then invited Joseph to speak and explain how they were to proceed with the takeover and eventually the final dissection of the consortium and all its divisions.

The room was still.

Fairfax stood up from the table to address everyone.

"Gentlemen, the details on exactly how our plan is to work are really quite simple, so I will keep this speech the same. The details are here."

He lifted up the documents for all to cast their beady little eyes upon and then gently placed them back down in front of him.

"All we have to do is inflate what our profit margins are for the first quarter of this year. Investors will then rush to put their money in with us, increasing their shareholding. Then with this announced, we refute what we've said and that the figures were wrong and that we'd actually made more than we first calculated due to belated orders.....'.*bogus of course*'. This will cause panic buying of shares into the consortium. We then announce that we are to sell off each division, but, that each one of them will still be managed by members of this Board. Before anyone catches on or has the chance to investigate the dismemberment, we will all be controlling our own companies which will not be bound by the code of rules and regulations instilled by Jack Deer. We will be able to reduce the overhead costs of the different divisions by laying off staff, replacing them with workers who will be happy to accept lower wages, introduce term contracts with longer working hours …..and so we continue to make profits, only they'll be much larger than they are now….at least twenty percent larger."

"Gentlemen, it will be 'sky's the limit'. We shall own and be in full control of the consortium. We'll be able to influence government contracts and our limits will now almost have no bounds. So long as we remain firm, we can make this work."

Everyone sat grinning like Cheshire cats. A muffled rumpus ensued with quiet laughter breaking the otherwise intense atmosphere. Rothchild told Moore what a fantastic plan it was. Moore looked to Fairfax and gave a thankful nod, cracking a sly grin out of the side of his mouth. Rothchild looked coldly across the table at Fairfax.

Rothchild was, and always had been envious of Fairfax. He could never stand the way in which he had always been on the right arm of Jack Deer. Now he was the right-hand man of Moore. He believed that he was above his station and that he still wasn't to be trusted, especially considering how he'd been best friends with Deer for the past twenty years, and yet, at the drop of a hat, was willing to knife him in the back. His mistrust strengthened with the speech he'd made twisting the knife and pushing it deeper. Any further and it would have burst through the man's chest.

The clash of the two personalities was just impossible to contain and as always, the cheap points were once again trying to be scored by Rothchild.

Once the euphoria had died down, there was a quiet lull in the room. As always, Rothchild had to make himself heard.

"So, doing the donkey work again, hey, Joseph ?"

The room turned cold and then it froze. All eyes were upon Rothchild, everyone giving their undivided attention.

"What do you mean by that Simon ?"

"Well, let's face it ! One minute Deer's grinding the organ and now Charles is. You, meanwhile, are still the monkey, dancing to the tune."

He'd betrayed Moore's confidence in letting Fairfax know that they'd obviously been discussing him.

Fairfax, waiting, knowing that such a derogatory comment as this was inevitably going to come from Rothchild, replied in a calm cool tone. He was always ready for Rothchild in instances such as these. Fairfax's oratory skills were out of Rothchild's league. He gave his reply in a style all of his own.

"Well, Rothchild, if your analogy is true and I'm a monkey dancing to the tune played by Charles here,"

he turned to Charles with his arms spread out towards him as though he were a game show host introducing his guests and then putting his arms back down, turned to face Rothchild,

"Then what are you ?"

Smiles lit up the vast majority of the room. They all knew what was coming, some even chuckled. They knew that once Fairfax turned from the defensive to the offensive he meant business. From previous clashes with Rothchild and a number of other would-be upstarts, who eventually faded away, Fairfax never came out worse. He continued,

"After all, both Jack and Charles have seen fit to entrust me with their plans, yet you always seem to be on the receiving end of decisions. Plans are made without your consultation or input. If your analogy is to be believed Simon, then you are addressing everyone in this room, because this is Charles' plan."

Fairfax lifted the documents he'd been reading from and waved them in the air, he continued,

"And in your eyes, me telling everyone what it's all about, is like me feeding nuts to monkeys. But I'm sure that all of us here resent the analogy to primates, including myself and I'm sure that you regret this comparison. After all you must obviously be comparing all of us here, as we are all colleagues together and all working towards the same goal. I'm sure neither Charles, Sir Henry, Lord Andrew, Lord Arthur, William nor anyone else wishes to be compared to monkeys and I know that you must regret your analogy, seeing it in its true light and should now apologize."

Rothchild, now totally embarrassed in front of everyone, sat humiliated and stared scornfully at Fairfax, his alter ego brought down like a house of cards caught in a gust of wind. With all eyes upon him, he felt like an outcast, as though he were some kind of freak that had no place among them, let alone a part of them.

Rothchild would neither learn, nor accept that he couldn't beat Fairfax in either a verbal slanging match or a civilised debate. If it meant that he had to cut off his nose to spite his face in the 'one in a hundred' chance that he might just get the better of him, then so be it.

Fairfax was the most prolific of speakers and with his command of English could verbally bring down even the most ardent of intellectuals.

With all the room now on the side of Fairfax, the looks at Rothchild turned to glaring stares. Everyone was waiting for an apology, when Moore restored calm,

"Enough!"

At Moore's request, Fairfax sat down and nothing more was said by either of them. The scoring session was over and as always Fairfax came out on top. Charles' charismatic charm smoothing over yet another ugly incident. That eerie presence about him, chilled an atmosphere of disquiet. He was almost hypnotic when he spoke.

Once everyone had settled, he then told them that the road ahead would not be easy but if they followed the plan laid down to the letter, it could work.

When all present nodded their heads in agreement, he suggested the junior members should go back to their offices and work on how best to inflate their profit figures.

The key players remained seated as they always did, making idle chat. Some, like Warlton, began to light up their expensive Havana cigars taken from their top inside jacket pockets. Plumes of bluey grey smoke rose gently toward the ceiling and out through the silent extraction fans. As everyone sat waiting quietly, it was Rothchild yet again, who spoke,

"Fairfax !"

He knew typically what to expect.

"Yes !"

"How's your father doing, old boy ? Believe he's not been too well."

Rothchild had a sly smirk on his face, now indelible as his trademark.

"He died yesterday."

Rothchild was stunned into silence. The rest of the Board members just stared at Fairfax.

Fairfax said no more, but looked on at Rothchild impassively.

All were shocked at the news but more so with the way in which it had been announced. All were stuck for anything to say. Understandably, the situation was awkward and everyone was now making an excuse for escaping the room. Hurriedly making for the door, they quickly expressed their sorrow and sympathy, relieved to be getting away from the situation. Fairfax just nodded at each of them in acknowledgement as they did so.

Rothchild looked at Fairfax,

"I had no idea..... "

Fairfax interrupted him,

"You had no idea. Save it Rothchild. Please just save it."

"Joseph, I'm sorry I....."

"You're not sorry and you knew he was on his death bed. So you had every idea about what state he was in. I know you Rothchild, and how your mind works. Bringing up my father so that I sink into a sombre mood and then you come out with a *below the belt* remark, comment, or sarcastic question, so that you can have the last word. Well, it won't work, because for your information I made my peace with him just before he died and now I only have my fond and happy memories of him."

Rothchild felt as though he'd just had his heart and lungs wrenched out of his chest. He stood there, numbed into a state of paralysis. For as much as he was the slime trail of a slug, he was still human, and had feelings. He felt not just bad, but rotten about himself, and for the first time in a very long time, he really was lost for words.

Once out of the boardroom they all walked wistfully to their offices. Fairfax took a minute to look out of the window and thought of his father. He gathered his thoughts together and made his way to his own office.

He was on the phone when Moore walked in. He raised his finger to let him know he was just about to finish the call, at the same time saying to the person on the other end of the line he would get back to them and put the receiver down.

Moore sat down and looked at the phone and asked if it was anyone important.

"No, it's just the 'Pelican' hotel. It needs a few things doing and I'm personally seeing to it that they're done."

"You shouldn't be doing such menial tasks as these. Why can't your secretary take care of it? She's more than capable and suited to such trivia, Joseph."

"If I do it myself then I know it will be done properly."

Moore frowned, dismissing his behaviour as being the result of shock.

Moore sat down on the chair in front of Fairfax's desk and tried unsuccessfully to console him.

"Look, Joseph, we all know what Rothchild can be like and what an arse he can be sometimes but......"

Fairfax not wanting to hear, interrupted, saying,

"Charles, please don't patronise or insult my intelligence. We all know what Rothchild is like so please, don't try to soft soap me with that rational reasoning tone of yours, because you're wasting your time. Now I've got work to do and if you don't mind, I'd like to get on with it.....Please."

Moore stood up from his seat, straightened his jacket and told Fairfax that he was upset and that he should go home.

"Charles, I don't mean to be rude but I have to finish this, now more than ever. I made my peace with my father and I promised I would make him proud of me. So you of all people, will know what this means to me. I only need to accomplish this and then I can let my father's soul rest in peace."

Moore looked at Joseph and nodded his head accordingly. He turned around and without another word walked out of the office. He met Peterbough in the corridor. He asked if Fairfax was alright. Moore looked coldly at him,

"Yes, he's alright."

Peterbough looked to the door of Fairfax's office. Moore told him to leave him be and not to bother him, saying that it was best if he was to get over it in his own time.

Chapter Three

Day Three - Saturday

Jack was still acting rather peculiarly. He was answering only selected calls to the house. When he did speak it was only privately behind closed doors. Anyone would have been forgiven for thinking Jack was paranoid. He trusted no-one, not even his two most loyal employees, Mary and Tel and they had worked for him for the past twenty-two years.

He had instructed one of the consortium maintenance vans to be delivered and left at his house. Also delivered were a number of wooden boxes, which were neatly piled in a corner of the hallway. They all had 'FRAGILE' stamped on them and symbols indicating the correct way up plastered all over in bright red ink.

A strict instruction had been given by Jack to Mary and Tel to leave the boxes where they were and that neither of them were to go near them.

He then disappeared into his workshop at the back of the house. It was like Aladdin's cave. There was a lathe, shaper, drilling and milling machine. He had everything a handyman could want and more. Running the length of the workshop was a long work bench that had seen better days. An abundance of work tools pockmarked the walls and situated prominently in the corner was a drawing board.

These were all relics from the early days when Jack had worked as a 'hands-on' tradesman. He'd never forgotten his roots nor tried to deny them.

He would occasionally lock himself away in the workshop, his own world, to work on different things as a hobby. It was he who had designed and built everything. Nothing had gone amiss with Jack. He thought back to the day almost twenty years ago when on the drawing board in the corner, it was he who designed the emblem for the consortium. If he could build, construct or make something himself, he did. Jack's hands still had calluses on them from all the work he still did with his tools. Tools he had faith in, tools he could rely on, tools he could trust. Attributes the Board members had demonstrated they certainly did not have.

Jack stripped himself of his expensive clothes and carefully hung them up on a hanger behind the door. He swapped them for a pair of overalls that had been hanging from the same hanger. He finished off his new attire by putting on a pair of old work boots that had also seen better days.

To the bewilderment of Mrs. Briggs and Tel, he emerged from the workshop and started loading the mysterious boxes from the hallway into the van.

"Here, let me help you with that," said Tel.

"No, leave it." Jack snapped back at him. "I will do it !"

Startled by his aggressiveness, Tel stood back from the boxes.

Watching from the landing was Mary who caught Jack's eye.

He stopped to look at her but she just moved her head away from his gaze and headed back to the bedroom where she was taking care of Sammy. He knew what she and Tel were thinking, that there was no need to be so quick. He also knew that they were bemused as to his behaviour. Things weren't normal and neither did they look it.

A common work van at the front of the house, expensive and fashionable clothes exchanged for a pair of overalls, mysterious boxes not to be touched. Things certainly were not at all normal.

Jack knew their thoughts must have been that he was in trouble with the business somehow, and with Sammy *'taking a turn,'* that he must have flipped and didn't know what he was doing. But Jack knew exactly what he was doing. Time was of the essence and it wasn't on his side.

He didn't go upstairs to say goodbye to Sammy before he left. Remembering what the doctor had said, he knew her seeing him in overalls would only disturb her. She would be curious and start asking awkward questions that he just wouldn't have time to answer. Instead, he finished loading the boxes and gently drove off down the drive. He left a note for Mary telling her to inform Sammy that he would be gone for the day, maybe two, on important business.

Mary walked downstairs, saw the note and read it. Tel closed the front doors as Jack disappeared out of view into the small wood. Nothing was making sense. What possible business could Jack be on, dressed in overalls and carting mysterious boxes around in a work van? It didn't add up...things were strange.

Mary was putting the note into her pocket when Tel asked,

"What do you think his game is, then? Has he flipped or what?"

"He's certainly not himself. Whether it be about the business, Mrs. Deer, or both, I don't know, but he's not right."

"You can say that again. Has Mrs. Deer enlightened you by any chance or told you anything?"

"No, nothing. Not a sausage. She just lies there staring at the family picture of them all in Disneyland."

They both continued to speculate what Jack was up to, guessing wildly as they walked to the kitchen to get something to eat. Once they were both tired of the subject, which was some considerable time later, they started to discuss the important matter of the latest village gossip. In the middle of their chronically important discussion, a call came over on the intercom system. It was Sammy.

"Mary !"

"Yes, madam."

"Could you bring me up a cup of coffee and a light snack please, I'm feeling a little better now."

"Coming right up, madam."

Mary, with a rather delighted look on her face, turned to Tel who was smiling,

"Well, how about that then ? 'His Nibs' walks out the door and 'hey presto', she gets better."

"Well, I'm glad she is, maybe she'll be able to tell you what's up."

Tel's curiosity was getting the better of him. Mary just looked at him as she took food from the fridge and made a fresh cup of coffee.

Once Mary had made a couple of freshly cut sandwiches and a pot of coffee, she took it up to Sammy's room. Mary knocked gently on the door and pushed it open. The air had a slight musty edge to it.

Sammy was wearing her silk pyjamas and sitting upright on top of the bed, her back supported against the headboard by a couple of pillows. As Mary entered the room, she turned and patted them...she was half out of breath.

Mary walked over to Sammy's bed and placed the tray down across Sammy's legs. In a rather frail and tired voice Sammy said,

"Thank you, Mary. I'm feeling a lot better today."

She didn't look it. Her face was still pale and drawn and her hair dull and dishevelled. It was an improvement, but she still wasn't herself. Mary smiled, walked over to the curtains, opened them and then a window to let in the fresh air. Sammy squinted with the light.

Mary sat keeping her company as she ate her snack. She crossed her legs and biting into one of the sandwiches looked to Mary,

"Thank you Mary, it's just what I fancied."

"Oh, it was my pleasure. Now you just sit there and enjoy. Don't want you doing too much just yet, madam."

From out of her apron pocket Mary passed Sammy the note that Jack had left. As Sammy began to read it, Mary left to make some phone calls.

First she rang the doctor, to keep him informed of developments as he had asked her to do. The advice was to ensure that the citalopram tablets prescribed were dispensed with and that she should now be left to recuperate without them. He also told her that he would look in on his patient when he had the chance.

Then she made two long distance telephone calls to Hong Kong and Australia to inform Laura and John about their mother. Although against the specific instructions of Jack she felt it was the right thing to do and in her heart she had wanted to call them on the first day. Now that Sammy was getting better, she could always say that although Jack had told her not to inform John and Laura that their mother was ill, he never said not to inform them if she was getting better. Mary always had an uncanny knack for distorting the truth, that's why she was *'chief rumour spreader'* in the village and why Tel badgered her for more information on different things considering that she would have mastered in 'Gossipology.'

Mary called Laura's special 24 / 7 number in Hong Kong. She gave a special code word and explained who she was. She was transferred to Laura's mobile number. She was in Paris closing out a deal with clients. Mary told Laura everything including that Jack had told her, not to say anything. Laura explained that all her business had been concluded early that day and that she was taking the opportunity to pay her mum a surprise visit. But she was the one who was surprised. It was unbelievable luck that she was in the departure lounge of Charles De Gaulle airport waiting to catch a plane to Heathrow. Laura said she would be home in the next four hours or so, and she promised she wasn't going to say a word to her father until she was home.

Mary then called John's office in Australia. She was told that he'd left on a plane for Oslo, Norway and that the plane should be arriving just about now. Just as with Laura she explained who she was and was transferred to his mobile number. John was being greeted by an entourage of executives and company reps when he received the call. He, too, said that he was dropping everything and would make his way home immediately and promised not to say anything to his father. He would be home within half a day.

Satisfied in the knowledge that she had done her bit and another good deed ...all in the line of duty, as she saw it, Mary continued about her business.

Day Four - Sunday

Peterbough had stopped by the office. It was on his way to the Marlborough Club. He arrived at about ten thirty. There really wasn't any need for him to be there. It just made him feel good, it fed his ego. The only thing he ever had to do was sign a few pieces of paper here and there. This, and only this, was his function in the great on-going, ever-turning wheels of the consortium. He was a minuscule cog of no real consequence, in a machine that was larger than life itself. After pottering around for a couple of hours he left for the Marlborough Club.

He didn't have to tell his driver where to go. The routine was now a ritual. Peterbough only had to give a quick nodding flick of his head sideways and his driver knew exactly where to go.

His expensive custom-built Mercedes pulled out of the car park and made its way to the club.

Once there, he made the usual small talk, laughed at unfunny jokes, and agreed with the various views and politics. He never did have views of his own, this could probably explain why he'd survived so long. Peterbough was a follower. So long as he had a hole in his bottom, he would never be a leader. If by some miracle he did become a leader of any description, it would only be to lead in the path of following others.

Finally tired of the nauseating rhetoric spouted, he gave the nod to the deputy manager.

A phone call was made and within a few minutes Peterbough was having a private conversation, with him being told the details. It was all very efficiently run.

The manager's deputy was the 'pimp'. If you had already been with one of the prostitutes, then simply giving his or her name was enough. If you required some fresh meat, then, depending on your choice, male, female or both, an arrangement was made to escort these people through the back entrance of the Pelican hotel. Then they would be shown to the usual room, reserved for the sole purpose of these secret rendezvous, and hence sex sessions. The only thing you had to do was either accept them into the room or not. It was as easy and as simple as that. Nothing in writing, no photographs to pick and choose from, nothing incriminating, should it fall into the wrong hands. The members left it all up to the 'pimp'... even his phone calls were cryptic. If ever the phone was tapped, then it would appear as a perfectly innocent and decent phone call.

Peterbough had his chauffeur take him to the hotel.

The car pulled up outside the front steps where he was met immediately at the reception and shown to a room by a bell boy.

When they got to the room, Peterbough commented that it wasn't the usual room that he normally had and started to demand why.

As he did so, the bell boy, saying nothing, opened the door.

The room was a complete overdose of luxury.

"So, this is what Fairfax must have been arranging."

Peterbough thought to himself.

A four-poster bed was the centre piece of the room. It had purple satin sheets, with matching pillows and mirrors on the ceiling above. There were a pair of vulgar looking cupid statues either side. Beneath his feet was a sea of thick red shag pile carpet. The high ceiling had a crystal chandelier hanging from it. Peterbough shut up and walked into the room, the bell boy closing the door leaving him to admire this colourful, loud and gaudy harem.

There was a wide screen television in front of the bed. In the magazine rack, instead of newspapers and magazines, were what looked like girlie magazines. Peterbough picked up one of them and began to flick through its pages. Every conceivable sexual activity was covered, whether heterosexual, homosexual or bisexual, all to the delight and excitement of Peterbough.

He took off his coat and laid it on the bed, continuing to look at the pictures. Placing the magazine on the bed, he then played one of the many DVD's neatly stacked in their stands.

Peterbough lay on the bed watching one of these films when there was a knock at the door. He quickly turned the TV off and answered it. Standing before him was a young man of about eighteen or nineteen. He had dyed blonde hair, bright blue eyes, pale skin, a thin build and was very effeminate-looking.

"Come in my boy, come in," Peterbough said, grinning with his yellow nicotine-stained teeth.

He showed him to the bed and asked if he would like a drink.

"Whatever you're having Mr. Peterbough."

"Please, call me Tiger."

"OK …. Tiger…. whatever you're having."

Peterbough sat on the bed and turned the TV back on. He then asked questions about the boy.

How old he was ?

How long had he been a rent boy ?

What was his favourite kinky thing ?

He was extremely nervous and his nerves were getting the better of him. Asking for the TV to be turned down, he answered all of the questions loudly, clearly and by repeating the question. Peterbough, seeing that the young man was obviously nervous, stroked his hair, telling him not to be and that everything was going to be alright. Peterbough then started to undress in front of him, leaving his clothes to fall on the floor. His body was like that of his colleague Warlton. A blubbering mass. Peterbough was so obese that his belly hung so low, his genitals weren't visible. The young man took off his clothes. Then they got down to business.

When Peterbough was finished, he gave the young man two hundred pounds and told him that he would ask for him again next time. The young man took the money, said nothing and left the room. Fully satisfied, Peterbough left half an hour later after taking a shower. This was standard procedure, to avoid being seen leaving the room together by anyone, for obvious reasons.

Peterbough made his way out of the hotel to where his car was waiting. Once in his car, Peterbough told his Chauffeur to take him home. All through the journey, he just lay back thinking of the young man he'd just been with. It was almost as though he was in love. The car pulled up outside his house. He was greeted at the door by his ever-loving wife, Helen, who was blissfully unaware of her husband's 'other side.' She kissed him on the cheek and put her arm in his.

"I've given the maid the night off so that we can be together......alone."

His mind went into overdrive. Why was she being so affectionate ? It came to him in a flash, it was their wedding anniversary. He smiled,

"That's wonderful darling. Just you and me by the fireside. How lovely."

His deceitfulness was enough to make a person vomit. He was a bastard to the core. Walking into the lounge whilst his wife disappeared into the kitchen, he looked at the photograph of his twin son and daughter over the fireplace and sat down. His kids were the same age as the young man he had just been with. He thought of him again. His wife emerged from the kitchen with a couple of cocktail drinks in chilled glasses. She gave him his glass and sat on the floor at his feet. She raised her glass to him and wished him Happy Anniversary followed by a heartfelt 'I love you darling.' He merely repeated the same. They both sipped from their glasses and placed them on the table next to his chair. She began to take off his shoes and asked him how his day had been. He spieled lie after lie about the office that day and how it was the usual drink at the club to get to know new clients and to keep in with the existing ones.

Lies, lies, lies. There weren't any clients at the club, only his old school chums and acquaintances. With his wife sitting on the floor and leaning on his legs, she once again told him that she loved him. He got a rush, knowing that she didn't have a clue about his double life. The dark and sinister Mr. Hyde of his personality.

They both sat in front of the log fire. His wife aglow with the fact that they were together, alone. He just sat there and kept thinking of the young man. Staring into the fire, she told him that Charles had called.

Peterbough's eyes lit up and in an almost elated manner he asked,

"Oh yes, and what did he want?"

"I don't know, he wouldn't say."

"What do you mean he wouldn't say, he must have wanted something."

"No, he just asked where you were, and when I told him you weren't around he just assumed that you must have been at the club."

"Did he say anything more?"

"No, he just hung up."

Peterbough jumped up from the chair and went to the phone in the hallway, closing the lounge doors behind him. He dialled Moore's number, making sure that his wife hadn't followed him and that she couldn't listen in on the conversation. Like a small child always trying to impress the teacher at school, he told Moore about the new room and what a fantastic job Fairfax had done, keeping the secret about him and the young man a closely guarded one. He went on to tell him about the magazines and films when Moore interrupted.

"What the hell are you talking about William?"

"You know. The job that Fairfax was going to take care of himself. You told me that yourself the day before yesterday, in the corridor outside his office. Well, this must have been it."

"I called to see how your department was getting on."

Moore put the phone down. It didn't make sense. Either Fairfax was in deeper shock than he had at first thought or he had completely snapped. Moore couldn't help but think to himself that if William was correct, what the bloody hell was Fairfax doing sorting out the decoration of the Pelican when everything they had to gain was on the line?

Day Five -Monday

The next morning, Moore went to see Fairfax but he wasn't in his office. Asking Peterbough where he was, he told him that today was his father's funeral. Moore said nothing as was usual for him and walked back towards his office. He was like a robot, showing no emotion of joy, sorrow or anger. He was always calm, cool and collected. Not once had anyone ever seen him lose his temper. He was as cold as ice in thought, body and soul.

Rothchild was working in his office on how best he could manipulate the figures to increase his department's profit margins when Moore came in to ask how things were going. He quickly turned the computer off.

Startled, he looked up at Moore.

"How's it going Simon ?"

"Oh, fine, just fine. I was just finishing off actually."

Moore could see that for some reason he was nervous but dismissed it as Rothchild's apprehension at deliberately lying about the quarterly quotas.

"Well, remember, we not only have to portray the inflated figures in a believable form to the shareholders and general public, but once they have been announced, a week or so later, we then have to buff them up again announcing even greater profits."

"Yes, Charles, I fully understand, that's what I'm working on right now."

"Good, then don't let me stop you. Please carry on. There's going to be a meeting at the end of the week to see how things have developed in all departments."

"Right."

Moore left the office and Rothchild sat back into his chair relieved that he'd gone. Turning his computer back on, he then copied everything he'd been working on onto his memory stick.

Rothchild was not only cooking the books to give false information about his department's figures, he was also cooking the books for his own personal gain. He was personally taking care of his department's figures instead of letting the accounts department take care of it just as he had always done. This was the last chance he was going to have to greedily rake off millions for himself, something he believed he'd managed to do when Jack Deer was in charge. But Jack was no fool, and knew what Rothchild was up to. The very first time Rothchild tried it years previously, Jack secretly organized a small team of accountants to cross check every single figure....over and over and over again, all unbeknown to Rothchild. However, Jack strangely, always allowed a significantly smaller amount of money to be embezzled by Rothchild. But this wasn't so strange in the scheme of things. If Rothchild remained focused on his own account, Jack had him right where he wanted him – preoccupied and out of the way, rather than looking to try and embezzle money from other accounts. Plus Jack could backtrack and prove irregularities.

Rothchild was the definition of 'greed'. He would stop at nothing to increase his own bank balance. He would sink to all depths of secrecy and to the pits of hell, if he had to, to pull off such underhanded stunts. He would risk all to gain little, if it meant one more penny in his name, rather than the consortium's or Jack Deer's or anyone else's for that matter. He was pathetically helpless. The greed he had was like a rotting, festering cancer that couldn't be stopped. He had more than most men, already a millionaire, he could never have wanted for anything more ever in his life. However, the thought of more and more money drove him like a secretly possessed madman. For years he had cleverly hidden his kleptomania, never on the outside showing any signs of his unjust gains from his embezzlement. He was just plain *'good old Simon.'* His plan really was quite simple.

Rothchild being as familiar with computers as he was, had a direct link into the database of the accounts department. He had helped set it up in the first place. He helped set up the programme that ran it all. When all was proven to work correctly, he then initiated a system whereby through a password that only he knew, he could access the system and fiddle the figures. When auditing the accounts, he simply installed a system whereby any figures that came into the consortium as payments from different clients were rounded off. Before they were actually seen by the auditors he had any odd 'tail-end' amounts of money sent directly to his personal account. If a client sent in a payment of £257,267 he'd worked it so that the odd £267 pounds was directed to himself instead of rightfully going to the consortium. This rounded off all the figures evenly and made everything work out perfectly to the last penny. The programme would issue an acknowledgement letter for the amount they had correctly paid. He would sign it and post it onto them so that they never came back to enquire if the payment had gone through. A second letter was printed showing the adjusted figure and it was this that the auditors saw. Playing everything so close to his chest meant that no-one ever 'cottoned on'. And due to the fact that there was money coming into the consortium from all over the world and from so many clients, to discover what was really happening was near impossible. Rothchild was the only one with the password to the 'raking programme'.

Moore looked in on Sir Henry, the laziest of all the Board members, who let others do absolutely everything for him. He was the personification of sloth. The fact that he turned up at the office at all, could be considered a miracle. He usually slept in and only ever emerged from his pit to meet other Board members, his old school chums and associates at the Marlborough club. His attendance at the office might well have been considered as guest appearances.

Remaining in his chair, puffing on a Havana cigar, he addressed Charles.

"Ah, Charles and what can I do for you?"

Charles hadn't come into his office to make polite conversation. He came straight to the point, doubting whether Sir Henry had done anything at all.

"How are you coming along with your figures, Sir Henry?"

"They're ready, Charles. I've had Simon in to have a look at them and he's done a fantastic job in buffing them up. We've got no worries where my department's concerned, none whatsoever."

"Good. Then you'll be ready for the meeting at the end of the week will you?"

"Yes, we're all ready now."

"Right then, we're 'OK' with your figures, are we, Sir Henry?" Moore said, still doubting him.

"Yes, everything is hunky dory."

Moore just nodded and quietly left the office. Warlton remained seated in his chair, puffing on his cigar, so full of himself he could have burst.

The truth of the matter was that the figures were ready and that all was in order for the forthcoming meeting. The figures had been cooked by Rothchild and a portfolio had been created in readiness, by Warlton's staff. What Warlton, nor any of the others knew, was that Rothchild had cooked the books so well, he had once again been able to transfer funds from Warlton's department into his own personal account. Even if Warlton was to have known this, he wasn't going to bother himself because he was just too lazy to do anything about it. It wasn't his money and it wasn't his consortium, so why should he bother? Instead, he just took the easy way out, sitting back and letting others do everything for him, taking his obscene salary, bonuses and share dividend payouts.

Jack returned to the house later that afternoon. As he drove up the gravel driveway, he could see two sports cars at the house. It was John and Laura. Mary sprung to mind. On hearing the news, they had both boarded consortium cargo planes making their way back to London. Upon their arrival they had the consortium helicopter take them home. After seeing their mother they had both taken their cars for 'a spin.'

Jack hadn't wanted either of them to know what had happened with the business or that their mother had been taken ill. He knew this would only alarm them, disturb their mother and that he'd probably end up in a confrontation with John.

His two kids had had everything. They were both blessed with having high IQ's and coming from such a privileged background, their lives had had many doors opened for them, providing many opportunities. It really was 'sky's the limit' for anything they wished to pursue.

They had been to the best schools and had been taught all the things that Jack and Sammy had only dreamed. Both were fluent in French, Spanish and Arabic. Laura could also speak Russian. They could both play a number of musical instruments from the classical violin and piano to modern guitar and bass. John was a demon drummer too. They had both majored in business and commercial studies too.

Not surprisingly, they were 'au fait' with computer technology and communications, since they had grown up with it all as part of everyday life.

They could pilot light aircraft, navigate the family's yacht using traditional sextants rather than modern satellite equipment, although they could use these too.

They had the inheritance of their father's business to look forward to in later life and not a worry in the world. Most importantly of all, they had loving parents, who ensured they had had a stable and balanced upbringing. Unlike many other parents of the day, Jack and Sammy were never afraid to chastise them if there was call to. Even now, in a verbal rather than physical sense, they would still be corrected should they fall foul of the guidelines their parents had brought them up to respect. They had been looked after extremely well, yet surprisingly, due to their parents' background and the values that they were brought up to respect, they weren't spoilt brats.

John worked for the gardener during the summer holidays and when old enough, was taken to work at different building sites to have a better appreciation of what the consortium was all about.

Laura, too, was not exempt from hard work. She was taught and made to cook proper family meals at weekends and during the summer holidays. She was even made to clean and polish the house from top to bottom to help Mary out with her chores. When she was old enough, she was taken into the main offices and worked as a secretary for different managers in various departments of the company. This was followed by site office work.

They were both instilled with a true moral upbringing, with a sense of self-respect and respect for others. They were encouraged to constantly strive to better themselves, but at the same time, not to look down on those who were not as fortunate as themselves.

Everything they had, they had had to work for. There had never been such a thing as a blank cheque book for either of them. They were taught from a very early age that money didn't grow on trees. If they wanted anything they had to work for it and earn it themselves.

But for all this, both John and Laura were just like Jack, headstrong and stubborn. They arrogantly pursued their ideas if they believed themselves to be right. Neither were shrinking violets, they would stand their ground in any argument and never succumb to either browbeating or peer pressure. If anything, this made them more determined to win their argument....just like Jack.

Jack had done just about everything possible for his kids, but as a sacrifice to get where he was, he had never done anything with them. He had paid for all their private schooling and he had private tutors live at the house for languages and music. During so-called *fun time off* he had the captains of the private jet and yacht teach them their skills. But he himself was always too busy and preoccupied in keeping the business alive and successful. It was the business and its success that kept everything going. It kept everything alive. It meant wealth, power, the lifestyle, all simply accepted as the norm by John and Laura. They had never known any different.

Always working and striving for more and bigger contracts, Jack never really did anything with them, he only ever seemed to provide for them.

Now twenty-five and twenty-four, John and Laura were part of the business but not on the Board of Directors. Jack was only to allow this when they had both worked continually for a period of not less than ten years before being granted a place on the Board. As Jack saw it, they too, must show true loyalty before they were to be given such a prestigious position.

This had always been a bone of contention. Both John and Laura thought that they, more than anyone, deserved a place on the Board. But Jack had always remained adamant that the temptation to sell-out would be overwhelming for the two of them, if given this position too soon.

If they went on the Board at a stage in their lives when they themselves had contributed something into making the consortium even stronger, then they would be far less likely to sell-out for thirty pieces of silver. This was how Jack saw it. Why after all the hard years and sacrifices that he and Sammy had made should their kids be able to walk into a boardroom and announce that they were to sell-out and give it all up. So Jack had seen to it that they were to work from the ground floor up. They were never in contact with any of the senior executives, as he always knew that familiarity always bred contempt. His conviction was, that they too, would have to work their way up, and aspire to the ranks of the Board. Only then would Jack feel safe in the knowledge that everything would be in order, and that he could retire knowing that all was in very capable hands.

The van pulled up outside the house and Jack was cursing Mary under his breath as he just knew it must have been her who had told them. He was greeted on the steps by both of them.

"What are you two doing here ?" Jack said knowingly.

"Why didn't you tell us mum was ill ?" Laura said, in sheer disbelief that neither of them had been told of their mother's condition.

"Who told you ?"

"Mary."

"I thought as much."

"What exactly is going on dad ?" asked John.

"Look, it's a long story and I don't have time to go into it right now."

John, upset and totally put out by his father's attitude would not relent,

"What do you mean you don't have time ? Mother's lying up there in a bloody trance almost, and you don't have time. Its just like when we were younger, you've never had any bloody time."

Jack stopped and looked at the two of them. He said nothing and made his way into the hallway. He'd only taken two steps when John added,

"That's right !...Walking away again, always bloody walking away."

Jack was deeply hurt by what was just said but didn't answer back.

Laura made her way upstairs to be with her mother, followed closely by John.

After Jack had showered and changed, he made his way to the bedroom to see Sammy. As he entered, he could see both John and Laura sitting either side of her. She was sitting upright and holding their hands and smiled at Jack as he entered. Five days had passed and finally she was slowly but surely getting over the shock of losing it all.

"How are you feeling, love ?" said Jack.

"Oh, a lot better, now we're all together."

"You're going to be just fine, mum, just fine," said John to reassure her.

"Yes, we're all here to look after you. You're going to be up and about in no time," Laura added.

Jack walked over to Sammy and kissed her on the forehead. Sammy smiled at him and looking to both Laura and John asked,

"Do you both remember our trip to Disneyland ? That was the most fabulous holiday of my life. We saw all the wonders, Mickey Mouse, Donald Duck the Magic Palace and......"

Before Sammy could say any more, John erupted,

"Yes and dad left half way through the trip to come back home on business. Yes, I remember it alright."

Jack looked at him scornfully, but said nothing. For as much as he wanted to correct him, he knew a confrontation with him in front of Sammy would only upset her. Besides, it was true, he had left to go back to work. Something that neither John nor Laura had forgotten or forgiven him for.

Sammy put her head down. Laura told John to shut up. Mary came into the room with a cup of tea and something to eat for Sammy. Nobody said any more. The atmosphere was tense. As Mary sorted the bed table for Sammy, John and Laura stood up and said that they would see their mother later. Kissing her on the cheek, they made their way to the door. Jack winked at Sammy, following them, leaving her in peace to eat her meal and to have Mary as company.

Outside, John started at his father again. This was the confrontation Jack had been waiting for. There was always one when they were together. Somehow they always seemed to get their reunions off to a bad start, their characters were too alike in every way.

Jack gripped hold of John's shirt. Face to face, Jack, gritted his teeth and whispered,

"Shut your big bloody mouth. Can't you see your mother's not well. What the hell are you trying to do, make her worse ?"

John's face dropped. He knew he'd overstepped the mark this time. He stood wide-eyed, looking straight into his fathers' eyes. He knew then that things were more serious than he or Laura had wished to believe.

Knowing that he had no choice but to tell them what was going on, Jack asked them both downstairs so that he could explain.

"Come with me, both of you. I'll put you in the picture."

Without any hesitation or further ado, they both quietly followed their father downstairs and into the lounge. They sat either end of the sofa. Jack asked if they'd had anything to eat. The answer was, 'No' but neither of them was hungry anyway.

"How can you think about food at a time like this ?" Laura asked. Jack said he had a lot to tell, an awful lot. He closed the lounge doors, sat down in the armchair, and began to tell them all that had happened. How the Board had connived against him and how it was, that they were to finally take away his empire at the end of the month, only eleven days away. How they had made it impossible for him to ever contest it because they'd seen to it that through falsified documents and accounts, he could never prove either his innocence or his honourable reputation.

They sat in total disbelief and bewilderment as to how this could have happened. Jack continued to tell them the facts. Jack was only telling them as much as he wanted them to know. He omitted plenty from the tale such as ....How exactly he planned to turn things around. And that he had someone on the inside helping him. And he and his insider had hatched their plan in advance of the Board's takeover, only three days before the Board decided to make it's move.

When he was through, Laura asked,

"So what are you going to do ?"

"How are you going to get it all back ?"

"Can you still get it all back ?"

John sat there thinking. He was the image of Sammy. Especially now he was in deep thought. Jack looked at him. After a few seconds, John asked if he was going to nail them for what they'd done.

Jack smiled, he knew that his son was thinking along the same lines as he. He looked to Laura and back to John,

"The answer to all your questions is, 'yes', I am already doing something about it and 'yes', I can and will get it all back."

He paused for a moment and looked at them both. Remembering when they were little and how he'd done everything he could for them except to be there with them. He had a small lump in his throat. It was obvious that John and Laura were never going to stand aside and let him tackle this problem alone. Jack knew he would have to involve them in some way, otherwise they would ruin the plan. For the first time ever in his life, he was going to call on the help of his kids, whom he knew would do everything they could, not for the consortium or their own best interests, but for him, their Father. Clearing his throat he looked at them both and said,

"I can only get it all back with your help."

"We're here to help dad, whatever happens," Laura said in support of her father.

"We may have our differences dad, but as a family, we'll fight them." John said flaring his nostrils.

It sent shivers down Jack's spine. Finally he was to do something with them, instead of for them.

Mary knocked on the door to tell them that their dinner was ready in the dining room.

"Thanks, Mary," they all said, as they made their way out of the lounge and into the dining room. John, stopping in mid flow, asked about Joseph.

"Oh, don't worry about him. He'll get his just desserts for what he's done and what he's now helping the others to do. I personally will see to it, and take great satisfaction in doing it."

Joseph had been his friend for over twenty years. He had helped Jack get into the circles of big business makers. Jack owed a great deal to him. A chance meeting had brought them together, when the finer details of a joint venture building project were being thrashed out. Jack was impressed with Joseph, and so invited him to join his company, promising great prospects if he did. Joseph thought it over for a few days and joined him. Through his connections, he introduced Jack to more and more business contacts. He had helped Jack get an incredible amount of work over the years. He had always been faithful and always advised Jack about whom he should trust and whom not to. Even members of the Board had sometimes been chosen on the judgement of Joseph.

Joseph had been richly rewarded. Amongst many things, Jack had a house built for him as a heartfelt 'thank you' for his solid loyalty through the years. He was made Jack's right-hand man. Now it seemed as though he must have been the key factor in helping Charles Moore turn against him. He was now Moore's right-hand man.

The three of them entered the dining room, and sat themselves down at the table. Each place was laid out with the best silverware on a fine oriental lace cloth, with the best crockery money could buy. This was the norm to both John and Laura, but Jack appreciated it all more than anyone. Looking to the doors and pointing to them with his knife he said to them both,

"It's alright now, she's gone."

"You seem apprehensive of Mary all of a sudden, dad. It's as though you're suspicious of her," Laura said holding back.

"Look, it's taken me nearly thirty years to get where I am today and in the space of two weeks I'm to have it all taken away from me. I can't afford to trust anyone. The less she knows the better. I specifically told her not to tell you about your mum so as not to panic you and what did she do ?......Tell you. It's not that I don't think she can be trusted, it's just that I think the less she knows the better or anyone else for that matter. This is not the sort of subject for village gossip. The only people I have to trust are my own and that's you and John. I've been foolish enough to let things get to where they are and that's been through being too trusting. With the help of you two and only you two, I have a chance of getting it all back. But should either of you let me down in anyway, then we stand to lose it all.....'*if we haven't already*'. We can't, in anyway, discuss anything outside of this room with anyone. There must only be ourselves in on this."

"What about mum ?" said Laura in anticipation.

Jack snapped back at her,

"She, most of all, is not to know what's going on. I thought that she was going to be strong, but look what thought did."

He couldn't help thinking that her shock had come from what he had told her. Laura, saddened by her father's feelings about the whole thing, put out her hand to his and held it gently.

"Don't worry dad, we'll help you the best we can and we'll follow your instructions to the letter. You can trust us, we won't let you down, we promise."

"Yeah, you can count on us, dad, we promise." John said backing up his sister.

Now that they were fully aware of what had happened, Jack told them that in the morning he would go over the details of how exactly he planned to regain control of the consortium.

They all smiled at one another and continued with their dinner.

When they had finished Jack suggested a good night's rest, as they had a lot to do in the next fortnight.

Chapter Four

Day Six - Tuesday

In the morning Jack, as always, was first up. He made his way downstairs to the kitchen and started to make John and Laura a full English breakfast. He wasn't on his own for long. John and Laura joined him within five minutes. Just like their mother, they both took their coffee black with no sugar.

They were both greeted with a 'Good Morning' by Jack.

John, with his long blond hair, looking as though it had been caught in a whirlwind and with his dressing gown hanging over his shoulders with the cord belt not tied, looking as though he'd been dragged through a hedge backwards stared at his father,

"What's so good about it?"

Jack just smiled and turned to continue attending to the fry-up, glancing at the bread in the toaster.

Laura's immediate thought was of her mother,

"How's mum this morning, dad?"

"Oh, she's a lot better than she was a couple of......here she is now."

Sammy came into the kitchen not looking much better than John. In a tired and dreary voice, she greeted everyone 'Good Morning'.

"How are you feeling, mum?" Laura said softly.

"A lot better than I was, thank you love."

John looked at his father who was looking back at him. He quickly shook his head as a sign for him not to speak of what they had discussed the previous evening. The toast popped out of the toaster. A convenient distraction for Jack, who snatched all four rounds and started buttering. Laura hugged her mother as she sat down. Polite conversation was made and the subject of the business was not brought up by any of them, no-one daring to speak for fear of upsetting the other.

There was a turning of keys in the lock to the back entrance of the kitchen. It was the ritual of Mary turning up for work. At the same time, at the same place, Monday to Saturday, week in, week out. It was more than just routine to Mary, it was more that just habit, it really was a ritual.

"Mrs. Deer, what are you doing up? You shouldn't be out of bed surely. Don't want you overdoing it now."

Mary said, astonished that Sammy was out of her bed considering that the doctor hadn't yet called.

"Oh, it's alright Mary, I feel fine."

Mary, stood with her back rod-straight, both hands on her hips, and with her lips puckered as she looked doubtingly at her.

"Honestly Mary, I feel fine."

Still, Mary kept her stance.

"Please, Mary, I'm OK honestly. Now please stop worrying, I'm O.K."

"Well, if you say so madam, but if I catch you doing anything too strenuous, you'll have me to answer to, do you hear?"

Everyone just smiled. An unknowing air had been lifted from the kitchen.

Mary really was a caring and devoted member of the family. She looked on them all as being helpless without her. In her mind this was her second family and she not only had a deep sense of fondness and loyalty to them all, but she loved each and everyone of them in her own special way. *"God' have pity on anyone who hurt them in any way."*

"Here, let me do that Mr. Deer," she said, trying to take the pan from Jack.

"No, it's quite alright Mary, I can manage."

She knew that they all wanted to be together and so hung her coat up and went off to do her chores, whilst everyone sat to eat their breakfast, all still making polite conversation.

Once finished, Sammy said that she was going to take a shower and get dressed. Everyone else just stayed perched around the table and said OK. When she had gone, the real serious business of Jack's plan was revealed and discussed.

Jack told them that the only way to foil the Board, was to have both John and Laura at the very heart of the plot, among the Board members, to get into the main office and not just work in there but to work for them. This way they would get to find out their every move.

"How can we do that?" asked Laura puzzled.

"Well, the first thing that we have in our favour is the fact that neither of you are known by the Board members."

"Wrong!...What about Joseph?... He knows us very well, he's been like an Uncle to us. The minute he saw us in the offices he'd smell a rat and the game would be up before we'd even started."

John was intent on looking for every conceivable pit fall.

"Yes, I know, but he won't be there."

"Why?"

"He left to go on business to Chicago for the week. In fact, he should be arriving there around about now."

"How do you know?" asked Laura.

"I've an informer telling me what's going on but I can't tell you who it is just yet."

"Oh that's just great! We're here to help and you don't trust us. How are we supposed to...."

"John, please! I can't tell you everything just yet, you'll just have to trust me. I know what I'm doing and exactly how it's to be done."

Laura told John not to be so impatient. He nodded in agreement and apologised to Jack.

"It has to be my way or I know we just won't pull it off, O.K."

They both agreed and Jack continued.

"When I found out about this....'mutiny' I was told that there were to be new staff recruited into the consortium. These would be junior executives who would replace the existing ones."

Laura and John both sat there frowning trying to make sense of what their father was telling them. Both were trying to fathom out the story before Jack had a chance to tell it to them.

"Once the Board takeover moves into operation, the new executives would all be in favour of the dismemberment of the consortium because they would have more to benefit from it."

"How exactly ?" said Laura still frowning.

"Well, being part of the system as it is now, the existing people are going to expect to still keep all the benefits that they have at the moment such as their company cars, mortgages taken care of by the company, holiday flights paid for and so on. But when the Board members takeover, these benefits will cease to exist. This is going to be one of the first things announced."

"They won't stand for that," said Laura vehemently.

"Yes, I know that and so they'll kick up a fuss. Half of them resigning, moving onto firms that will come somewhere near the benefits that they have all been used to."

"But won't that be a bad light on the consortium and so give bad publicity ?" John asked inquisitively.

"No, on the contrary. The bastards will turn this all around and call it 'streamlining'. If investors see this then they will put their money into the consortium hand over fist. The fewer outgoings in the form of expensive overheads, the greater the profit margins, the more they would get in returns. Think about it, if you were an investor and your money went on their perks you wouldn't be happy about it, would you?"

"So why did you give them in the first place if that's the case?"

"Because of their loyalty. They were devoted to serving the company. It was only right that they be rewarded in some way and as you both know it was tiny in the scheme of things."

John and Laura both knew he was right and so became quiet. This was their father speaking, but more than that, it was a man of conviction. In awe of the sense he made they sat and listened. Now truly convinced in their minds that whatever their father said, they would follow his instructions to the letter.

"The Board's plan is really quite simple. All they have to do, a week or so later, is announce the dissection of the consortium. The investor, since this will only boost his dividend returns, will pour even more money into the deal. Those bastards will then appoint themselves head of their own little empires and be made for life. But the stumbling block will be time working against them. They will have to pull off the stunt before a government investigation could be put into operation."

"Why would the government have anything to do with it?" asked Laura.

"Because whenever anything of this size is dismembered, there always is. Don't forget, we've done a phenomenal amount of business with not only our government but many others too. Our government has sanctioned investment into the consortium as being sound, on the basis of it's set-up and the way in which it was run. Now suddenly, in the space of only a couple of weeks, profits will be made to look as though they have soared, soared again and then all of a sudden, they take a knife to it and carve it up. You only ever do that if divisions are making a loss. The government would certainly be involved and to dodge this, they would have to move quickly to avoid being exposed."

Laura shook her head from side to side,

"I still don't understand how could they avoid this exactly." "Well, they'll certainly need the help of the junior executives, to do all the donkey work for them," said Jack.

"But you said that they're to be shit on, too. How could they help ? They quite rightly would have left. You just told us that two minutes ago."

"Yes, I know, but what you've missed, is the fact that the 'new' helping executives are to work alongside the existing ones whilst everything is as it is. This way, they get to find out how the system all works, so that when the existing juniors get stabbed in the back, its of no consequence. It's all part of the plan, because they'll have an immediate replacement work force that comes in and takes over before the existing ones have had a chance to protest, hand in their resignations, or they've even had a chance to leave the building."

"What a bunch of bastards," John said with disdain in his voice. The expression on his face was a carbon copy of what Jack's would have looked like twenty years previously. Then the penny dropped. He raised his eyebrows and with a wry smile on his face looked at Jack,

"I get it now, what you plan to do, is have us as two of those executives."

Laura was delighted at the prospect of personally being involved in sabotaging the takeover plan.

"Exactly," said Jack with a knowing nod.

"Brilliant. But how will we do it ? I still don't see how that can be made possible. It's not as though we can just walk in there unannounced and declare that we are two new executives to work for the company."

John, yet again the ever *'Doubting Thomas'* was searching for loopholes in the plan.

"Simple !...You know I've an informer on the inside ?"

"Yes."

"Well, he has arranged that you should work for two members of the Board directly."

"How could he? We only arrived yesterday and not even you had knowledge of us coming here. In fact, it was only last night we knew of all this and we agreed to help you. Furthermore, we weren't even part of your plans until last night, so how can anyone have known?"

"When you went to bed last night I made a phone call and informed my little helper about the two of you. It was decided there and then about your recommendation and so you'll be starting tomorrow."

"Bloody hell, dad, you didn't waste any time did you?"

"No son, I didn't, I can't afford to. Time is the one thing even I can't buy and its working against me."

"I don't believe it, so we can just start work with the company and remain incognito, disguised as somebody we're not. Fantastic."

"But what about Joseph? If he should come back for any reason..." John threw another obstacle in the way.

"Well, if that's the case, you'll both have to get out of there pretty sharpish. I couldn't bear to see the whole thing fail, now that I feel confident I can stop the Board from taking over."

Laura asked exactly what it was that they would be required to do and in what capacity. Jack told them that they would more than likely be involved in refining the final announcement of the Board's plan to the public and media on his resignation. And that they would probably be checking and rechecking the figures of the company's inflated profit margins before any announcements were made. He also told them who they would be assigned to, John to Lord Andrew Barron and Laura to Lord Arthur Cavendish. He told them that he would fill them in on all the details once they'd had a chance to shower, change and freshen up.

Mary was in the hallway and seeing them come out of the kitchen, she automatically stopped polishing and went into the kitchen to wash, dry and put away the dishes. Her sense of tidiness was almost obsessive. Tel in the meantime had arrived to wash and polish the cars and to be on standby, should Jack wish to go anywhere.

The doorbell rang as Sammy was making her way downstairs. She answered the door to the doctor who had come to check-up on her. Surprised to see her up and about, he asked if she was feeling better. She answered him and then invited him in for a cup of tea. He accepted her invitation and told her that he just wanted to make sure that she really was fit and getting over her shock. Sammy asked Mary to do the honours whilst she and the doctor chatted for a while and he made a quick and brief examination. He gave her a clean bill of health, warning that she should still take things easy for a little while.

Mary came in with tea and biscuits for the doctor and a cup of coffee for Sammy. He advised Sammy that a change of scenery wouldn't be a bad thing because she had been cooped up in the house. When she started to dismiss the idea, saying that she just wanted to be with her family, Mary butted in, saying that the doctor was right and that it would be a good thing. Just as she was in the middle of giving her unasked for opinion, Jack walked into the room.

"Hi doc, come to check on her ?"

The doctor replied and then they both started to talk about Sammy as though she wasn't there when Mary poked her nose in again.

"Yes, and he thinks it's a good idea if she were to get away for a while and quite frankly Mr. Deer, so do I. She's been cooped up in this house for....."

"Yes, thank you, Mary...." Jack said authoritatively. He wanted to hear what the doctor had to say.

When the doctor confirmed this to be the case, Sammy told everyone to stop talking as though she wasn't there. Mary was asked to leave and the three of them decided that it wouldn't be such a bad idea after all. The doctor asked if she had close friends or relatives she could stay with, saying that a change of surroundings would be far better than any medicine he could administer. Jack suggested she should visit her parents, as a healthy change of environment, and stay with them for a week or so. She agreed, but only on the condition that Jack promised he wouldn't send the kids off around the world on business ventures. Sammy explained that it was they who had made her come to her senses. The doctor looked inquisitive. It was obvious he was waiting to be told the reason she had gone into shock. Jack could see this, but it had nothing to do with the doctor and so promptly gave his word to Sammy. The doctor finished his cup of tea, thanked them both and said he must be off. He was shown to the door. No sooner was the front door closed, than Sammy asked about the business.

Jack, ignoring her questioning took her arm,

"Come on, we'll get you ready. Mary, will help you pack."

Refusing to be palmed off, Sammy insisted that he answer her.

"Look, love, I have a chance of saving the business and that's what I'm working on at the moment but I won't have time to do anything if you refuse to go to your parents and end up moping around here. If you go to your parents, it's one less thing I have to worry about and I know that it's for the best. Even the doctor says so, after all, he suggested it."

Jack had convinced her that she was doing the right thing and Mary was called to help her pack. On the way up the stairs, they met John and Laura coming down.

"I'm off to your Gran's for a week, for a change of scenery. The two of you can come with me if you like."

Jack was standing at the bottom of the stairs tapping his foot impatiently. They declined the offer saying that they needed time to rest and settle in after their journeys, but that they would both see her in a week or so. Sammy just nodded her head in disappointment that neither of them were to join her and so continued on her way to her room.

Jack walked back into the lounge to call Tel on the intercom system to ensure that the car would be ready to take Sammy to her parents. John and Laura got to the bottom of the stairs feeling really bad about themselves. They wanted to be with their mum but under the circumstances knew they had to help their dad.

Jack, seeing they were all fresh and spruced up, called them into the lounge to talk.

"Right, first things first. First appearances always count. John, you're going to have to get your hair cut, get your beard trimmed and wear a charcoal grey three-piece suit."

"Oh, come on, dad! I haven't cut my hair since sixth form and I don't even wear trousers, let alone a suit. Besides I don't have one."

Jack wasn't in the mood to debate the subject. Glaring at him, he repeated himself in a low and quiet voice. He only ever did this when he was mad. John backed down in agreement. Laura began to smirk but not snigger, she never had the chance. She too was given instruction,

"Laura, you're going to dye your hair red, wear bright red lipstick and wear all the sexy regalia you can buy."

"What and look like a tart?"

"Yes, and look like a tart....so long as you don't act like one, then the plan should come off."

The smirk on her face turned into a despondent look of insult. They both asked why it had to be this way and why they just couldn't be themselves. Starting with John, Jack went on to explain.

"It's the old school tie network we're dealing with here. If you walked into the office with your hair down to your knees, covering up the holes in your jeans, questions would be asked about where the bloody hell you had come from. It's only going to take one smart arse to do some investigating and you're going to be revealed for who you really are. Whereas if you go in, dressed and looking like 'them', in a suit and with a short and clean-looking hair cut, then they won't think anything of you. You'll be as they are, and blend in perfectly with them."

Jack looked John up and down and spoke from his own personal feelings.

"In other words, you won't look like a hippie from the sixties but an executive of the nineties."

He looked to Laura, who felt insulted that she now had to parade around as though she were a red headed hooker.

"You have to dye your hair because Cavendish has a fetish about red heads. He also can't resist women in sexy gear and loves to ogle it. So it's a high split skirt, stockings and suspenders, wonder bra.....pointy out pieces at the front as though your nipples are..."

"Ok, Ok, I get the picture," snapped Laura. She looked to the ground shaking her head from side to side as she continued,

"This is so sexist, it's beyond. How do you know all this anyway dad ?"

"I make it my business to know. If you call him 'My Lord' you'll be in straight away. With your red hair and suspenders showing, he'll be drooling all over you within the first minute of meeting you. Act classy, as though you're a tease, he likes that sort of thing. The fact is, that you'll be a challenge for him to try and get in your knickers."

"Dad !....I don't believe this, it's so chauvinistic. It goes completely against the law of sexual harassment."

"Maybe so, but this is the real world. This is what has always gone on, does go on, and will always go on, whether you like it or not. That's life, and so long as there's a pretty girl around, there will always be a Cavendish to take full advantage."

"Just so long as I don't have to sleep with him."

"Never. Cavendish will come onto you heavy….real heavy. If he comes onto you too heavily, and you feel as though you're not in control, just walk away. I don't want you to do anything like that on my behalf…….ever. Do you understand?"

"Yes, dad, I understand."

"Good, then I think the two of you had better prepare for tomorrow."

Jack told John where to get his hair cut. He also told him where he could buy a good quality, ready-made suit. It was to be bought from one of the tailors the other juniors went to but must not be tailor-made. This way he would look authentic, as a junior executive, looking smart but not yet in the big league able to afford tailor-made suits costing a mint.

He advised Laura the opposite. To go into town to buy the most modern and fashionable lingerie at the top stores. Jack specified stockings, suspenders and a high, uplifting bra. He told her that when she'd bought these, only then was she to purchase her pastel coloured suit. When trying it on he wanted her to ensure that when she walked in it her breasts looked proud and when she sat her suspenders showed. She was to have her hair done at the best salon she could find, apart from the one at the Pelican, to ensure she wasn't noticed. Her good looks were hard not to notice to begin with, without one of the Board members who might just be in the hotel noticing her if she were to walk in. He also told them that they must appear as though they had money, but that they didn't smell of it. The sports cars would have to be exchanged for more suitable and fitting ones. A small car for her and a year old production saloon car for him. Jack was again doing everything, moulding them into exactly what they were to be, down to the smallest detail.

Jack said that they had better go and say goodbye to their mother but not to tell her what they were up to. They both said that they were fully aware of the situation and that they too didn't want their mother to start worrying about anything and that they wouldn't *'let the cat out of the bag'*. Jack nodded his head and so both Laura and John followed him upstairs to the bedroom. They could hear both Sammy and Mary laughing. Sammy really was making a recovery, Jack thought to himself. As Jack entered the room, both became quiet as they looked at him with smiles they found impossible to mask. They looked at one another, sniggering and then they burst out laughing. It was obvious that Jack was the brunt of their humour.

"What's so funny?" Jack asked with a smile on his face.

"Oh, nothing." Sammy said, still sniggering.

Both Laura and John started to laugh as they were shown a picture by Mary.

"Here, let me see that."

It was a photograph of Jack from 1972. With long hair, bell bottom trousers and platform shoes. Even Jack began to laugh. The atmosphere was a happy one and the best way in which Sammy could have been sent off. All packed, Jack and John carried the bags downstairs to the car that was waiting at the steps. They all said their goodbyes, hugging and kissing Sammy as they did so. Tel then drove off down the drive. Jack called Laura and John back into the lounge to go over what it was they had to do that afternoon.

Once Jack was satisfied that they both knew exactly what was expected of them, he walked with them as they made their way out of the front door to where their cars were parked. Annoyed, he called them back,

"What was the first thing I told you?"

"It's OK, dad, John's going to take me to the local second hand car garage in his car. Then we'll drive back here. Me in my 'new' car and John in his. Then I'll give him a lift back to the garage and he'll pick-up his 'new' car.....'simple.' We're going to buy ourselves the cars you told us to. Don't worry, we know exactly what to do, we know to follow your instructions to the letter."

Jack just smiled. He knew that they weren't dumb and that they wouldn't let him down.

Knowing all was in safe and good hands, Jack smiled at them, wished them good luck and closed the door. He then made his way to the kitchen, poured himself a glass of milk and walked out of the back entrance and into his workshop.

Here he started to prepare documents as a strategy for them both to work to. Sitting at his drawing board, he mapped out a plan of operation onto paper. He already had the plan in his head, it was just a matter of doing this for John and Laura. This was his way of making sure everything was going to be crystal clear and unambiguous. Once the plan was completed and neatly drawn up, he went to a filing cabinet that was situated in the corner of the room. He unlocked it and opened the top drawer. He then lightly fingered through some files arranged in alphabetical order, which filled the cabinet drawer from front to back. There were files on every single member of the Board, past and present. He lifted the first two folders out of the drawer. Each had the surname of a Board member on the side of it with a photograph stapled on the front. Barron, Lord Andrew and Cavendish, Lord Arthur.

As he pulled them out of the drawer the face of Fairfax's photograph stared at him. Jack looked at the folders in his hand, curled his lip and said "Bastards" aloud to himself. Then he slammed the drawer closed and walked back to his drawing board. Slapping them down on the surface, he said aloud,

"Right, Cavendish, let's start with you."

Flicking open the front cover of the dossier, there was a full-size picture of Cavendish, eight inches by eleven. A ginger-haired man, with red rosy cheeks. His nose was bluey purple in colour with thin red veins running all over it. It was, bulbous and pitted. It was grotesque. All due to a lifetime of heavy drinking. To top it all, he had a horrible looking wart on the left-hand side of it. His eyes were a dull blue, the whites of them, a tainted yellow. He had a smile that emphasised his slightly goofy, protruding front teeth. He was not photogenic by any means.

All the details about him were there. Birth certificate, schools he attended, firms he'd been associated with and so on. There were many things in the folder about Cavendish but the most intriguing was the birth certificate. It showed all the details that you would expect, date, birth place, and so on. However in the space for the father's name was the name 'Lord James Barron.'

His dark and shameful secret was that he was an illegitimate son of the gentry and the half brother of Lord Andrew Barron.

Cavendish's biological father, Lord James Barron had fallen in love with his mother, but she was married to Lord Frederick Cavendish through an arranged marriage. They had an affair. Cavendish was the result, and he had been keeping it a secret. Coming from the background he did (and with a bestowed title of 'Lord,') for this to ever get out in the open, would destroy him. Even in this day and age, when nobody really seems to care or would be bothered about such a thing, to the hierarchy of the system such as he was a part, it would mean total ruin. If people were to discover that he was the misbegotten son, 'a love child' of the elite, then he would be stripped of his title and shunned by high society. He would no longer be part of the elite, 'the set', he would be out in the cold with nowhere to go and nowhere to hide. It was a dark and menacing secret he carried with him.

Lord Frederick Cavendish, who had raised him, didn't even know that he wasn't Arthur's true biological father. In fact, nor did Arthur himself, until he was twenty years of age. Discovering his secret when innocently rummaging in the family attic for nostalgic photographs and the like, he stumbled on his birth certificate. Understanding what it all meant should it ever get out, he turned to drink,......now, a hopeless alcoholic.

Barron was an only child and so was Cavendish. Cavendish was younger than his half brother by one year. This meant under the new inheritance laws, Barron being the elder, would have claim to the title and legacy that had been left to Cavendish by his 'adopting' father, Lord Frederick Cavendish.

It was a stupid law, an unjust and cruel law, but it was the law.

Whether Cavendish liked it or not, Barron was the rightful heir to all his inherited fortune.

If this skeleton was ever taken out of the closet and aired, it wouldn't just take away the foundation stone and pedestal that Cavendish had put himself on, but it would cause such a scandal that it would raze him to the ground. He would not only become bankrupt, he would be ruined and never be able to make anything of the fragments. He would also be banished by all, into oblivion.

Jack had got his hands on the birth certificate and other documents on the other Board members through his confidant. It was always a case of ask no questions and you'll be told no lies.

Cavendish had fallen into another one of his drunken stupors and was near collapse, when he was offered a lift home by a 'friend' at the party. Cavendish's driver was off sick and Jack had let Tel go home because he knew that the party would probably go on to the early hours of the morning.

Once home, the friend tried helping him up to his bed. Singing and stumbling all over the place, Cavendish refused to co-operate unless they had one last drink together, the infamous 'one for the road.' It was an impossible situation. His inhibitions gone, Cavendish started to talk about himself and unlocked his birth certificate from his bureau and started waving it around. He was ranting at how unfair the law was, how Barron didn't know and how it was going to remain a secret to his grave! The whole scene was pathetic and laughable. But no-one was laughing. Cavendish's companion said that he didn't care and asked who gives a toss anyway? Cavendish, out of breath, told him he was a good man.

He was helped to his room, where he collapsed onto his bed and fell into a deep sleep. He was then undressed and rolled over on his side to ensure that if he was sick, he didn't choke on his own vomit. Cavendish's friend then went back down stairs to Cavendish's study cum office.

He looked for the copying machine and turned it on. Grabbing hold of Cavendish's birth certificate, he made a copy. He put the birth certificate back in the bureau and left the office exactly as he found it and rejoined the party. No-one was any the wiser as to what information he had just netted and, if he could help it, nor would they.

When Jack spoke to Cavendish the next morning, he didn't remember anything, least of all being taken home.

The 'friend' gave the copy of the birth certificate to Jack's confidant who had it verified by Somerset House. He then handed it to Jack. Jack knew nothing about what had happened nor what he was being given. When he started to object, his confidant assured him he may well need it in the future. With reluctance, Jack locked it away for safe keeping in his workshop.

Jack, busy making notes on all these facts, despised himself for what he was doing. As he sat back from the table to take a break from writing, he gazed at the tools adorning the walls of the work shed. He couldn't help but think of all the blood, sweat and tears that he had endured to make the consortium what it was. He had physically and mentally busted his guts to get where he was. 'They', he thought, have been handed everything on a silver platter. His thoughts began to turn to anger as he thought how they had turned against him and how they had connived to steal away his empire and fortune. Squinting his eyes and shaking his head, he calmed himself down. He knew that he had to play the game by their rules. Only by being cool, calm and collected was he to beat them all, otherwise he knew that he would fail in his efforts. He said to himself that if they wanted to play dirty, they could play with filth from their own back yards. They would be given so much filth from their own pasts, that they would be like hippos marooned in a mud pit. Still this all went against his nature but he had to think and act with his 'business survival head' and not his heart.

Jack, then leant forward and flicked open the folder on Lord Andrew Barron. His photo also adorned the front inside cover. A blond-haired man with blue eyes, light complexion and goatee beard. He looked in appearance as though he were typically Victorian. In contrast to Cavendish, he looked quite handsome. He had kept well with age. Not being a heavy drinker like Cavendish went a long way. All of his details were here in this dossier.

Just as with Cavendish, it had all the information relating to his history. The schools he went to and how he performed, what firms he had worked for and what he had done for them and in what capacity. Everything seemed normal until his personal life was scrutinised.

He had developed violent tempers which were a bad progression on tantrums he threw as a child. His parents and teachers were unable to correct them. He was sent to be analyzed secretly by psychologists and psychiatrists. They advised that he should undergo regular consultations at all stages of his childhood and if necessary into adult life, for anger management. The exercise was in the hope that he could vent his anger verbally, to relieve himself of the way he thought towards people who had either upset or annoyed him in any way.

But Barron had a dark and sinister side.

He had been married and divorced three times. Although now single, he was always to be found in the company of call girls. There was nothing new in this. But Jack wasn't going to use this against Barron, as he had something far more damning instead.

He had documents relating to Barron's third and last wife, Lady Jane Mortimore. Their marriage had been one of the usual and seemingly blissful types, with roses on the outside and the warmth of a well-to-do family man on the inside. This was not the case. In fact, it was so far from the truth, it made it all look like a pantomime. The real marriage turned out to be a Punch and Judy show.

At a ball held by the Earl of Dewsbury, Barron got drunk and started to get abusive. He was asked to leave and then became violent. A fight started and Barron was ushered into his car with his wife. When they got home, Lady Jane continued giving him grief about the whole thing. Barron's temper erupted and he began battering her.

In a scramble, she had managed to lock herself into one of the bathrooms. Barron tired himself out by trying to knock the door down and worn out with booze, collapsed on his bed to sleep it all off. In the meantime, Lady Jane had waited until the coast was clear, crept downstairs and called for the police.

The next morning Barron found himself waking up in a police cell with charges of G.B.H. brought against him. The evidence against him was overwhelming. Statements by guests at the party, his chauffeur and his wife all corroborating. Her statement could be read from the state her face was in. It told the whole story. She had two black eyes, a broken nose, fractured cheekbone, split lip and torn ear. She also had bruised arms, legs and ribs from the assault. She was black and blue all over.

Jack had in his possession a full-size police photograph of Lady Jane and the injuries that she had sustained from the attack. He also had copies of all the statements given by all witnesses who had seen them together that night.

Lady Jane never pressed the charges though. An out of court settlement was made between his family and hers. It gave her half of all the fortunes his family held at the time and the rights to have half of all his future income until such time as she should marry again, in which case it would be reduced to a quarter. Barron also ensured a quick divorce that only took two months to be drawn up and finalised. It was a hefty price to pay, but it avoided a public scandal and total ruin. This way he would be able to keep something of what his forefathers had amassed, his title and his 'respectability'. The divorce papers all legally signed up and the documents appertaining to their divorce agreement were witnessed and placed in the hands of solicitors and the charges of assault were quickly dropped. Only a handful of people were actually aware of the full details of what had happened and Jack was one of them.

Jack knew all the people of influence....And so did his confidant. It was his confidant who passed him Barron's record...police record. It was all there. How Barron had also beaten and battered his two previous wives in the same way. Charges were never brought against him then either, due to pay-offs and so saving public scandal. That was the name of the game.

Jack had no intention of releasing any of these files to the general public or media. However, if pushed, he would consider it an option.

Jack had something on everyone.

Just as in the case of the cleaner woman in Hong Kong and the Indian workers, it needed to be repeated to those who just dismissed him that,

"Jack made it his personal business to find out everything possible about people he came into contact with, or in whomever he took an interest. No matter who, or what they were, he made it his job to get to know everything about them".........but it was his confidant who supplied the dark stuff.

Jack looked at his watch, it was five thirty. He knew that both John and Laura would be coming in from their shopping trips and so he put everything back as he had found it. Locking the filling cabinet door, he patted it and again, speaking aloud to himself said,

"Well boys, your pasts are about to catch up with you."

He returned to the house with only his notes and photos of both Barron and Cavendish. He placed the information he had, on top of a cabinet in the kitchen, *'out of sight, out of mind'* just in case Mary should walk in. As he pulled his arm away from the top of the cabinet, she did just that.

"Will Laura and John be coming back to the house, Mr. Deer ?"

"Yes, they should be home within the next hour or so."

"Right, then, I'll put their tea on for them."

"Thanks, Mary, but if you wouldn't mind, I'd like to do it myself as a surprise for them."

"OK, but if you need a hand or want help with anything then please don't hesitate to ask now, will you ?"

"I won't. Thanks Mary."

Jack was trying to recall old times. His son was now a man and Laura a woman, but in his eyes, they would always be his kids. And that without him, they would be lost and he was making sure that whatever he did, it was for them. Even the futile gesture of making them 'tea' was his way of believing in himself that he was doing something for them, that it was he, who was putting the food in their mouths and that it was he who was rightfully playing the fatherly role. This was just the way Jack thought and the way in which he was easing his conscience. He was on a guilt trip as he thought back to when they were little and how he had never been around for them because he was always working. Now, by doing such small and seemingly insignificant things, like making them 'tea,' made him feel a whole lot better.

Mary continued about her household chores as Jack prepared something to eat. As all the ingredients were placed on the worktop and all the utensils, pans and cutlery laid out, the Manor gates were opening for John and Laura. Laura called the house on her mobile to let them know. Jack went to the front door to greet them.

A smile almost split his face from ear to ear, as he watched them pull up. John was in a two-year old, five door Vauxhall hatchback and Laura was in a Ford Fiesta, which had a number of extras. As they both pulled up and got out of their cars, Jack chuckled to himself. He could hardly believe his eyes. Before him stood his two kids who had undergone such a metamorphosis that he could hardly believe it. He stood staring at them both.

Laura stood before him. She had red hair that had a beautiful and healthy-looking glossy shine to it. It had been styled into a French bun. She had put on make-up that bordered between a classy, executive look and that of a tart. She wore black mascara and rouge which highlighted her high cheek bones. Ruby red lipstick cloaked her lips with such a gloss that it looked decidedly 'tarty'. Ironically, you knew it wasn't, because anyone of taste and distinction knew that what she was wearing was expensive and classy-looking. On Laura with her natural beauty it was chic. She wore a light blue suit with a brooch of the consortium on her right lapel. Being an employee in Hong Kong, she had been given one as standard issue. The suit was tight fitting, but not so tight that she couldn't breathe or walk around in comfort. It was the perfect fit to show off her high and proud breasts. Her skirt hugged every contour of her waistline. It had a split up each side that stopped halfway up her thigh. She twirled round for him, asking what he thought. He could see how the skirt was almost like a second skin on her behind. He also noticed her matching high-heeled shoes that were the same colour as her suit. She had walked a fine line between looking expensively classy and that of looking cheapish and 'tarty'. She had managed to get the balance just right, greater than Jack could ever have hoped for, exceeding his highest expectations. As she stood in front of him smiling, he smiled back, he stepped towards her, wrapped his arms around her and hugged her tightly, then he kissed her on the cheek telling her that he loved her. He gently stood away, looked her up and down and said that she had done him proud. They both then turned to focus on John.

He was standing on the gravel, looking up at them both. They looked like a pair of Cheshire cats.

His hair, instead of resting on his shoulders, making him look like a Viking warrior, was cropped into a traditional but stylish short back and sides. It was exactly how Jack had asked it to be. His beard was gone.

Dressed in a charcoal grey, double-breasted suit, he looked immaculate. His black brogue shoes gleamed. His college tie from Cambridge, made into a perfect Windsor knot, fronted his pristine white shirt.

Jack stood back in admiration. He felt as though he was going to explode, he was so proud of them. Jack, stepping down to greet John, held out his hand to congratulate him on a job well done. As soon as John took Jack's hand, Jack pulled him towards him and told him that he loved him and that he was proud of him, just as he had done with Laura. Jack put his arm around John's shoulders, as they walked up the stairs. Jack put his other arm around Laura as they passed her and all three walked into the house.

Jack suggested that they should change into something more suitable, as he was going to prepare something to eat for them.

John and Laura both went upstairs to change. In the meantime, Tel had driven back from taking Sammy to her parent's house. He reported back to Jack, letting him know, and he was asked to wash and polish both John and Laura's new cars. Jack wanted them to look their best for tomorrow. Without any hesitation, Tel promptly obliged.

Tel wasn't married, nor had he ever been. He didn't have any family either, so his life was working for Jack. Although he was in essence, only his driver, Jack, because of Tel's service and devotion, made sure that he was not only paid a handsome wage but in other ways he was handsomely rewarded too. This way, Jack knew that anything asked of him, at anytime, within reason, would most certainly be done.

Mary meanwhile, greeted both of them in the reception hallway and commented on how different and wonderful they both looked, especially John. It was years since she'd seen him with short hair.

"In fact, the last time you had a proper hair cut, you were in short trousers," she commented.

Both of them just laughed and they all continued about their business. The meal was prepared and ready as they both entered the kitchen, showered and changed. They all sat down to eat. When they had all finished, Jack then asked them both into the lounge. He was going to prepare them for the day ahead.

The first thing he did was to tell them what their new names were to be, 'John Hammond' and 'Laura Briskel'. They were also given false documents relating to different fictitious firms where they had previously / supposedly, been employed. Jack went to the cabinet in the kitchen and retrieved the folders he had placed in there earlier. The folder on Cavendish was given to Laura and the folder on Barron to John.

Both John and Laura were informed that they were to do exactly as they were told and not to use any initiative whatsoever. There was always the danger that they might do or say something that ironically only they would have known, such as telephone numbers of offices around the world, or names and addresses of subsidiary companies which worked for the consortium, which if they were fresh into the company they could never have known.

They sat and asked questions relating to their task, all of which were answered down to the finest detail by Jack. One of the most prudent was by John, asking where the details had come from about their false identities. Jack just explained that they were prepared by his informer. The only thing that wasn't asked was what the plan was to be and how it was to be executed. Nor did either of them ask the name of the informer. They were told in no uncertain terms that their roles at this stage in the game were purely observational and that the spy Jack had on the inside would be watching over them.

They went over the way that they were to conduct themselves time and time again, each getting it right every time. Jack then suggested an early night as they all had a long day ahead of them. At that, John and Laura retired to their rooms and went to bed. Jack went to his workshop and put back the folders on Barron and Cavendish in the cabinet drawer.

The next day was going to be their first real test to see if they could infiltrate the Board successfully. Jack's planning was to be put to the test. He knew that if they failed him now, they would probably ruin any chance he had of ever getting back his empire.

Chapter Five

Day Seven - Wednesday

It was 6.30am when Jack rose from his bed. Before his usual routine of toilet, shave and shower, he knocked on the doors of John and Laura, ensuring that they would both be up at the same time. The ritual for Jack in the bathroom was the same as any other day except today, he didn't shave. When he had finished in the bathroom, he made his way downstairs. Jack, as always being first in the kitchen, started preparing something to eat. Fifteen minutes later, both John and Laura entered the kitchen in only under-garments, cloaked in their dressing gowns.

"What's this ? Haven't changed your minds, have you ?" Jack said in dismay, expecting to see them in their new attire.

"What's what ?"

"Your clothes."

"Think about it dad, if we spill some milk or splash some fat onto our clothes, then that isn't going to look very good is it ?" Laura said sarcastically.

Jack smiled and thought to himself,

"My God, I've thought of just about everything that could go wrong and something as trivial as that..... Laura, what a girl !"

Still smiling, he nodded his head in agreement and looked at John who sat down not looking at anyone or saying anything.

"How are you feeling this morning son ?"

"Same as I always feel in the mornings, tired."

"Hope the two of you still feel up to it."

"Yeah, course we do. We promised that we wouldn't let you down and we won't."

Laura was the spokesperson for the two of them. Even as a child, she had always been the one who woke in the mornings fresh and ready to meet the day's events head on. The events of this day, more than any other, were waiting to be greeted with a mixture of apprehension, excitement and caution.

"Good, then you'd better get this down you."

Jack placed bowls of cereal and tall glasses of pure orange juice in front of them whilst he continued to make a fry-up.

Just as they had finished and were about to leave the table Mary's daily routine began as she entered by the back door.

"My, we're all up early this morning," she said sprightly looking to John and Laura.

"Will you be helping your father out whilst you're both home?"

John and Laura just looked at one another, neither of them wanting to say anything, knowing what their dad's thoughts on the matter were. There was a pregnant pause before Jack answered her question.

"No, Mary, they're not. They're to work in the offices of a rival firm on the far side of town. As I'm sure you can imagine, the offices that John and Laura have worked in have their own unique way of operating. Hong Kong, Australia, the States and everywhere else, all have their own set-up which is different from what we have here in Britain. It wouldn't be fair to throw them in at the deep end, so they are going to work for another company to get to know how the system works here in this country. Until they have gained that experience, they are not going anywhere near my offices."

Mary looked gormlessly at him. Jack might as well have spoken in Chinese to her. She didn't have a clue what he meant or what he was talking about. Jack's intention was to spout off a load of verbal, so that she wouldn't ask anymore awkward questions or wonder why everything was as it was. Mary replied,

"Mr. Deer, I haven't got a clue what you're on about but I'm sure you know what you're doing."

Laura and John were both then asked to get ready for the big day ahead. They went to their rooms to change.

Mary continued about her normal business and Jack told Tel to get the Bentley ready.

After half an hour or so, they all met together in the hallway. Jack was the most casually dressed, whereas John and Laura were well turned-out in their business like attire. As he saw them off and wished them all the best, he called to John,

"Well, son, this proves that you've never had an inkling to dress or look smart and presentable of your own accord."

"That's rich coming from you....'Silver Whiskers'. State of your face, blunt razor was it? So, what's the matter with the way I look then?"

"Nothing ….. at the moment. But I'd just like to show you a simple trick that any self-respecting executive knows."

"Yeah, so what's that then?"

"You look perfectly smart and presentable to me but there's just one problem. In the space of only a few hours your collar will have an ugly-looking scum mark on it."

"How's that?"

"Because you're all hot and clammy now, the sweat will soak into the collar. If you loosen your tie, undo your top button and take off your suit jacket in the car, then when you've cooled down you make yourself smart again and your shirt collar will still be pristine white at the end of the day."

John did exactly as his father advised and Laura was told that she shouldn't sit down too hard for fear of splitting her skirt further than it already was. They both bid their father goodbye and drove off down the driveway. John led the way, Laura following close behind. Jack meanwhile, made his way to his car where Tel was, as always, standing at the back door waiting to open it for him. He hadn't told anyone but Sammy where he was off and nor was he about to, but that night he had packed a suitcase and had Tel help him load it into the car.

Once at the offices, John and Laura made their way over to the receptionist. They told her who it was that they were to report to. They were told to go to the conference room on the twenty-fifth floor. They made their way to the glass pod lift, looking in admiration at the magnificence of the decor. They knew their father had instigated it all and they had seen it all from photos but they had never actually seen it for themselves. They couldn't help noticing how everyone looked the same. Although this was the case, they still managed not to look bland or clone-like, instead they all looked 'uniform smart.' There were a number of other executives standing at the bottom of the lift waiting for it to descend. When it did, the operator waited until everyone in the lift got out before allowing the others in. Another futile effort on his part because everyone was civilised enough to wait until the lift was empty before getting in anyway. He asked which floor people wanted to get off on. There were only five of them in it and they all said the twenty-fifth. Making only two stops on the way up, the lift finally stopped at the twenty-fifth floor. Laura asked the operator where the conference room was and he obliged. Looking calmly at each other, John and Laura made their way to the room. They stopped outside the doors and John looked to Laura, took a deep breath and said anxiously,

"Well, here goes !"

They entered the room. The first thing that struck them was the magnificent and breathtaking view over London. Before them was the ebony conference table, the length of which seemed to run forever. The Board members were all present and sitting in their now usual seats. All, that is, except for an empty seat to Moore's left. Fairfax wasn't there. The other seats were, as usual, taken up by the junior executives who sat around the table as though they were barnacles on a rock, seemingly immovable from their seats. It was as though they had been super-glued to them. All faces were upon John and Laura, staring as though they were freaks in a circus. All was quiet and they felt quite uncomfortable. The first to speak was Cavendish, seeing her red hair, bright red lip stick and low cut top he knew from his notes exactly who she was.

"Ah, you must be Miss Laura Briskel."

"Yes, that's right, and who might you be, Sir?"

She knew full well who he was.

"I am Lord Arthur Cavendish."

Not bowing her head but slightly dipping it and not a curtsey rather flexing of her knees as though she had a cramp pain running through them, she replied.

"Pleased to meet you 'My Lord'. "

His face lit up immediately. She had done exactly what her father had told her to do, sent him on an ego trip by seeming to be impressed by his title and so calling him by it. Cavendish, meanwhile, sat there with a pompous look on his face, as Laura took an instant dislike to him. He made her flesh creep. She knew that as he was looking at her, he was mentally undressing her. But she also knew that this was how the game was to be played and that he was falling for the set-up. She wanted to egg him on as part of the plan and so giving him a sultry look, smiled at him. Cavendish just sat staring at her all the time, thinking to himself how he was to bed her. No more was said. Laura went to take a vacant seat which happened to be next to her counterpart, Miss Helen Auldrich. She took an instant dislike to Laura, seeing how she was dressed, how pretty she was and her general appearance, mannerisms and polite way. Helen saw her as undue competition instead of someone she could side with and strike up an alliance. She totally ignored Laura and so

not to be outdone, Laura ignored her also and did not take
the seat. Instead, she took one of two vacant seats at the
end of the table. She already knew that she was in
Cavendish's good books and as her father had told her, she
knew he was already thinking of how he could bed her.

John stood as a solitary figure in the room. No-one spoke
or asked him who he was. He coughed to clear his throat
and then said loudly and clearly,

"Lord Barron is the man I have been assigned to work
with gentlemen. May I ask which one of you is he ?"

"I am, my boy."

Walking over to him, John held out his hand to shake
hands with him.

"Who the Dickens are you ?"

Sniggers and smirks could be heard coming from around
the room.

Barron looked at him in sheer disgust, as though he had
just been insulted. He hadn't, it was just another morning
aftermath of one of his drinking binges. With eyes like
piss-holes in the snow and a stench of whisky emanating
from his mouth, he just sat there, ignoring the offer of a
hand shake. John acted embarrassed and uncomfortable and
looked to the others as to what he should do next. He
wasn't at all overawed, he wanted to give Barron a feeling of
superiority. This was part of what his father had told him to
do and how to play the game with Barron. Then Barron
stood up and put his hand out to John saying,

"Ah, I remember now, you're the one sent to help me
to......"

Moore interrupted him saying,

"I'll take it from here. Thank you, Andrew."

He wanted to say sit down, shut-up and sober-up but
Barron just looked at Moore and without saying another
word sat down. John sat in the vacant seat next to Laura.

Moore looked to John and whilst idly pointed to one of the junior executives 'Stephen Williams,' he said,

"You'll be working with him."

The junior executives were so self-conceited. John introduced himself to his counterpart, who in contrast to Barron was very civil and polite. Looking at his tie and then at John, Stephen said,

"Cambridge !"

"Yes."

John looked at his tie,

"Kings college !"

"Yes."

They both smiled at one another and sat themselves down. All the time, both John and Laura couldn't believe how right their father was. Telling them down to the most minute detail all of what would happen, how the people would behave and react to different things. How even the most trivial of things were held in great esteem. Did it really matter what school, college or University you went to ? So long as you could and did do what was asked of you. More importantly, was how you were as a person but these values meant nothing here and almost immediately, John and Laura were finding this out for themselves. But whatever they thought, they had one great advantage over the whole situation. Only John and Laura knew the Board were in for a rude awakening. All the Board sat making private small talk and jokes as other 'replacement' executives arrived and sat down. Once all were present and ready, Moore looked at Peterbough. He was to be the spokesman in Fairfax's absence. Standing up, he began.

"Gentlemen," he said, before correcting himself. He was not a prolific speaker as was Fairfax.

"Sorry,.....Ladies and Gentlemen, we are gathered here today to start the process of forming a new infrastructure for the consortium."

He really might as well have been addressing a church congregation. He was a tautologist. He was painful.

"Plans have been drawn up by us....'the Board', who have drawn up these plans to let you know how the restructuring is going to be done. First and foremost, the new executives are to be assigned to work with the existing ones. The road ahead is going to be a long, hard, arduous one, and it is impossible to expect our present executives to carry all the burden of such a mammoth task on their shoulders alone. Therefore, they will be given the help of you, new and keen recruits to train under them, all chosen because of your aptitude and tenacity. It should only take a period of a full seven day week before you are familiar with the system and how it is set up. You'll be 'au fait' with how it all pieces together and operates. Then starts the process of the restructuring in which 'some' of the existing executives are going to be promoted and made Board members."

Peterbough didn't even flinch telling them this downright lie. Peterbough lied and was deceitful to his wife about his other side, his, 'Mr. Hyde.' These people meant even less to him. In his eyes they were lower than dog dirt on the sole of his shoe. Why should he worry or be bothered? He kept a straight face and without even batting an eyelid, continued. "The new recruits here today will then walk into their positions."

Being one of the more astute executives, Stephen asked the question,

"Sir, you say that 'some' of the executives, will be moved onto the Board. What will happen to the others?"

John had taken to him straight away and wanted to answer his question, but circumstances dictated his actions. Peterbough answered,

"I'm just coming to that," Peterbough said dismissively,

"Obviously, there won't be places for all of you. So those that perform the best and are the most successful in training the new executives will be the ones moved onto the Board.

Those of you who do not perform well will be asked to leave."

There was an uncomfortable silence. Many felt betrayed. Their performance was to be judged on how well the trainees did, regardless of how they themselves were as employees. But almost all were going to fall over themselves in ensuring their appointed underling was up and running with all they had to know before the end of the week. A tall, if not impossible order, but they were going to try.

The Board had been very clever in their manipulation of all present. They had instantly set up an atmosphere of such eager competitiveness that all would quite literally go out of their way to ensure that their trainee came out on top. All of them were too ambitious for their own good. They were all the calibre of person that proved the point that ambition can be bad for 'somebody else's health,' as they would stop at nothing and destroy anyone who stood between them and success. For every rung of the ladder they had climbed, they had ruined somebody else's career. They would sell their own grandmother to have a place on the Board. They would all stab each other in the back for promotion.

They would work night and day to train up the new executives but unbeknown to them, they would all be terminated at the end of the week regardless of their efforts, and replaced by the new executives for less pay and benefits. The only winners of the whole scenario were to be the Board members. It was an ingenious plan, but no-one could see the wood for the trees. They all genuinely believed that they were in with a chance of promotion onto the Board. They could all see a vision before them, of reaching the pinnacle of their careers. They had all unwittingly been lulled into a frame of mind where the best man would win. The trouble was, the vision which they saw before them, was only a mirage and there wasn't to be a best man. With all of them being so young and energetic, the Board knew that they would put their hearts and souls into doing exactly what they wanted them to do. They also knew that the new executives would also work themselves into the ground to ensure that they, too, would have a place in the company when the results of who were staying and who were going, were announced.

The existing, serving executives were asked to leave the room and prepare themselves to train their prospective trainees. The new ones were asked to stay as the Board members wanted to put them right on a few things. With a suppressed eagerness, the executives stood up from the table and made their way out of the conference room to their respective offices.

Once the existing executives were out of the room, Peterbough began to speak again.

"Right, now we'll get down to the truth of the matter."

'Truth' was an alien concept to him. He couldn't tell the truth if his life depended upon it. He was about to spurt out more lies.

"The executives we have at the moment were very efficient and proficient when they first started, but have become lazy. Also, it has come to light that a number of them have been deceitful and informed our competitors of our every move and contract. Therefore, at the end of this week, we shall be dismissing them, putting you in their place, on the conditions that are laid out in these contracts."

They were all given a contract to sign, spelling out what it was they were to be paid and what benefits they could expect to receive. It was in vast contrast to what John and Laura knew the existing executives had been given. They had been told this would happen by their father.

"There is a clause, however, that at the end of this week you yourselves, will all be assessed. If it is shown that you haven't grasped or learnt what is expected of you, *i.e.* to take the place of the executive you're here to replace, then I'm sorry to say that you will be one step behind them walking out of the door. This company has carried too many people for too long, and this restructuring programme is going to see to it that those left can carry their own weight."

A cry of "Hear, hear!" could be heard coming from Warlton sitting opposite him. Why he was agreeing with Peterbough was a damned cheek. He and the rest of the consortium, except Fairfax and Moore, had been carried all the way by the others, as all knew the only reason they were there was due to either their title or contacts. It was lie upon lie that flowed easily from Peterbough's mouth. None of the serving executives had ever given away company secrets. On the contrary they were all dedicated employees who had a sense of honour to the consortium, although they'd stop at nothing to get on. It was all lies to lull all the new people into a false sense of security about their own positions. Now they were blinded by their own ambition for getting on in the company.

The plan had been a masterful one. The Board had succeeded in setting everyone to work vigorously together and yet at the end of the week the only winners were going to be the Board members themselves. The existing executives were to be kicked out and the new ones would be in their positions for less pay and benefits, and double the workload in setting the consortium up for dismemberment. All that the Board had to do was oversee it all.

When all were in the picture as to what was going on, they were told to join their respective counterparts for what was going to be a long week. They all stood up from the table and waited for the Board to leave first. On the way out of the boardroom, Cavendish gave a sickly smile to Laura. He really did give her a churning gut feeling. She was sick of the sight of him already. He repulsed her, making her flesh crawl at an instant. She forced a smile back at him. Then he winked. She had to look down and pretend to be slightly embarrassed, otherwise her smile would have turned into a snarl and that would have undoubtedly put a dampener on the whole plan. The only person who had caught onto the gestures made by Cavendish was John. As Cavendish disappeared from sight out of the doorway, John gripped her arm as she walked to the door herself. He whispered into her ear, "I saw what happened and don't worry, I'm here for you if the going gets too tough. Remember dad said that it wasn't going to be easy."

Laura said nothing, but just smiled and nodded to him then gently gripped his hand.

Everyone made their way to their respective offices, walking through the sea of carpets, along corridors adorned with paintings. Just as with the offices in Australia and Hong Kong, nothing was ever cheap. Everything always had an air of excellence about it.

Stephen showed John into his office sat him down in the chair opposite his desk and asked him direct and straightforward questions.

"OK, John ?"

"Yes."

"Who appointed you to work with me ?"

John immediately became suspicious and began to smell a rat.

"The Board appointed me."

"Who, exactly ?"

"I'm not at liberty to say."

"OK, here's the deal. I'm not stupid and I know, that come the end of the week, we're all going to be fired. I'm correct in that assumption aren't I ?"

"Look, I'm not at liberty to say."

Stephen shaking his head in despair, knew he wasn't going to get anything out of John. He tutted, curled his lip and looked straight at John,

"It would be easier to get blood from a stone wouldn't it ?"

John said nothing, he wasn't going to be swayed or intimidated into giving anything away. He knew that Stephen was right and wanted to tell him so, just as in the conference room, but he also knew that his father had a lot more to lose than he did, and so said nothing.

"Well, my friend, you're going to have to find out about the system yourself."

"What do you mean?"

"Work it out for yourself!"

John was left sitting in his chair as Stephen turned to his computer and started to type on the keyboard. John remained seated, looking at him, suspecting correctly what he was doing.

"It's your resignation, isn't it?"

"Bingo, you've got it in one! There's no way I'm going to put you in my position after all the hard work I've done in getting this far in the company and earning this post. Whoever has chosen to put you in my place after I've 'trained' you has underestimated my intelligence ...No, insulted it. What did he think I was?......'a bloody fool'. I know that come the end of the week you're going to take over this office, I'll be fired and that all this will only be for the benefit of the Board and nobody else but them. Things were better under Deer, I know that they've stabbed him in the back, but there's no way I can prove it or that I'm going to let them do it to me."

John said nothing, although he was, yet again, tempted to tell him that he was right in everything he said. But remembering the long discussions he had had with his father, he knew that he had to trust nobody and that he must say nothing. The worst danger of all, was if Stephen was putting on a charade and that his conviction was all a show and that he might be trying to trick John into telling him all about himself, the plan and everything. But he knew that he was getting carried away with himself and that he was in danger of becoming paranoid about the whole thing. He knew in his heart that Stephen was genuine but just couldn't tell him anything. Even as he sat there, he too, wondered who it was that had put him to work with Stephen which was not to be. John knew that it had to be his dad's informer, but just who was he?

John then said that he was going to get himself a cup of coffee and asked if Stephen would like one. He was totally ignored. When he returned with his drink, Stephen was gathering a number of personal items together and placing them in the corner of the room. John couldn't believe the ferocity with which he had packed everything away. He admired his conviction and glad Stephen could see what the Board members were all about.

"So, true to your word then, you're going."

"I was a fool not to have seen what they were up to in the first place. Still I know now and as the saying goes, 'it's never too late'."

"Well, I can only wish you good luck."

"I don't need it from the likes of you, thank you very much. You and the others are helping to spoil a great thing that Jack Deer started. I can only hope that you all drown in your own shit."

At that, he made his way out of the office and without looking at John snarled,

"I'll be back to collect the rest of my things later."

He flung open the office door and stormed out of it and into Barron's office. Seconds later, he emerged red-faced with anger and rage at the way he had been treated. John knew that to go and speak to Barron at this very moment in time, would be a waste of time. He decided he would wait until tomorrow, in the hope that by then, he would be sober enough to be civil. He then got onto the computer to see what files were held on it. After a quick preliminary look through them, he then studied the folders on the shelves. Some contained copies of different contracts which the department had set up, others were about the restructuring programme with a basic outline of what needed to be done.

As John stood studying these, the door was flung open. It was Barron.

"What's happened to him, then ?"

"Don't know, he's just decided to quit."

In a mood swing, Barron shouted at John,

"DON'T GIVE ME THAT. WHAT DID HE SAY, HE MUST HAVE SAID SOMETHING. HE DIDN'T JUST LEAVE BECAUSE HE FELT LIKE IT."

It was almost as though he was embarrassed by the whole thing, that it was only his personal assistant who had decided to leave. John, seeing the situation, took the opportunity to jump on it and swing it in his favour.

"He was probably frightened of me showing him up and therefore got out whilst he could. I've already had a look through the files and the restructuring programme and I must say, that even without him, I'll be able to do the job effectively and efficiently without help from anyone. Who knows, I may even be able to help some of the others."

"You think so, do you ?"

"No, I know so."

In a complete turn round of mood and temperament, Barron smiled at John in a truly, happy way.

"I like your confidence, my boy, I like it. I want you to work on the programme today and let's see what you come up with tomorrow then, shall we ?"

"Why not this afternoon ?"

Barron just continued smiling. He really did admire his gusto. Nodding his head in approval, he told John that tomorrow was just fine with him but if he didn't come up with the goods then, he was out. John replied that the task ahead of him would present no problem.

Laura meanwhile was in her office with her counterpart Helen Auldrich. She was the opposite of Stephen. She wanted to get on so badly, it was like a pining to clamber up the ladder of success. Like the Board members, she would stop at nothing to get on and further herself. Which is a big difference from bettering yourself, although in this particular game there is a fine line that separates the two. She was the type Jack had warned them about, the type that really would sell her own Grandmother for the chance of 'getting on'. She would stop at nothing, if she believed that she could and would get on. Her attitude too, was in total contrast to Stephen's. She wasn't polite or courteous to those she evidently believed were either below her or of the same status. In that case, she would attack verbally to create a class distinction of 'I'm the boss and you will do as I say.' Laura had read this a mile off and was just waiting for it to happen, and when in the sanctuary of her own office it did.

"Right, I know what your game is !"

"Excuse me !"

"Your hair is obviously dyed, you're wearing all the 'tarty' make-up, even down to that glossy red lipstick and the slits up your skirt so as to entice Cavendish into your slit."

"You cheeky, disgusting cow."

"Don't give me that. Someone has told you what he's like and what he's attracted to. I know what you're up to and believe me when I tell you that you're not going to have an easy ride into this position......my position. You're going to have to work for it. And you're going to get me on that Board."

"Oh, am I now ?"

"Yes, you are. If you think that simply allowing him into your knickers is your meal ticket to the top you can forget it, girl."

"Speaking from experience are you ?"

"And what's that supposed to mean ?" Helen asked indignantly.

"Exactly what I've just said, but I shall spell it out for you.......'Girl.' You've got where you are through hard work and knowledge, obviously. Hard work on your back and ....

'carnal knowledge', of every boss you've had on your way up the ladder."

Helen squinted her eyes. She was being played at her own game and she didn't like it. Laura was serving back harsh comments which both knew had a foundation of truth. It was a hell of a start to their working relationship with neither of them giving an inch on accepting the other.

There was a pause, both of them looking scornfully at one another, like two tomcats in a stand-off fight, each waiting for the other to show a sign of weakness and back down. It was clear that neither of them were going to.

Flicking back her head and looking Laura up and down as she did so, Helen snarled,

"Right, I'm going to have you out of here before you know what's hit you. You may have Cavendish fooled but I can see right through you like a pane of glass. You're nothing but a common tart and you're not going to work with me so long as I stand a chance of getting on that Board."

"So long as you're sleeping with him, you mean."

"Right, that does it."

Helen barged passed her and made her way into Cavendish's office. Laura stood shaking like a leaf. She was overcome with nerves. It was not the first time that she had ever encountered conflict, but it was the first time she had encountered such a bitter and venomous personal attack. Her knees were turning to jelly so she sat down before she fell over. She could hear herself breathing but couldn't help herself. She felt like crying, but over her dead body was she going to give that malicious cow the satisfaction of knowing that she'd got to her. This, she knew, would be seen as a sign of weakness, and exactly what she was vying for. Laura couldn't help but think that already she was going to be dismissed before she had even started.

As she sat trying to control her feelings and not to cry, Helen was having an intimate chat with Cavendish. Cavendish had been startled at her entrance into his office and was amazed at her lack of decorum and etiquette, like a fisher-wife, she started at him,

"Why the bloody hell was she sent to work with me ?"

"What do you mean ?"

"Come off it, Arthur! You know exactly what I mean."

In an instant, it all clicked with him, and he could see she was emerald green with envy. This was another opportune moment for him to take advantage of the situation.

"Look, you are the prime candidate for getting on the Board. You will be the first woman to do so. Furthermore, because I've constantly kept the Board informed of all the good work you've done, they have been watching you very closely. If you continue to behave as you are now, then you'll not only ruin it for yourself, but also for me."

He grinned at her with his slightly buck teeth,

"After all, I couldn't let your rendered services go unrewarded now, could I ?"

She had obviously slept with him on the promise of getting on in the company. She hadn't moved up in the promotion stakes, because ever since she'd been in the position of his personal assistant, she had been made promises that had never been fulfilled. Through excuse after excuse, she had been let down. For all her intelligence, she really was blinded by her own ambitions. Cavendish had always dangled the carrot in front of her and like a dumb mule, she had always followed his lead. He stood up from his chair and walked around his desk. He held out his arms as though to embrace her. Although he made her flesh creep, as he did with Laura, she obliged by putting her arms around his fat waist and rested her head onto his chest. The scene was pathetic, it was as though they were in a film from the thirties. She was playing the hard-done-by daughter and he, the ever-present father figure, in whose arms she could always find comfort. The trouble was, in reality, she was one step up from a whore, who was sleeping with him to get on as payment. He was one step down from a paying customer because he only ever paid her in false promises.

He started to stroke her hair with the palm of his hand. In a patronising tone continued,

"There, there now, don't you worry about a thing." He was leading up to asking her to sleep with him again, although his thoughts were on bedding Laura.

"Look, I suggest that you go back in there, make the peace with her, whichever way you can. After all this time you will be made up to a Board member, even if she should succeed in being able to takeover from you. And as I've already said you're still the hot favourite."

"How can I face her now? It will seem as though I've backed down."

"Don't worry, I'll go in with you."

"No, I can't."

"Look, don't worry, leave the talking to me and I'll handle it. You just follow my lead."

"But I can't just walk in there and say sorry. Besides I'm not."

"You won't have to if you pick up on my lead."

"OK, then. Promise we'll get rid of her at the end of the week and replace her with someone that I approve of."

"I don't have to. You'll be on the Board. But will you do something for me tonight?"

"For you, anything."

He was going to bed her again for the umpteenth time.

They both then made their way back into her office. Laura looked towards the door as they entered.

"Well, my dear, you've passed our little test with flying colours."

"What do you mean Sir?"

"You were set up here by Helen, to see if you could pass our first test and you have with flying colours, my girl. You spoke up for yourself, answered back and stood your ground. I admire that in a woman. All you have to do now is prove to Helen and myself that you can produce the goods, so to speak. Isn't that right, Helen?"

In a completely changed mood and smiling as she chuckled Helen added,

"Laura, it was a set-up. I never meant any of the things I said. It was all a show to see if you were the right calibre of person to do the job in hand.....honestly. We can't afford to have shrinking violets on our team, and you're certainly not one of those, are you?"

Laura wasn't fooled for one minute. She knew that everything Helen had said had come from her blackened heart. But she knew that for her dad's sake, she had to pretend that she had been taken in and that it was all a misunderstanding on her part and a test on theirs. She started to grin, smiled and then let out a laugh that sounded genuine.

"Well I never! So it was all a trick to see if you would have me?"

Cavendish had a sinister, crooked smile tarred to his face and in a demeaning tone continued,

"Of course it was. We don't want just anyone to work in our department. We can only cater for the best my dear."

They all then pretended to laugh, acting as though nothing was wrong and that all was well, Cavendish and Helen truly believing that Laura had been fooled. But it was Laura who had them fooled. She walked over to Helen and offered her hand in friendship, while thinking "you slimy slut." As they shook hands, Laura looked at Cavendish and thought to herself that Helen was no more than his personal sperm bank rather than his personal assistant. Laura made no false apologies for what she had said to Helen. She meant every word.

"Well, ladies, I shall leave you both to it then and remember that you two are the hot favourites to move into the top positions at the end of the week."

Laura wasn't fooled by him for one minute, whereas Helen, as always, was taken in by his every word.

For the rest of the day and early evening both John, Laura and all the other helpers were to work hard in achieving their own personal goals. It wasn't until about eight-thirty that the die-hards were to call it a day and leave to go home to rest. Time was of the essence and all parties were working ferociously to meet their deadlines.

Whilst all this had been going on, Jack had made his way to the airport that morning and boarded a flight to New York. Before leaving the house he had paid a visit to his workshop cabinet. He fingered passed Barron and Cavendish and pulled out the folder on Fairfax. Looking at it he muttered to himself, 'Right, let's get you sorted.' He sat at his drawing board and placed other selected folders from the drawer inside the folder he had on Fairfax. He beavered away doing what he had to. Forty minutes later he was ready.

He was chasing up on consignments of cargo the Board had shipped out to New York two days previously. It had cleared customs. This was not the only place to which they had had consignments of cargo delivered. They had been sent to all the major offices of the consortium throughout the world. They were sent to Dubai, New Delhi, Kuala Lumpur, Beijing, Hong Kong, Sydney, Houston and San Francisco, Brasilia and Buenos Aires, all of which had 'FRAGILE' and arrows showing the correct way up plastered in bright red ink all over them.

Jack knew the Board's every move. All the information coming from his informer on the inside, whose identity Jack wasn't going to disclose to anyone until the crisis unravelled itself and it was safe to do so. The Board, however, was not aware of what he was up to.

The plane arrived in New York. Jack cleared customs and immigration and went to the hotel where he'd made a reservation and booked himself in. He wore a baseball cap and sunglasses. The cap was so that the receptionist never saw the true colour of his hair. Not that she would have specifically remembered him anyway, considering she checked in anywhere between fifty or sixty people a day. But Jack was taking no chances.

Jack placed his travel rucksack on the bed and unpacked his toiletry bag and took out the usual items of toothbrush, toothpaste, shampoo and so forth, but no shaving items. He also took out a hair dying kit. He then proceeded to dye his hair, just as he had asked Laura to dye hers. Although for her, the reason was to entice Cavendish, his was one of disguise. He would have dyed it in London before he left but there was the problem of passport control. He had no option but to leave it until now. It was all so mysterious. Why was it that he wanted to look so different? Only he knew.

He already had a slight beard from not shaving that day. He was the type of bloke whose facial hair grew so fast that he'd have a half-decent beard by the morning.

With the dye now soaking into his hair and although tired, he made a few phone calls. One was to contacts, who were to meet him at a designated warehouse where the consignments were being held, and another was to arrange for a consortium van to pick him up at the warehouse at eight in the morning.

It was all so mysterious. No-one knew he was going to New York, nobody knew about the consignments that had been shipped or what the Board was intending to do with them. No-one, that is, except for Jack and his informer who had planned these moves.

Jack, contented that everything was in order for tomorrow, was now ready for a good night's sleep. But he had a few other things to do first. He made a long distance telephone call to John and Laura. He didn't tell them where he was but just that he was playing his role in the scheme as he and his ally had planned. Neither John nor Laura pushed the matter any further. They chatted on about how he was right in everything that he had told them, about the way in which the Board had planned the take-over of the consortium. Also how the executives were all to be replaced with ones that were prepared to work for less money. They also spoke of his description of how Barron and Cavendish were going to behave and conduct themselves, not to mention their personal assistants. Jack just told them to toe the line and keep him informed of any developments.

Then he made a call to Sammy. He told her not to worry and that he had kept his promise in not sending John and Laura off around the world on company business. Not strictly the truth, a 'white lie,' a half truth but it was for the best, all things considered. He reassured her that if she wanted to see or speak to either of them that they were at home and could be reached on the telephone. He also said that should she wish to break her stay with her parents, then they would be at home for her. He persuaded her that this wouldn't be a good idea for two reasons. One was that the doctor had specifically requested that she should be there to get some real rest. The second was that both John and Laura were helping him in following up on a lead that might help them salvage something of what they stood to lose. She agreed and wished him good luck. They ended the conversation by telling each other that they missed and loved one another. The day ahead was going to be a test for all of them.

Chapter Six

Day Eight - Thursday

The day started with Jack getting a wake-up call. He'd only had a few hours sleep but that was all he ever needed regardless of the fact that he'd travelled for fourteen hours straight. He showered but did not shave. He put on his work overalls and work boots, which looked like training shoes. There was a knock on the door. It was room service with his breakfast. He'd only taken one mouthful of his cereal when he suddenly thought of his father.

"If only he could have visited and seen places such as these, maybe he'd have had a different outlook on life."

Jack couldn't help but think of their humble background. How, as a kid, a trip to the seaside was the major event of the year. How, if his mother was bought a new dress, it was only ever due to his father getting enough overtime to be able to afford it after spending the other half in the pub and in the bookies. As he looked around, he could see how plush and luxurious everything was. This was how the rich folk lived.

"If only he could see me now," he thought to himself again.

I can fly to any sun-drenched beach in the world, bathe in the crystal waters amongst the tropical fish, the sort that his father had only ever seen on a nature programme. How buying new and wonderful clothes need not depend on 'overtime.'

Jack shook his head, with the last thought in his mind being of his beloved mother.

"She deserved better, but she was happy with dad and that's what mattered.....it's the only thing that mattered," he thought to himself.

With his breakfast finished, he looked at his watch. Five to seven. He made a phone call to the people he'd arranged to meet at the warehouse. They said that nothing had changed and that they would be there to pick him up at the arranged time. Jack then rang the hotel reception to ask for a taxi to meet him at the main doors. Nothing was too much trouble.

He put on a rain coat which draped down to the middle of his shins. The collar was turned up, the lapels were turned in, all the front buttons were done up and the belt was tied loosely around his waist. He checked his appearance in the mirror. Jack was ready.

In the foyer, he confirmed the receptionist had ordered a taxi for him. She called to one of the bell boys to show him to the car. They both walked through the revolving glass doors and out onto the decorative marble slabs at the front of the hotel. The bell boy then pulled open the door of the waiting cab, coughing as he did so, a gesture for him to be given a tip. Jack greased his palm with a twenty dollar bill.

Jack had important things on his mind. His mind was abuzz with a hundred and one things, but only one objective. The bell boy closed the door and the taxi pulled away from the sidewalk.

The taxi driver asked where he wanted to go.

"The warehouse on George Street."

"OK. No problem."

On hearing Jack's un-American accent, the driver decided he was going to try it on. He proceeded to talk drivel as he drove. Looking towards a road on his right, as they passed it, Jack asked,

"You do know where to go, don't you ?"

"Yes, man, I get you there, no problem."

"Yes, there is a problem, you should have turned right just then."

"No, man...."

"Look mate! I'm no dumb bleedin' tourist, right. I've been here before…..many times and you should have taken that turning back there."

The driver had been had.

"Yes, boss. Sorry boss." The driver made a 'U' turn in the middle of the road, after checking in his rear view mirror. Jack had to put out both arms to either side of the vehicle doors to stop himself from being thrown about all over the show.

"Hey! Take it easy, will you?"

"Yes Boss. Sorry Boss."

"I need to get to that warehouse before eight."

"Yes boss. No problem."

The driver hurried through the streets to the warehouse. He arrived in good time.

The car pulled into the warehouse car park and stopped at the main entrance. Jack got out and paid the man what he knew was due. It was different from what the driver had asked for. The driver had deliberately left his meter off when he'd heard Jack's accent but had forgotten to turn it back on when he'd been found out. The driver didn't argue with him as he could see that he'd be onto a loser and so said nothing.

"OK!" Jack said expectantly as he gave him his money,

"Yeah. OK."

"Here!" Jack handed the driver a tip. He was pleasantly surprised and smiled. Jack patted the roof of the cab twice and stood upright from the cab as the car gently drove out of the car park and back onto the hectic streets.

Jack looked at his watch. Ten to eight. He entered the warehouse reception office, took off his coat and hung it on the back of one of the chairs. He sat waiting for the people he'd called on the phone, to come and pick him up. He helped himself to a cup of coffee from a dilapidated vending machine precariously placed on an uneven floor which sloped down from the walls. He had no sooner taken a sip from his cup, when he saw one of the consortium's vans pull up into a space in the car park. Without any hesitation, he threw the cup into the bin and made his way outside. Muttering under his breath,

"Thank God. That was howling. I might have had to have drank that."

He was greeted by the two men with whom he had arranged to meet. They introduced themselves to Jack. Jack introduced himself to them as Jack Henley. Once the preliminary formalities were over, Jack told them that they should sign for the goods to be released from the warehouse. They asked what they were and why it was that they had to sign them out. Jack only answered their second question, saying that he was only a subcontractor and that the property belonging to the consortium could only be signed-out by the employees. This was true, but Jack could just as easily have signed for the goods himself. He could have proved that he was from the consortium but he didn't. He was travelling incognito, under the guise of being not with the consortium but with a subcontracting firm which was doing work for them.

The two men shrugged their shoulders and then followed him to the foyer of the warehouse. Jack led the way and on the back of his overalls was a symbol of a satellite with the words 'Global Television Productions' written on it.

"So, that's what's in there is it, satellite equipment?"

"Of course. That's what I'm here for, that's what it says on my back, isn't it?" Jack replied candidly, playing it coy.

Again, the two men just shrugged their shoulders and proceeded to follow Jack. They signed for the consignment and loaded it into the van which was of an ample size to accommodate the goods, just as Jack had specified in his conversation the night before. Once fully loaded-up, the three of them made their way to the offices of the consortium down town.

They pulled up at the rear 'tradesman's entrance' of the offices. A number of labourers sent by an employment agency were waiting for them. Jack got out of the van telling the helpers to load the boxes into the lift. He then told them that one of the boxes contained a satellite dish which had to be taken to the roof, assembled and installed. The other boxes were to be loaded into the main conference room. Without objection or asking questions, the helpers obediently carried out every instruction. The other two men asked if they should then assist him in the installation of the equipment. He just said thanks for their help but that he had other help coming and that they had done enough.

Jack accompanied the first consignment up to the roof. He was running the risk of being recognised by using the lift but what other option did he have? It wasn't as though he could get the gear up to where it was needed any other way. He just had to hope and pray that the lift didn't stop on the wrong floor. He looked completely different but there was always the chance that he'd be recognised by someone. His face wasn't exactly unknown as it had appeared on numerous consortium news bulletins. But he needed to look different. He could not afford to be recognised, hence the reason for dying his hair, growing a beard and wearing overalls instead of a suit. Only in magazine articles with pictures of Jack twenty plus years ago would anyone from the consortium in New York have seen him in overalls.

He told two of the helpers who had gone with him to carefully unpack the boxes, ensuring that any paperwork i.e. the instructions, were to be kept and put to one side. Again, without a word, they did exactly as they were told. Jack then went back down in the lift to collect the other boxes which were in the basement area of the building. As the lift descended, it was brought to a halt on the seventeenth floor. The doors opened and Jack's worst fear dawned. Getting into the lift was Bradley Rainier, who was friendly with Moore. Their eyes met briefly as Rainer stepped into the lift and turned to face the doors.

Jack had completely changed his appearance. Different hair colour, beard and even his clothing. He really was a different man. Despite this, Rainer's mind was racing. He knew he had seen Jack's face somewhere before. It was familiar, but he just could not place it. He gently shook his head, not able to think and so dismissed him as probably having seen him around as what he was, 'a maintenance man.' Jack fearing that Rainer might turn around to look at him, quickly dropped to the floor as though he was tying his shoe laces. He was, but only because he'd deliberately pulled on one of the laces undoing it. And 'boy' was he making a meal of tying it back up again. He knew that he would have to stand up again otherwise the whole scene would have just become too suspicious. He pulled out a handkerchief from his pocket and as though he had a cold, pretended to blow into it to cover up his face. He'd got this far and the last thing that he needed was for Rainier to recognise him and so ruin his plan.

The lift went directly to the tenth floor without stopping and Rainier got out, much to the relief of Jack. He then used the handkerchief to wipe the sweat from his brow. The lift arrived at the basement where the other helpers were waiting to load the rest of the goods. Jack directed them to stack the equipment in a column in the lift so that he could hide behind it just in case he should find himself in the same situation again.

The lift stopped at the seventeenth floor and Jack helped the labourers out with the consignment as they loaded it onto the trolley. He was stopped in mid-flow by one of the inquisitive office personnel. She questioned him. What was he doing ? And who were the people with him ? Jack gave her a scornful look as he knew that she was no more than an interfering 'busy-body'. He pulled out a slip of paper from his pocket, and pretended to read from it,

"Listen, love, I've got a job to do for a Mr.......Rainier. Now he has ordered this stuff and wants it in by the end of the day and if you have any authority over him then I will do as you say. But I don't think that that's the case. So, if you don't want me to advise him that you've been hindering me and obstructing my progress, I suggest that you stand aside and let me carry on."

The girl gave him an indignant look. She was more embarrassed at being corrected in front of the labourers than anything, saying nothing for fear of reprisals, especially from Rainier, after all, he was the main man in New York, she quietly walked away. A number of other people saw and heard what had happened but daren't approach him, as they had heard Rainier's name mentioned and so with Jack's aggressive attitude, they knew that if they were to challenge him, then they would more than likely be reported themselves.

Jack then led the way to the main conference room. Although it was five years since he was last there and it was all of three thousand miles away, nothing had changed. Everything was just as it had been when he was there previously. The table was the same as the one in London and so were the chairs. The suits of the men and the outfits of the women were all uniform smart. The general decor was identical, carpets, wooden panelling, pictures on the wall. The only thing different was that the lift didn't have an operator.

Jack held open the doors of the conference room as the helpers bundled in the equipment. As they were busy doing so, an entourage of four men entered the room. They all wore the same overalls as Jack.

"You Jack Henley ?" said the leader.

"Yes, that's me."

The man then introduced himself and the other men.

"Hi, I'm Joe, this is Pete, Phil and Andy."

Shaking hands with each of them, they all said the usual greeting of 'Pleased to meet you' and then got down to the serious work of installing the equipment with Jack taking the lead. He instructed each of them what was to be done. All agreed on how they were to do it. Joe asked the question,

"What do they want all this gear for anyway? It's not as though they can watch satellite television all goddamned day, is it? What's all this in aid of? Do you know?"

Again, playing it all candid, Jack answered him.

"Got no idea! It's probably so that they can keep in touch with stock markets around the world as they happen or something, that's the only explanation I can think of. I don't really know."

He knew exactly what it was for and that wasn't it.

The men just looked at him perplexed, they couldn't really think of a better explanation and just agreed with what he'd said. Jack left them to go down to the reception. He'd had a close call with Rainier, whom he knew had to be in on the scam, he hoped not to have another one.

Once in the foyer, he asked for the telephone extension of a Mr. Killen.

Killen had been with the company for twenty three years. He had worked his way up through the ranks to the position of Overseas Liaison Manager. He was charged with ensuring all new and current contracts ran smoothly. His informer had told him that this was a man whom they could trust in New York, probably the only one. He was truly a man of distinction. He had been asked to join the Board a number of times but had declined ostensibly because of the in-fighting and politics that would have gone with it. Jack had been told that the real reason he had rejected the offer was that he thought that the hierarchy of the management were a bunch of arseholes and there was no way in a million years he wanted to be associated with such people. Although Jack had never met the man, he just had to rely on the intuition, instinct and advice from his most-trusted colleague back in London.

The receptionist connected them, and told Killen who it was that wanted to speak to him.

"Hi, this is Jack Henley speaking."

"Yes, I've been expecting you. Would you like to come up to my office ?"

"No, I think it would be better if you met me down here."

Just as Jack had finished speaking, he turned away from facing the revolving entrance doors to the foyer area. Rainier had just come out of the lift and was walking towards him. Jack turned back to face the doors. He could hear the voice on the other end of the phone but wasn't listening to it.

"Jack, are you still there ?"

Rainer glanced at him, as he walked passed and out through the revolving doors into a waiting car parked outside.

With relief, Jack sighed,

"Yes, I'm still here."

"Is there anything the matter ?"

"No. Just meet me outside the building. I'll have a car waiting."

At that, Killen put the receiver down and looking at his watch saw that it was 1 p.m. He then told his secretary that he probably wouldn't be in that afternoon, as he had some important business to attend to. He said no more, even though his secretary asked where he could be contacted if needed. As he made his way to the lift, Jack had made his way outside. He ordered a taxi and asked the driver to wait whilst his friend came down to join them. To his dismay, it was the same driver as before. The driver felt the same way as Jack did. He didn't want him as his passenger but it was another fare. Frowning he grumbled,

"I can't wait here boss, I get ticket."

Jack had no time for this man. He simply told him that he would wait and if he got a ticket then he would pay for it. He ended by telling him to shut up, keep his eyes on the road and that he didn't want to hear another peep from him. The driver did exactly as he was told. It was only a couple of minutes later when Killen was outside on the pavement looking around for a waiting car. Jack called him. He got in the cab and the driver was ordered to take them to the hotel where Jack was staying. When they arrived, Jack put on his overcoat and told Killen to circle the block a couple of times, then to come into the hotel and go to room 137 where he was staying. Jack said that all would be explained once he was in his room. Killen looked rather puzzled at the whole thing but said nothing and did exactly what he was told. Jack then got out of the car and walked to the doors which were pulled open by the bell boy he had tipped earlier. Jack gave him a knowing nod and made his way to his room.

Jack waited there until he heard a knock on the door. Saying nothing, but looking through the spy hole, he ensured that no-one was with Killen. He waited. There was another knock on the door. He could see Killen looking around anxiously, to see that no-one was watching. For the third and last time he knocked on the door. Finally, he gave up and started to walk back towards the lift. When Jack was satisfied in the knowledge that no-one was with him, he carefully opened the door without a sound. He had done this just in case some one was standing to the right of Killen in Jack's blind spot. No-one was there. Killen was alone. Jack called to him.

"Looking for me ?"

Killen turned round, saw Jack and frowned. Walking towards him he asked,

"Didn't you hear me knocking ?"

Jack ignored the comment as he held the door open for him to come into the room, looking from side to side, ensuring that no-one saw him go in.

"What's this all about then?"

"Please take a seat."

Killen sat down in one of two chairs either side of a glass table. Jack then seated himself opposite Killen. Killen said no more until he knew exactly what was going on. Jack asked him what he knew so far. Killen then proceeded to tell Jack that someone in London had been in touch and that the Board had something heavy going down. Killen wasn't giving anything away. He was keeping it all close to his chest. Jack then asked the rather blunt question as to why it was that he had not joined the Board and why it was that he was still with the company if his principles were as strong as he evidently wanted people to believe them to be. At that Killen slowly took a deep breath and tilted his head back giving Jack one of the most disgusted looks he had ever had in his life. Killen felt insulted, but Jack wanted an answer.

"Actions speak louder than words, not looks." Jack said confidently.

"Look, how the bloody hell do I know you are, who you say you are? I mean, look at you! Overalls, hair, beard. I mean it's all a little farfetched, don't you think?"

"You'll just have to trust that I am who I say I am, regardless of my appearance."

Killen got up from his chair saying,

"I don't think so somehow."

He was making his way to the door, when Jack gripped him by his arm and pulled him back.

"Look, I've got everything to lose. And I need your help to stop that from happening."

Killen looked him in the eye. It was obvious for the whole world to see, Jack was desperate and needed help. Killen gripped his shoulder,

"Ok I'm prepared to listen."

Jack could see that he was talking to a deep man, not just some jumped-up know-it-all from nowhere. He knew from his intuition that this really was a man he could trust. Yet again, his informer had come up trumps.

Killen took a seat. Jack offered him a drink. He was expecting Killen to ask for a bourbon, or a Jack Daniel's but he asked for tea instead. Jack was surprised. Killen explained that he'd never drank, that he couldn't even stand the smell of alcohol let alone drink it. And seeing the state that some of the other directors in New York got into, he was surely glad that he didn't.

"Ok. No booze.....Tea! You're the first American guy I've met that prefers tea to coffee."

Jack put the kettle on and leaned against the dressing table, the edge pressing against his buttocks. Folding his arms he asked,

"How much have you been told and by whom?"

Killen was now confident that this was indeed Jack Deer. From looking closely at him and studying his moves as described by the contact in London, he opened up.

He told of how he knew about the plot to overthrow Jack as the Managing Director / Chairman of the Board. He also told Jack who it was that had been giving him all his information. He knew everything. Killen then asked him curiously,

"I don't understand some things though."

"Like?"

"If you know what's going on and who's behind it all, why don't you just come clean, declare your innocence and if, sorry, when, everything is proved in order and nothing is amiss, then you will be able to carry on where you left off. Surely?"

"No, I can't. For two reasons. If I did as you said, they would find anomalies."

Killen narrowed his eyes.

"What do you mean?"

"Well, for a start, they have fiddled the books."

"In what way ? Surely an investigation would prove all anomalies to be their responsibility."

Jack chucked as he knew that as with his son, Killen was trying to find every conceivable loop hole that there might be in their scheme.

"I don't see what's so funny."

Killen was a serious man who couldn't stand a lot of things….. the pretentiousness and at times the drunkenness of the Board members. Sniggering in his presence was another one of his bug bears, *but then again it would be for anyone.* He sat stone-faced. Jack could read Killen's thoughts so clearly that he may as well have stood there with a billboard displaying them.

"No, you're right, there's nothing funny about it at all. In fact I should be crying."

Jack looked at Killen and was about to answer but was distracted by the sound of the kettle turning itself off. Jack turned around lethargically to make Killen his cup of tea. Killen really was a sobering man. He wasn't impressed by small talk at all. He was a man who didn't mess around. He got down to the 'nitty-gritty', the crux of the matter, straight away, without any hesitation. As Jack made him his drink he again could only think of what it was he stood to lose. Tea made, he turned to face Killen and gave it to him. He was shaking his head in despair. But Killen was there to help. Looking at Jack he knew that if he had hit a low, then he must be strong to bring back a fighting spirit. Even if it meant showing no compassion, being brutally honest and totally cold and impervious to all human feeling, although his heart bled for Jack.

"Well, you haven't answered my question. Why don't you just come clean ?"

"As I say, they've fiddled the books. They have done it in such a way, so that all blame would and could be laid at my door."

"You're still avoiding the question with this drivel. If you want me to help, I must know how they've done what you say they've done. Please, just answer the question."

Jack had to pull himself out of his self-pity to explain. He wasn't dealing with someone who was going to mother him and tell him, *"there, there now, never mind! I'll kiss it better!"*

No, Killen was a shrewd, intelligent and most importantly, an honest man. He could and would help Jack, but he wasn't prepared to sit and listen to rambling babble from him. If he was to help, he had to be in full knowledge of all the facts.

"OK, what it boils down to is every time major documents and contracts are made with different firms or governments they have to go through me."

Still intent on getting to the bottom of things, Killen just sat staring at Jack awaiting the answers.

"So, as I'm sure you can imagine I would not, nor could have had time, to read through all that is placed in front of me."

"No, that would be quite impossible."

"Well, what they achieved was quite simple. They fabricated payoffs and shady, underhanded deals that were written into these contracts."

"Who's *'they'* exactly ?"

Thinking of the Board almost made Jack lose his temper. He paced around the room, waving his hands to help him talk and explain, he was talking from his heart, telling it as it was.

"*Who*? Those bastards on the Board. They've recruited the help of the executives who work under them. The accountants that all monies go through and the consortium solicitors. And before you ask how, I'll tell you, 'nepotism.' And before you ask why, I'll tell you....... greed."

"OK, now we're getting somewhere. I can understand all of that but you've just said that there was a second reason for not coming clean. What is it ?"

"If I was to encourage an investigation, I would be found to be soiled and blackened. If, by some miracle, I was exonerated of all blame and responsibility, just think what would happen to the investors."

"Why ? What do you think would happen to them ?"

Killen wasn't a dulled subservient listener. He was asking questions all the way. He wanted to know the 'ins and outs' of his mind. How he thought, what he thought. Only this way would he know how to tackle the problem and how he could best help.

"It's obvious."

"Is it ?"

Killen was relentless.

"I know you know it is. If you were an investor and you had money in a consortium, which had just hit a scandal, you would do two things. Firstly, you would pull out your money in case the allegations were correct and I can assure you, it will be made to 'look' that way. Secondly, with your money you would invest with the people that were in competition with the consortium, for the simple reason that they are going to be the people who are going to pick up your business when you start to crumble. I know that as well as you do."

"You're making perfect sense but you're still to explain why the Board would do such a thing."

"Isn't it obvious ?"

"No. It isn't."

"Do you remember when the declaration was made by me eighteen months ago that I was to take full responsibility for all of the consortium's actions ?"

"Yes."

"Do you also remember the conditions I set myself ?"

"Vaguely."

"The greatest one was the unprecedented step of allowing a vote of no confidence on the Board's behalf to remove me as it's President / Chairman if they should wish to do so."

"Yes, a very unprecedented move if you don't mind my saying so. What the hell possessed you to make such a declaration ? You built up the consortium to what it is today and look what happens, they do this. That never made sense to me at all. In fact, if you were to ask anyone who knows anything about the business world, they would have said that it was foolishly naive."

Jack was fired by his last comment. He was mad. In fact he was more than that, he was angry. With a rage in his chest and a red-angered face, he pointed a finger straight at Killen,

"You never complained about all the benefits it brought to you though, did you ?"

"What do you mean ?" Killen was almost smiling back at him.

"Listen, you smarmy bastard, that step was taken by me so as to bring in so much more business, the competition paled into insignificance. They hardly ever got an iota of business once that declaration was made. The orders and contracts poured in, we had so much work that we almost had to turn down orders due to over-stretching ourselves. But I restructured the company so as not to do that and it meant that you, 'Sir', had more benefits than you could ever have hoped for. Your salary, company car, mortgage help-out. So don't tell me I didn't know what I was doing, you..."

Killen started to laugh. Jack was so fired up he was just about to punch him when Killen asserted himself,

"Now, that's more like it ! If you don't keep up that fighting spirit then how do you expect others to have it ? That's what I want to see Jack, that arrogant and aggressive attitude. This is the only way that we can defeat them. I'm with you all the way. Now that I understand all of what's happening, I feel I can help. But you'll have to let me know how."

Jack had well and truly been had by Killen. He now knew that he had known the answers to his own questions all along but had to prove to himself that he was talking to a man who was indeed who he claimed to be.

Jack smiled at Killen, and then broke out into a hearty laugh. It was infectious and Killen started to chuckle. Jack walked over to him and patted him on the shoulder, nodding his head at him in elated approval that he had another man on his side whom he could trust and who was going to help him. Jack walked into his bedroom and sat on the end of his bed, clasped his hands together and leant forward. Killen stood by the door waiting for his instruction.

"OK. The way you can help me is easy. You probably don't know yet and wouldn't have known until it happens, but the Board here in New York and in the other major cites where the consortium is based, are going to have satellite equipment placed in them."

Killen looked at Jack impassively and unlike before, was going to listen to his every word until he'd finished before asking any questions. Jack had his full and undivided attention. He had expected Killen to ask what they were, for but he didn't, so he continued,

"This equipment is for the purpose of keeping in touch with the latest up-to-date stock market prices throughout the world. Or at least that's what you and everyone else is going to be led to believe. However, it's not going to be used for that reason at all."

Jack stopped and waited for a response from Killen.

"OK, so what is it going to be used for?"

"I can't say. But what I can tell you, is that I want you to be aware that in the next week or so a meeting will be called by the Board here, and it is essential that you attend it."

Again Jack paused, awaiting a response.

"I attend all meetings that I have to. Why will this one be so important?"

"Because it is. All will be revealed when it takes place."

"You mean, you've come all this way to tell me that? You could have told me that over the phone or in an e-mail at least."

"No. I couldn't. I had to see for myself what kind of a man you were. I had to know that I could trust you. Now that I know I can, I want to ask for your help face to face, man to man. It wouldn't be right to do it any other way."

Killen look impassively at Jack,

"I'll do whatever it takes."

"Thank you."

"No problem."

Jack opened his wardrobe and from the top shelf pulled down his briefcase, which he clicked open.

"At the meeting, I want you to present these envelopes to the people whose names are on them."

Jack handed him two A4 sized sealed envelopes with the names of two of the London boardroom members written on them. Killen looked at the folders in his hand and then glanced to the open briefcase. Fairfax's photograph was looking back at him. He raised one eyebrow and asked,

"How will I know it's the appointed time?"

"Trust me, you will. Boy, will you ever! These envelopes are another reason why I had to see you in person. I couldn't trust sending these in the post, they are far too valuable to be lost or to have gone missing."

Killen asked if there was a bag he could put them in. Jack gave him a duty free bag which he'd been given at London's Heathrow airport. This had been another part of his disguise as he'd used it to look like all the other travellers, with their cigarettes and drink purchases.

"There's something else I need you to do as well."

"Name it!"

Jack went back to his briefcase. He pulled out another envelope.

"I want you to fly to Buenos Aires and give this to a guy called Adam Younger. He will give it to the person whose name is written on it, at the appointed time."

"I suppose he will know when that is, will he ?"

"Yes, he will, because just like you, a meeting will be called, which he must attend."

"How do I tell him this. Furthermore, how do you know if you can trust him ?"

Jack pulled out a letter from his briefcase. Waving it up and down gently, he smiled and gave it to Killen.

"He will know because this letter explains it all to him. And we can trust him, because he's just like you."

Killen and Jack both shook hands and bid each other goodbye as Killen left Jack's room with the envelopes in an inconspicuous plastic bag. Jack lay on the bed. He was tired from all the travelling, jet-lag was beginning to set in and with the anxiety of it all, he was exhausted. But he was also happy and content that everything was going according to plan. Little did he know that in the next hour or so everything was going to be turned upside down, causing even greater distress. He would have to rethink and rethink quickly, another plan of action, literally standing on his feet. Near exhaustion, he was going to have to be rational, he was going to have to be logical and most of all, he was going to have to be competent enough to make the right decisions that only he could make. The next few hours were going to be the most critical of all for Jack and his quest of holding onto his empire. It was of paramount importance, that whatever happened, he kept cool, calm and collected and made the right and crucial decisions.

The sad thing about it all, was that as Jack sat back to relax he had no idea of the major upset that was lurking around the corner waiting to deal all his plans a devastating blow.

Chapter Seven

Day Eight – Thursday Afternoon

Fairfax, in the meantime, had been busy working on the overthrow of the consortium. He had been successful in Chicago and was now back in his Boston hotel room after having a very successful meeting that morning in the city. He had met with powerful business tycoons who were to back him in trying to break into the arms business. This was something completely different from what he or the consortium had ever done before. He kept secret that there was to be a dismembering of the consortium in only a few days time. He had met with all the senior executives, letting them know the financial commitments, which were incomprehensible sums of money! All the necessaries were laid out in front of them and every possible angle covered to keep arms production up. All this despite the end of the communist regime in Russia and Eastern Europe. How the selling of arms in African countries could be defended along the lines of providing a country with the tools to protect itself. And how arms gave a country the strength to up-hold a democratic government. How arms helped a country maintain its liberty, its free spirit, its 'freedom of speech' and ensured the spirit of free enterprise i.e. making money. How selling arms to Israel and all of its neighbours evened things out.

All that Fairfax had said made sense and he had everything going for him. He was of an educated and privileged background. His family history was a military one. But most importantly of all, he had money. He spoke with commitment and conviction. He was quite literally going to put money where his mouth was, not to freeload himself onto the arms manufacturers with nothing but goodwill gestures and cheap talk. All of the investors, without exception, were prepared to sign deals with Fairfax, giving him full running of the European operations, also a mercenary commission on what he could persuade the British government to buy from them once the package was finalised. Fairfax, never being one to gloat, had sealed the deal with the American arms syndicate. He knew that the arms manufacturers already had the likes of the military brass, Senate and Congress in their pockets. Many influential people were already on their payroll, lobbying for them in all the right political circles. Also with certain buzz words, such as Israel, Middle East and Communism, he had everything in his favour and had succeeded in pulling it off.

For as much as America and Britain might be friends, xenophobia soon set in, should such a case arise whereby it might be seen as a muscling-in tactic on Fairfax's behalf. He knew that the only real clincher was the money. If they were guaranteed no losses in the first year and knew that they could only make on the deal, then the agreement was all but signed. The people at the meeting were all taken to the most lavish hotels and restaurants in town, wining and dining were all part of the show before the finale of signing on the dotted line. He had finally broken into the arms market and the American one at that. He was now tired and weary from mental exhaustion and was getting ready for a relaxing afternoon's reading and a good night's sleep. But Fairfax would, in the next couple of hours, receive a shock phone call that would change everything.

Once again, Jack was going over the finer points of the plan in his mind as he lay on his bed. A hundred and one things kept cropping up again and again. He had to know that the men whom he had chosen in different consortium offices throughout the world, on the recommendation of his mole, could be relied upon to carry out his instructions to the letter, without question or hesitation. Could Killen really be trusted? Only time would tell.

Jack reached across to the bedside table and picking up the monthly magazine of the consortium settled down to read the news about how well it was doing in all departments throughout the world. Although each magazine was specific to the country it was printed in, there were always articles which appeared in all of them, no matter where they were printed. After all, it was still the same consortium, wherever you were in the world and there always had to be some kind of common denominating factor. Sometimes, it came in the form of history and how the consortium was first formed or profit margins world-wide rather than pinpointing a particular division of any affiliated company. As Jack flicked through the pages, he could hardly believe what his eyes were seeing in that month's ironic issue.

On a common article page, was a write-up on how Jack had built up the consortium, from nothing, by using quite literally, his bare hands. The articles had full-blown colour pictures showing some of the workmen he had worked alongside and some of the management team that later backed and supported him, breaking into the big league, and finally making the consortium what it was today. There were also members of the Board, including those who were now conspiring against him. Some were smiling such as Jack, Fairfax and Warlton, others with solemn-looking faces as though they were about to be shot, such as Moore and Barron. The picture was taken in 1972 at the London dockland complex where the main consortium office building now stood. In fact, it was a picture that was taken just as the building had entered the construction stage, after permission had been given for it's go ahead by the London council, after much controversy. Also in the picture was the now head of American operations in New York, Bradley Rainer.

Although the photographs had been taken as a public relations exercise, they lacked none of the common touch that Jack had always insisted upon. Instead of being seen as the others in their pin-stripe fashionable suits of the day with short hair cuts, Jack wore work boots, overalls and long scraggly hair and beard. He was not much different from the way he looked now, only age and hard work had carved a few of what some called 'laughter lines' into his weather-beaten face.

He took what seemed like an eternity, looking at each and everyone of them. He was so full of hate for these people, he surpassed himself in not tearing the magazine up into tiny pieces and flushing them down the toilet. He was mad at the very sight of them. His thoughts were on how they had been free-loading themselves onto him, how the consortium had carried them all this way for so many years and then for them to have stabbed him in the back. He breathed heavily out of his nose as he thought on. He would gain nothing by losing his composure now, even if he was alone in his room. He had to stop thinking the way he did every time he saw them in either the flesh or pictures such as these. If he let his emotions stand in the way now, then he would surely not only let himself down, but those he had entrusted to help him hold onto what it was he was seeking to regain, before it was truly lost forever. He read through the rest of the magazine without absorbing anything. He was, once again, understandably grieved at the fact that so many of the people who had supported with him in those early days were hell-bent on destroying him and everything that they had all striven to build.

He was saddened to think that against all the odds he had succeeded, even exceeding his own expectations and those of his competitors, but was now fighting the very people he had put on the Board of his company.

But Jack, just like Fairfax, would, in the next couple of hours, receive a disturbing phone call that would change everything.

There was someone else who was reading through the magazine that very same afternoon…Bradley Rainer. It was the third or fourth time Rainer had picked it up for want of some leisurely reading. More than that though, the pictures of those early days when the consortium was in its beginning were bothering him but he just couldn't put his finger on it. He looked long and hard at the pictures as had Jack, but nothing. He threw the magazine down onto the coffee table in his mistress's apartment to look at something else. She came into the room. She was considerably younger than he was. She was beautiful with a perfect figure but was as dim as dim could be. Her contribution to the relationship….. she was ready to have sex at any time….Rainer could not get enough of her. Scantily-clad, in no more than a see–through teddy, she placed yet another Jack Daniels with ice into his hand. She slouched back into the corner of the couch with her crotch-less panties staring Rainer in the face, as she sipped from a glass of the same. She began to tell him of her morning as the TV droned with the sound of pathetic game-show contestants, clapping themselves at every opportunity. How by amazing coincidence she had met a girl from the same high school that she had gone to. That they ate lunch in a restaurant that they had only ever dreamed of having a man take them to, and how they had both got on since leaving high school and what they were both doing now and so forth. Rainer wasn't the slightest bit interested. He was only nodding and grunting where he thought he should. His sole aim was one of just humouring her, to keep her happy and so avoid another one of their vicious arguments. She seemed unstoppable. Her chin was like a relentless jack hammer constantly on the go and now, almost making as much noise as the din coming from the TV. It was all tittle-tattle that Rainer just had to sit through and endure. His tolerance was just about to break when she announced,

"I recognised her straight away. She wore the same style clothes that we had when we graduated. She looked identical but for a few extra pounds on her fanny. A little weight she told me she was working on loosing, but other than that she looked just the same."

This made him turn and face her, sit on the edge of the chair and reach for the magazine once again. She continued for half a sentence before stopping in mid-flow and asking him what was wrong. He just sat there staring at the photograph that had been bugging him. Smiling with glee he said aloud,

"Got ya, you bastard, got ya !"

"Wendy, darlin', you're a dream."

She sat there, totally bewildered. He stood up from the chair and without lifting his eyes from the page, made his way to the telephone. Wendy followed after him, asking if everything was alright, when he told her to shut up and go into the other room, something that she did without question or murmur. He turned the TV off and dialled the number he had been given by Fairfax on his arrival so that he could be reached at any time, any place, anywhere. It was only ever to be used in a dire emergency or if anything should happen of the gravest nature. This was both and he knew that he had to get hold of Fairfax immediately and put him in the picture. The dial tone rang out only twice before it was answered.

"Hello, Joseph Fairfax speaking."

"Joe, its Bradley."

Joseph looked at his watch. It was 1.30 pm. He knew that for him to ring at all, it must have been of the utmost importance.

"....What is it ?"

"He's onto us !"

"Who is ?"

"Jack Deer. He's here in New York."

"What ?"

"Yep, that's right ! The one and only Jack Deer is here in New York. He's been into the offices and he must obviously be onto us."

The phone line had an eerie silence that spooked Rainer. He was just about to ask if Joseph was still on the other end of the line, when Joseph spoke. He was calm and cool and collected. His voice was soothing.

"You'd better be damned sure Rainer. How could you know it was him ? He wouldn't have, couldn't have, just brashly walked into the office building unnoticed. I would have been inundated with phone calls telling me that he had been there well before now. Are you sure you're right,

because we're both going to look incredibly stupid if you're wrong."

Rainer, although he could understand what Fairfax was saying and also see his point, remained adamant. It was indeed Jack Deer that he had seen in the offices. He could not, nor would he be swayed from his conviction that the man he saw, was, without doubt, Jack Deer.

"Oh, believe you me, it was Jack Deer alright."

"You'd better be right about this Rainier, because if you're not you'll be out on the streets, I'll see to it personally, I can assure you. You'll never work in this industry again. If the Board are made to look like jackasses because you've got it wrong then there'll be no saving you. Are you absolutely one hundred and one percent sure that the man you saw was Jack Deer ?"

"No !"

"No !"

"I'm a thousand and one percent sure. The man I saw was.....is Jack Deer."

"How can you be so sure it was him that you saw and what was he doing in there anyway?"

"You know this month's magazine has a picture of us all from 1972 and how we all looked, especially Jack?"

"Yes!"

"Well, that's how I know it was him. He looked identical but for a few laughter lines on his face. He's grown a scraggly beard just as in the photograph and he got into the building under the guise of a workman in overalls."

"But how could you tell it was him? His hair has greyed in the last thirty years and he's put on a few pounds, how can you be so sure? By the sound of it, your story doesn't seem too convincing at all. Besides if he was wearing overalls how could you know?"

"You remember how he always had to be just that little bit different to stand out from the rest of the crowd? Well I thought he looked different somehow when I saw him in the elevator. He had ripped off the collar and the sleeves on his overalls leaving only frayed fabric where they'd once been. This was the telltale sign. I looked at him but he hurriedly knelt down to tie his bootlace which wasn't undone......until he pulled it so. As I quickly glanced down at him, I could see that they were trainers of the type that Jack always wore. He couldn't look me in the eye, he was avoiding eye contact. He even put a handkerchief to his face so that I couldn't see him properly but I knew there was something familiar about him. As for greying, he's dyed his hair. I swear to you the man I saw was none other than Jack Deer."

"OK, Rainer, I'll buy your story. Now listen good and hard. He must obviously have some friends there so don't go round asking awkward questions, we do not want him to know we're onto him. Do I make myself perfectly clear?"

"Perfectly."

"Right. I'll inform London of the situation immediately, and you just sit tight and wait for instructions, OK"

"Right, OK."

Nothing more was said.

Rainer walked back into the adjoining room where Wendy was slouched on a different couch flicking through a woman's magazine. He told her he was going to treat her to a night out on the town. He would treat her to the best restaurant in town, night club, the works. She didn't know why he was so excited and she didn't care. She jumped up and said that she would wear something fantastic for the night......*like Rainer cared!* She would spend the rest of the afternoon getting ready. She took a long lying soak in the bath, happy in the fact that Rainer was going to spend some quality time with her rather than just bed her. Rainer phoned his wife to let her know that he was going to be 'out' late and would have to stay in a hotel down town......again. He spun her the usual story of entertaining business clients to clinch yet another contract.

Meanwhile, Joseph tried immediately to inform London of the situation. He rang Warlton's house only to have to speak to the maid who said that he wasn't at home. He surprised himself by asking if he was 'working late at the office'. She told him that he had informed her he wasn't going to be at the office from 2 O'clock and that if anyone wanted or needed him for anything she knew where to tell them he was.....the Marlborough Country Club. Joseph, without another word, slammed the phone down.

He looked at his watch once again 2 pm. He automatically calculated the five hour time difference with London. Warlton must have been in the club for the best part of four hours plus he sighed, tutted and said aloud to himself,

"That lazy bastard, I might have known."

Joseph, although now extremely tired, made another attempt to ring Warlton, this time on his mobile but there was trouble with the line. Frustrated, he made a few more phone calls, one of which was to the Marlborough Country Club. He asked to speak to the manager. The manager, recognising his voice, was obliging with answers to Fairfax's questions. Warlton wasn't there, he'd left. When Joseph asked where he could be reached he was told the Pelican Hotel. Surmising that he was probably already there, he called the hotel. He was told that Warlton did indeed have a room booked and prepared, but that he hadn't arrived yet. Joseph couldn't believe it, the one time he needed to get hold of Warlton to speak to him on a matter of the utmost urgency, he couldn't. However, he was informed that he should be there any minute as he had said that he should be there around nine. Hastily, he left a rather abrupt message saying that the second Warlton stepped into the hotel he was to phone Joseph Fairfax immediately and without delay, that he had to speak to him on a matter of the gravest nature. For the first time, Fairfax sounded anxious and there was panic in his voice, which was coming through to the messenger on the other end of the phone most clearly. Without having to say another word, Joseph put the receiver back on the hook and lay on the bed, exhausted. He was worn out from all the travelling, organisation and presentations he had done ready for the takeover of the consortium.

He felt like closing his eyes and falling asleep. But he doubted if Warlton would call back considering just how lazy he was. He doubted if he would even bother calling the next day even if he remembered to. Warlton would always put off today, what he knew he could get someone else to do tomorrow.

Joseph picked up the phone again and rang Peterbough's home number. His wife answered. She told him that he too, was at the Pelican. Joseph said that he would try and get him on his mobile but was told that he couldn't because he had forgotten to pick it up on his way out. Sighing, he then asked her if she would be kind enough to call the Pelican and ask her husband to give him a call, stressing that it was very important that he spoke to him. She was very accommodating and never even thought to ask why he couldn't phone the hotel himself. He was glad not to have to ring there again as he would have looked and sounded like a pest, something that he could do without, especially since at sometime, sooner or later, he would have to face the management. He lay back on the bed thinking to himself,

"I'll just relax here for a few minutes until either of them rings."

He fell asleep.

It was 4 p.m. when the phone rang. It was Warlton.

"At last, thank God I've got hold of you."

"Whatever is the panic dear boy? Whatever is the matter?"

Fairfax told him all of what Rainer had discovered. Warlton began to dismiss it, saying that Fairfax was at best getting carried away with it all and at worst, paranoid. Fairfax stood his ground and told Warlton that he had every reason to believe that it was Jack in New York and that he should inform the others. Warlton once again, tried vainly to dismiss Fairfax's claim but was abruptly told to warn the others that Jack was onto them. Warlton paused for a while and said that he would.

Fairfax said that he would see him on Monday when he had flown back. Warlton put the phone down with a wry smile on his face and shook his head. He then ordered a drink from the bar just as Peterbough arrived. Warlton called him over to join him for drinks. He took a seat.

Peterbough and Warlton had time to kill before they were to go to their rooms. A waiter came over to the two of them and presented Peterbough with a telephone telling him that his wife had called and that she had left a message telling him to call a 'Mr. Joseph Fairfax.' Warlton told him that there would be no need and waved the waiter away. Peterbough asked him what it was all about and so Warlton began to explain that he'd just that minute spoken to Fairfax and that it wasn't anything important. Peterbough waited for

Warlton to tell him what wasn't so important. He reminded Peterbough that Fairfax's father had just died and that this, on top of everything else, was another burden of grief that Fairfax hadn't yet come to terms with. Peterbough nodded his head, saying that Joseph had indeed been overdoing it of late and was in full agreement that he wasn't yet over the death of his father. Screwing his face up, Warlton went on to dismiss his conversation with Fairfax because of these very reasons, saying that Fairfax was overworking himself to escape the grief and was stressing himself unnecessarily in the process. And that a little 'illusionary' problem Fairfax thought he had, was nothing more than that, 'illusionary'. Warlton did not elaborate on what 'illusionary' meant exactly and Peterbough never asked. Warlton ended the matter by saying that with all things considered, Peterbough shouldn't call Fairfax back. Peterbough agreed and didn't bother to call. They sat there drinking and making small talk until they were both ready to go to their rooms.

Once in their respective rooms, they both made phone calls to reception asking if any messages had been left and that they were not to be disturbed under any circumstances. They both also made other calls.....outside of the hotel.

These weren't the only people who had received the shocking news of Jack's appearance in the New York offices. Jack himself received a phone call telling him that he had been spotted and that they were onto him. Jack's heart sank into his stomach like a lead brick. He felt queasy and was thankful of the fact that he was already lying on the bed, he felt sure he would have keeled over if he hadn't been. For the first time he was speechless, he didn't know what to say or do. The speaker on the other end of the phone took full charge of the situation, telling him he had had time to think and had come up with an idea, but that they would have to change their plans. Jack was dumbstruck. He didn't even think to ask who had seen him, or even how they knew it was him. He felt weak at the fact that they knew where he was and that he might just have blown the only chance he had of regaining the consortium. With a blank stare, his mind went into overdrive as the voice on the other end of the line assured him that all was not lost, to keep calm and not panic. Jack could hear the person on the other end of the line but it was a couple of seconds before he was actually listening. There was silence. The caller called to Jack,

"Jack ! ......Jack are you there ?.......Jack !"

Jack didn't say anything.

"Hello......Hello......Jack"

"Yes, I'm here. I'm just thinking" Jack said in a very quiet voice.

Jack apologised and asked him to go over the plan again. When it came to the part of being 'shopped', Jack seemed to come back to life.

The telephone conversation continued for about another hour whilst the two of them put forward every scenario on what could go wrong. And how they could manipulate the situation and circumstances, as they now stood, to their advantage. Jack paced up and down, up and down, slowly then frantically as a seemingly bright idea emerged then was destroyed, with obstacles Jack himself would throw in its way. Finally, they came to a new plan of action. It was mulled over at length and when Jack was satisfied, he said they would speak again,.......soon.

Whilst all this had been going on, two of the now crucial pawns in this dangerous game were unaware of what was to happen and the shocking instruction that one of them was to be given.

Tomorrow John and Laura were to start their third day at the office. They had both been making great strides in their achievements, impressing their respective bosses and most importantly, their father. They had excelled at what they were trying to accomplish, getting into the heart of the organization. The departments they worked for were none the wiser as to who they really were nor what they were up to. But all that was about to change.

Day Nine - Friday

An old-fashioned alarm clock went off and John's hand fumbled in the dark to stop the incessant ringing that it made. Looking at the time, 6.15am, he sat at the edge of the bed and rubbed his eyes as he sluggishly thought about making his body and mind kick into gear. He flicked on the light switch and turned the dimmer switch right down as the light hurt his eyes. Then he took a shower and dressed after putting on a pleasant-smelling aftershave, one that could have been bought in any decent high street store rather than one of extreme expense. Nor was it one that his father would ever have worn. This again was another one of the strict instructions left by Jack, as he didn't want even the familiar smell of his perfume on his son. However remote it may have seemed, it might just have caused a comment from one of the Board members, remarking on the fact that Jack used to wear such a scent, then maybe one of them asking where he had bought it, etc. It was all seemingly far-fetched and a little over-the-top but Jack had insisted,

"Why take the chance, doing it my way, such a thing will not happen."

All clean and refreshed from his shower, he made his way downstairs to the kitchen to get some breakfast. He was greeted by the sight of Laura, sipping on her cup of black coffee. "Morning," was the bright and cheerful salute she gave him as she looked at him with her big, round eyes, red hair and perfect, white smiling teeth. The response wasn't half as cheerful, but it was there.

"Morning."

"Why are you always like this in the mornings, John ?"

"Why are you always like that ?"

Laura just shook her head, knowing that to talk to John first thing was a mistake and so said no more as John proceeded to pour himself a coffee. As John placed slices of white bread into the toaster, Laura made her way upstairs and said that she would see John at the front door in twenty minutes. He just nodded his head. He sat down at the table and began to think. He couldn't get the problem of the computer programme he'd been working on out of his mind. The reason why he was more tired than usual, was that he'd been at the office until midnight trying to fathom it out. He was frustrated, because he just couldn't crack it, yet he knew that it just had to be something simple. He had surmised that it was probably someone tapping into the computer base at certain times to minimise the chance of being caught and siphoning money out of the consortium. Once done, the person or persons responsible would sever themselves from the mainframe accounting network and the system would continue as per usual, without anyone knowing a thing...except that is, for John.

Laura came down the stairs in all of her usual regalia ready for work, but to any red blooded man, let alone Cavendish, she was dressed to kill.

"Bloody hell, John, why aren't you ready, it's ten to seven."

"What ? Oh shit !"

He had been so engrossed that he hadn't noticed the time at all. He began to run up the stairs and Laura began to make her way out of the house when the phone rang. They both stopped in their tracks. It was either their mother or father calling at such an hour. More than likely their father. Laura answered it. It was Jack.

"How are you both doing ?"

Laura looked to John pointing at the phone saying it was their dad on the line. John immediately came down the stairs and went into the lounge and put the conversation over the speakerphone. Laura then put the phone down and joined him.

"So, how are you both getting on then ?"

Laura spoke first, telling her father how Cavendish made her flesh creep but that she was going to stay with it. Jack then asked to speak with John. John started to tell Jack what he had found to date, when Laura said that she would have to leave so as to try and miss the morning traffic. They both said goodbye and John continued telling of what he'd discovered and what he suspected. There was a pause for what seemed an age,

"Dad.....Dad....are you there ?"

"Yes, I'm here ?"

"What's the matter ?"

"You're right !"

"I'm right ! You mean you know. How long have you known ? Do you realise just how much money we're talking about here ? Do you realise how long this must have been going on ?"

John was shocked that his father knew what was going on. Why hadn't he done anything about it ? Why was he so calm about the whole thing ?

"If you know about it, you must have had something to do with it. Have you ?"

There was another pause as no answer came from the other end of the line. John's heart began to pump even faster as he knew that his father was keeping something from him. He started to get annoyed.

"Is it to do with the informer you have on the inside ? Is it the informer ?"

There was still no answer from the other end of the line. Still Jack said nothing. But John's mind was in overdrive. He was frantically trying to piece it together in his mind. There was a deafening silence ! Neither of them spoke for what seemed like an age. John broke the silence.

"I get it. You knew what was going to happen and to cut your losses, you designed this so as money would be drained out of the consortium leaving you with millions to fall back on. That's it, isn't it dad ? That's it !"

"John, calm down, I don't want you to give our game away."

"Then tell me what the hell's going on. Or at least point me in the right direction so that I can understand just exactly what is happening."

"You must promise to keep cool and act as though nothing has happened."

John erupted with elation. He'd cracked the plan and was now about to find out who the informer was.

"It's Rothchild isn't it ? Isn't it ?"

John broke into a little laugh.

"I knew I'd crack it. I just knew I would. So what do you want me to do ?"

Jack proceeded to give John his instructions. John asked if he should tell Laura but was told quite categorically to keep what was said between themselves and that it was on a need to know basis. John sat and listened attentively to all that Jack told him to do, until he was told to shop Rothchild. John was surprised. It didn't make sense. John asked why should he shop the only friend that Jack had on the inside ? Jack told him to do as he said, and not to question things. A plan of action had been formulated and was to be followed to the letter. The fact that the plan had been drastically altered from the original, due to a phone call, was unbeknown to John, however this was immaterial. John didn't utter another word until Jack had finished. John said that he had still to get dressed. Jack told him not to rush into work as he might have an accident in the car. He told him that he had the perfect excuse for not being on time anyway, as he had found out that there was a mole within the boardroom ranks, who it was, and what it was they had been doing. They said their goodbyes, both now happy in the knowledge of the next course of action.

Laura, meanwhile, had made her way to work and into the day's offensive while John was still on the road. Her day started with all the false normalities, with plastic smiles and "Good morning" greetings to both Cavendish and Helen

Auldrich. The only thing Laura thought good about the morning, was that it was yet another day when neither of them knew who she really was, nor what she was up to. It made her queasy just to look at them, especially Helen, creeping around Cavendish like some sleazy slut off the streets, out to make money from whomever she could. And Cavendish, just the mere sight of him, fully-clothed, made her flesh crawl, but to think that Helen, who was a very good-looking woman, could lower herself to sleep with such a man, made her dislike the woman even more. Cavendish staggered into the room and went over to where Laura was sitting at her computer while Helen was showing her how her database was structured and how to access certain pieces of information. Cavendish smiled at them both. Helen smiled back with her eyes fixed on his, but all that Laura could do when smiling back was to keep her eyes glued on the ugly-looking wart to the left of his nose. He reeked of booze and it was only 9.45am. It wasn't the smell you might have after an all-night drinking session, it was too powerful even for that. He'd obviously hit the bottle the minute he arrived in his office, as he so often did, even though he had been out the night before drinking heavily till the early hours. He was now so full of booze that he became obnoxious, telling them how great they were. He rambled on. Cavendish then asked to see Laura in his office for a little chat. She promptly replied, "Yes, Sir." and stood up from her seat and made her way to his office as Helen stood scornfully looking at her and then indignantly at Cavendish. She knew what his game was and what he was about to try and do. She was racked with envy, but daren't create a scene as it might just be the excuse that Cavendish would need to get rid of her, totally destroying any chances that she would ever have of aspiring to a higher post. She had suspected for some time that Cavendish was getting rather tired and bored with her and so of late, had become a slave to his every whim. Giving him an escort when he wanted one and having sex with him whenever and wherever he felt like it. Trouble was, she was right, Cavendish was bored with her.

Cavendish was after something new, as this would give him a challenge rather than getting what he wanted, carte blanche. He liked the idea that he had to chase for the admiration of a woman and not be given it on a plate. Trouble was, he never realized women only ever slept with him because of his title, money and position. Never had he been with a woman because of his charm, looks or charisma. Helen, in her eagerness, couldn't wait to get on by what she thought pleased him, dropping her knickers and letting him park himself in her at anytime and any place. Flirting with Laura in her company was bad enough but stopping to wink at her, as he followed Laura out of the office, just added insult to injury. Helen puckered her lips, frowned and made her way rather hurriedly over to her desk to continue work. She was livid and seething with anger. She deserved an Oscar for not letting her emotions erupt to the surface as she had done two days earlier, when Laura first started.

Once in Cavendish's lair, Laura stood by the side of a chesterfield armchair opposite Cavendish's desk. Cavendish closed the door, as he thought quietly behind him, but in fact it was slammed shut instead. Laura jumped at the noise as Cavendish made his way over to her with a pissed smile showing his buck yellow teeth once again. Looking at her, through his dull blue eyes he asked her to take a seat. She smiled back at him and sat down resting both her elbows onto the arms of the chair. Her breasts stuck out from her chest in a most provocative way. Her cleavage could be seen as her short low cut dress hugged every contour of her voluptuous body. Her good looks, make-up and her bright red hair tied up in a neat French bun, instilled a lustful desire within Cavendish to take and have her right there and then. Laura sat facing his desk, expecting him to sit down.

Instead, however, he made his way round the back of Laura's chair and, with both palms of his hands spread-eagled out in front of him made a cheap and clumsy lunge from behind to grasp and feel her pert breasts. Laura shot out of the chair quicker than Cavendish could stop himself from falling awkwardly onto it. He lost balance and fell onto the floor. She didn't know what to do next. Should she slap him good and hard walk out of the room never to return, and tell her father? Should she laugh aloud and humiliate him or should she bite her lip, help him up and carry on as though nothing had happened? What would her father want? Every answer involved her father's approval. She couldn't stop thinking of him and although she had been warned of things like this happening, she was never really going to be ready for it, or know how she was going to react until it happened. In a flash, all of these thoughts had gone through her mind, before Cavendish hit the floor. Before even he knew what had happened, she was kneeling at his side, checking that he was OK and helping him up to his feet. He was out of breath and had to use both Laura and the chair to get himself into an upright position. Puffing and panting, he pulled Laura to him and put his face in hers, as his mouth opened to give her a French kiss. How she contained herself from being sick, she didn't know but she was able to push him off. He stumbled into the chair once again. This time, she really didn't know what to do. She was tempted more than ever to make a beeline for the door, walk out of the building and never cast eyes on such a horrible bastard again. Instead, she looked at him, smiled and told him that she wasn't that cheap nor that easy and if he had such intentions, he might at least ask her out a couple of times. Then flicking her head back and looking him up and down rather provocatively, she said that they'd see where it took them from there...perhaps a bedroom and not the office floor, although who knows, when they got to know each other better, who could say where they might do it. She could not believe what she was saying, nor how she was saying it, nor how she had kept her cool. She had frightened herself with all that had happened and was bothered, shocked and disgusted with herself for what she was doing. But on reflection, it was for her father and not herself that she did what she did and it was this factor which was her saving grace every time. She never wanted it said that because of her, her father had lost everything. With this in mind, she opened the door and walked back into her office to continue as though nothing had happened. Not five seconds later the door opened with a rather disgruntled-looking Cavendish popping his head round asking her to have lunch with him that afternoon. Thinking of her father and all that he'd coached her on giving Cavendish the run around and presenting herself as a bit of a challenge for him to conquer, she replied,

"Yes, that would be lovely."

He grinned pathetically at her and closed the door. Helen glared at Laura, suspecting more than ever that it was the beginning of the end for her in the favouritism stakes with both Cavendish and possibly the boardroom. Laura was now dreading each passing minute as time slipped effortlessly away like sand in an hour glass, counting down the seconds before she'd once again be in the company of Cavendish. Cavendish was happy as he knew it would only be a matter of time before he could deposit himself in her.

John arrived at the offices and was asked where he'd been by Barron, who was not the slightest bit amused at the hour he had decided to show his face.

"What the hell do you call this boy, a guest appearance ? Now get to work."

John wanted to give him a mouthful but instead, kept calm and tried to explain that he'd been in the office till midnight working on a problem of the gravest nature. It all fell on deaf ears. Barron, being of the arrogant nature he was, shouted at John, telling him that he didn't want his excuses and to get to work. John was incensed and called to Barron.

"Lord Andrew,"

"What ?"

"I'm not your boy, and don't you ever forget it."

Barron cracked an ugly grin, he liked the spunk of the man. He ignored the last remark, happy in the fact that he had ruffled John's feathers.

John sat at his desk and got to work. He had presentation papers to prepare. He couldn't help but think of Rothchild as he sat there. He couldn't approach him nor could he say that he had been cooking the books without proof. He had to get his hands on the memory sticks that Rothchild had in his office. He had been told by Jack exactly where to find them, in a drawer in his desk, that would be locked.

He had to break into his office drawer and grab the sticks, check they were the ones he was looking for, and then present them to Moore.

It was 12 O'clock. Laura's heart sank into her stomach as John waited for Rothchild to leave for lunch before making his move. Nearly all of the office staff had gone for their ritual Friday liquid lunch, only a few still remained in the office and those that had gone, wouldn't be back before two. John seized his chance. The chances of someone walking in and catching him were slim, at best.

Laura walked down to the basement car park with Cavendish, who was stumbling about all over the place. He was an embarrassment to be seen near, let alone be with. He summoned over his driver who held open the door for them to get in. Cavendish stood behind her as he drooled,

"After you, my dear."

She bowed her head and stepped into the back of the car as his hand patted her round, pert and seductive bottom. Her low cut dress rode up her thighs to almost reveal the colour of her knickers as she sat down. Cavendish attempted to get into the car. He tripped and was quickly caught by his driver, so avoiding falling onto the floor. He had been hitting the bottle .... all morning. As he finally sat next to Laura, reeking of alcohol, he tried to catch his breath wheezing, coughing and spluttering. Laura thought he was going to die in front of her there and then. No such luck. As the car sped away, he tried to make yet another indiscreet and clumsy advance on Laura. He placed his hand roughly onto her leg and tried to run his hand up her black stockings to her sensitive area. It was out of bounds for Cavendish, it was strictly a 'no go' area. She quickly grabbed his hand and snapped,

"Not here, not now" and that he "shouldn't rush things," Cavendish loved it. The idea of the chase, the wanting, the thought of getting what he wanted. The pursuit and timing,.... Cavendish wallowed in it all. Failing to have his own way there and then but knowing that the day was yet but young, he helped himself to the drinks cabinet in the back of the car. Pouring himself a grossly out-of-proportion whisky and water, he asked her what she wanted. For all of his upbringing, he still didn't have the manners to ask a lady what she would like first. He was drinking himself into a stupor, but Laura never once hinted that he might have had too much to drink. When she asked where he was taking her, he just grinned and patted her on the knee telling her that it was somewhere special and that she wouldn't be disappointed. Shrugging her shoulders and smiling back at him, she said that she couldn't wait. Cavendish thought that he was her knight in shining armour. Truth was, he was Laura's idea of an oversized pig in a suit.

John, meanwhile, seized his chance to get hold of the computer memory sticks he knew Rothchild had been using to drain money away from the consortium. Carrying some of the presentation papers under his arm, he walked up to the doors of Rothchild's office and let himself in without any problems. None of the office doors were ever locked and his secretary had also gone for lunch,....it was Friday. He quietly closed the door behind him and made his way over to Rothchild's desk. Standing behind it he bent down to pull open some of the drawers. They were all locked, just as Jack had told him they would be. He looked around the room for something to open the drawers with. He couldn't find anything. He tried his own keys in the locks, in the vain hope that they might just fit. He turned his keys in the first lock, then the second, third and then the fourth. Nothing. Then he tried the keys in the lower fifth drawer. It turned slightly and in his anxiety John inadvertently twisted the dammed thing so hard in his now ensuing panic to get the thing open, he had only succeeded in jamming his key in the lock. Time seemed to be racing away as John, for the first time, started to panic and lose control of the situation. What if somebody should walk in? What if the memory sticks weren't there? What if he couldn't get his key out of the lock? What if he couldn't even get the drawers open? What if? John's breathing began to get heavier and heavier. Adrenaline pumped through his veins. His senses were magnified. Suddenly his worst fear raised its ugly head. He heard a cough from the corridor, then a humming. It was Rothchild.

The door suddenly burst open and although John was waiting for him to enter, he jumped with fright.
"What the bloody hell are you doing in my office?"
John stood there clenching his chest with his right hand and holding the papers he had brought with him in the other. Rothchild, understandably, was not amused at the sight

of John in his office without his knowledge. Rothchild stood waiting for an answer as John 's forehead let dribble a bead of sweat. John was to 'shop' Rothchild and this was scene one. Rothchild's umbrage was so convincing. John couldn't help but admire him for playing the part so well. He was convincing. John quickly calmed down and said that he was putting work on his desk for his review. Rothchild without further ado, walked round to his desk and told John to move out of the way. John looked up and could see people at the other end of the corridor, watching. He quickly looked at Rothchild. The key that had jammed in the lock was now safely in his pocket. He'd managed to pull it free moments before the door had been flung open. Rothchild opened the top right drawer and then quickly closed it again. Was this him telling John in the most discreet way he could, this is where the memory sticks are ? He looked at the papers on his desk. "Anything else ?"

Rothchild asked dismissively.

John just stood there. He was lost for words. He couldn't make him out. One minute he's hinting at where the memory sticks are, then he's putting him on the spot and embarrassing him into leaving his office after closing and locking the very same drawer. John thought that his father must have told him to play it all as though the two of them didn't know they were both on the same side and with the door to the office wide open Rothchild didn't really have much choice in the matter anyway. Still, John didn't like the way this particular game was being played but if that's how his father wanted it, then so be it. Rothchild looked around the room and asked if John had taken his letter opener. John looked at him with a puzzled look upon his face and said,

"No, I haven't."

Then it suddenly dawned on him. Get hold of a letter opener and use it to lever open the lock.

John returned to his own office and quickly found a letter opener.

Meanwhile Rothchild had tidied his desk and was off to a business lunch. He'd worked hard. He'd been in for two hours straight!

John re-emerged and once again entered Rothchild's office. Using the letter opener he was able to easily flick open the lock on the drawer. With one swift movement the drawer was open. Low and behold there were two memory sticks staring him in the face. Rothchild had let him know exactly which drawer they were in and what to use to open it. John kept whispering the word 'yes' over and over again to himself.

Leaving the drawer as it was, he made his way to the computer in his own office. Without any hesitation he promptly put the memory sticks into his computer and eyeballed what was on them. The programmes they contained appeared incredibly complicated to the ignorant, but to John, who'd majored in computer programming, they were very simple by programming standards. The memory sticks proved all that John had suspected to be correct.

The memory sticks were used at any time Rothchild chose, to take over the accounting process of the consortium. The memory stick ran the mainframe computer, rounding off all monies paid. The remainder was directed to banks in Switzerland, Germany, America and Canada. The minute the memory sticks were disconnected from the system, even if they were pulled during an illegal transaction, the main frame computer programme kicked back into operation. Everything carried on as though nothing was wrong and all monies went on being paid rightly into the consortium account. The fact that Rothchild had supreme control over the accounting system via mere memory sticks was just mind-boggling. But even more startling was the ingenuity and simplicity of the programme. John couldn't help but admire the sheer genius of it all.

In the middle of all this admiration he thought of his father. The fact that he had let it go on, because all the time, he was behind it all getting his own money back anyway, thus minimising his losses. John just sat there, whispering to himself again, only this time he kept saying,

"Brilliant, bloody brilliant."

He thought of how he was to spill the beans and tell Moore about what had been going on. This, above all else, simply did not make sense. Why he had to shop Rothchild, he couldn't work out at all, or come up with any logical explanation. This was a mystery which was harder than trying to crack the puzzle of the computer programme, of which he'd made correct assumptions and posits. But he knew his dad was running the show and considering his genius so far, who was he to argue with a man who had manipulated the situation so aptly for his own gains. His, was not to question why. He was now more than ever in awe of his father and what he had done in trying to prevent the loss of his massive empire. John was going to play the game to the rules and instructions of his father. All he had to do now was to see Moore.

That afternoon Rothchild was going to be exposed to Moore. How would he react? What would he say? What would he do? And how was John going to explain everything to Moore without letting on that he was Jack's son?

Chapter Eight

Day Nine – Friday Afternoon

Laura was sitting for the main course of her meal in the stagnant company of Cavendish, who was indulging in another bottle of wine. The conversation was all one-sided, with Cavendish telling her and slurring his words as he did so, how he was the 'King pin' in all operations. If it wasn't for him, the consortium wouldn't be what it was today. How he had personally helped Jack Deer to achieve and aspire to the greater heights of the business world. How Jack had lost the plot. Laura was incensed. She just had to say something. She was coming to the end of her tether with this self-centred, sanctimonious bastard and her patience and endurance of the man were on a razor's edge.

"But if it wasn't for Jack Deer, you nor any of the others would have a position on the Board, because there wouldn't be a consortium boardroom seat to be had. And whilst we're on the subject, I do believe that one of the many talents of Mr. Deer, was in actually helping to build the consortium offices with his bare hands and more than that, he actually helped in it's design. Surely all the credit that is due, lays at his door,....doesn't it ?"

Cavendish kept looking into his half-empty wine glass.

"Now, my dear, I don't know where you've got all these stories from."

Laura frowned. She wasn't going to either let him off the hook or slag off the good name of her father. She was trying her hardest not to let her temper get the better of her but it was beginning to surface. She knew that if he persisted with his verbal assassination of her father, she was going to erupt like a volcano. What was worse, was the idea that once she did blow, there would be no going back. She couldn't take this arse anymore. She did, however, manage not to raise her voice or cause a scene, conscious of the fact that it would only be a matter of minutes, or indeed seconds, before a drama might be made of the situation. She had had enough and for as much as she had bitten her lip and put up with this pig, she just could not take any more. It was inevitable that she was going to explode and spew a molten lava of home truths at him. In defence of her father, she had to say something.

"I don't think so. It's all there, in this month's magazine and from the stories I've heard about him."

"No... No... No, that's all a PR exercise, and as for the stories, that's just what they are, stories, my dear. How naive you are."

Cavendish couldn't have been more patronising.

That was it. She stood up from the table with a scornful look on her face and a raging anger within her soul, as her high-spirited character was now about to let rip. She was all geared up and ready to put Cavendish in his place, when he suddenly closed his eyes, grunted and keeled over onto the table. In a flash, every vengeful thought left her mind as she quickly stepped over to him, asking if he was alright. People were now starting to look over at them, and she was panicking, thinking that he might have had a heart attack. The manager walked quickly over to their table, clicking his fingers at two of the waiters as he did so. The manager sighed, clicked his fingers hurriedly at the waiters once more, pointed to Cavendish and then quickly pointed again to the reception area. Laura asked what was wrong with him. Not waiting for an answer, she tried to explain,

"One minute he was drinking, then the next thing I knew, he'd passed out."

The manager wasn't listening to a blind word she was saying. He was only interested in getting Cavendish out of his restaurant. Laura could see that he didn't want or have to say anything to her. After all, she knew that she must have looked like another of Cavendish's 'escorts.' He told the waiters to get him out of there and that he had done this for the last time. Laura was taken aback. Rather indignantly, the manager took Laura to one side and spoke to her.

"Tell Lord Cavendish that his custom is no longer wanted or required in this restaurant or any other of my establishments. He has done this little party trick for the last time."

As he walked off towards the reception desk, the two waiters were standing either side of Cavendish, his arms strewn over their shoulders, with his head bowed, sunk into his chest. As he was held in this pitiful, crucifix position for all and sundry to see, Laura couldn't help but blush. She followed behind the manager with her head held low and feeling so ashamed. She could have died there and then. Struggling behind her were the two waiters, who were almost dragging Cavendish to the door. He was like a pathetic well-dressed rag doll. The manager had summoned a taxi to take him and Laura off the premises. She tried to apologise but the manager would hear none of it. It was hard to tell who was the more embarrassed about the whole thing. A taxi pulled up to the doors of the restaurant. The manager couldn't open the door quickly enough. As the waiters threw the carcass of Cavendish into the back seat, the manager went round to the driver and told him where to take them. Cavendish's house. Laura said nothing, she just wanted the ground to open up and swallow her whole. She daren't look up from where she sat. The manager then paid the driver in advance and told her that it would all be added onto Cavendish's account......final account.

Laura was so pleased and glad to be out of the place where so many prying eyes had gazed upon Cavendish and her. Everyone knowing he had passed out through alcohol and how they couldn't help but think that she must be his latest bit on the side. How shameful. She felt disgusted with herself. What made it worse was that she didn't even get the chance to defend her father. She didn't dislike Cavendish, she didn't hate him, she didn't even loathe him.....she despised him. What topped everything, was when the driver turned around to her, when he had to stop at the first set of lights and said that if Cavendish was sick, she would be charged for having to get the cab cleaned and the loss of earnings whilst it was being done. She then started to question herself,

"What the bloody hell was she doing in the taxi with him anyway ? Why hadn't she got one of her own ? Why hadn't she called Cavendish's driver on the telephone ?"

It was all in hindsight, it was now all so clear what she should have done, but it had all happened so quickly, there had been no time to think. She was about to tell the driver to stop the car and that she would get out, when the driver said that it was a good job she was looking after him. And that he was going to get home alright, otherwise he might just have choked on his own vomit. She couldn't help but wish he would. As the car trudged through the mid-afternoon traffic of London, Laura had mixed emotions. She felt like crying, was angry and shocked at herself, in total and utter disbelief at what had happened, what was happening, and what would happen when she finally got to Cavendish's home. Looking out of the window, she was unable to believe the present situation. She was pleased that she hadn't blown up in a rage in the restaurant and given Cavendish a mouthful, as this would surely have resulted in her being dismissed or at worse, ruining everything. She sat there, not knowing what to do, but had made up her mind that she would see Cavendish home and then get the driver to take her back to the office where she would pick up her own car and drive home.

John, meanwhile, was in Moore's office, telling him of his findings and demonstrating them on the computer on his desk. Moore was sceptical of John at first, telling him that if he wasn't correct in his allegations against Rothchild, he would see to it personally that he was prosecuted for slander and breaking into his office and stealing private property. John had to go to great lengths to prove to Moore that everything he was saying was true and that as much as he didn't want to believe it, he just couldn't ignore this damning hardcore evidence. Moore was visibly stunned and shocked, not only at the fact that Rothchild had indeed been fiddling the accounts, but at just how much money was involved. He was speechless. The total amount that he must have drained out of the consortium was in the hundreds of thousands, possibly even millions. Moore, in total disbelief, asked John to run through the programme once more with him so that there was no ambiguity in his claims of Rothchild's fraud and deception. John obliged and went through the procedure slowly and methodically so that Moore was left with no doubt in his mind that John was correct and that Rothchild had indeed been stealing money. John, in his eagerness, even set up a demonstration for him. He rang through to the accounts department and asked them what the computer printout had on it regarding the latest instalment payment from the Chinese government for a road and dockland development they were in the process of building for them. He showed Moore what it should have been, then ran the programme. The expected monthly instalment for the project was £253,854. But when the programme was run, the money actually paid into the account was £250,000. The sum was accepted and authorised by the programme to be the correct amount due and printed this out as being so. The other £3,854 was seen to be transferred into a bank in Switzerland. John explained to Moore that although this was an insignificant amount of money by the consortium's standards, it must be noted that such transactions happened several times a day, everyday, and if this had been going on for a period of years, as he evidently believed was the case, then the amount of money stashed away in unsuspecting banks throughout the world, would be phenomenal. This was the simplicity of the programme that John couldn't help but admire. No-one knew, no-one suspected and no-one would ever have known if it hadn't have been for John stumbling onto it by accident and then having it confirmed by his father. Moore thought slyly to himself that considering the Board was to announce record profits then say that they had got it wrong and that the profits, were even higher than at first claimed, that if this money was retrieved, their figures would have some credibility. Moore, now convinced, congratulated John on his findings and called to his secretary to ask Rothchild to come to his office. Ten seconds later, he was told that he wasn't in when the doors to Moore's office were burst open.

"There you are, you thieving little bastard!"

It was Rothchild. He was enraged. He had come back from his business lunch to find his desk drawer had been broken into. Because he saw John snooping around his desk just before lunch, he had correctly assumed that he was the.... 'thief' who had stolen the memory sticks from his drawer. Moore stood up from his desk and intervened.

"So, you admit it then, that these are your memory sticks and you've not only been stealing from Jack Deer but you were planning to continue robbing us?"

Rothchild's expression was halfway between a perplexed frown and an angry grimace. The room went quiet. Both Moore and John looked at him when he spoke.

"I don't know what you're talking about."

"Let's not play games here, Rothchild, you've been stealing from us all and you had no qualms about stealing from me when I take over."

"Oh, 'you' are taking over now, are 'you'? So what happened to 'us' taking over?"

"You're out Rothchild! When I show this to the fraud squad you'll be doing at least ten years behind bars."

"Can't you see it's a set-up ? I've been framed for God's sake....by this little bastard."

Moore pointed to John and asked Rothchild,

"Why do you call him a thieving little bastard ? When these sticks are yours ?"

"Because he was mooching around my desk before lunch. I've only just this minute come back and found that he's broken into my drawer. I didn't check to see if anything was stolen, I just wanted to catch him still here in the building. But instead I find him in here with you saying that he......*'found'* those in my drawer, which is a downright lie. That little runt is trying to frame me and I can only think of one reason why."

He looked to John who was saying nothing.

"You're in this with Jack Deer."

John's heart stopped. Why the bloody hell did he have to say that ? That surely would only bring his father to the forefront of Moore's mind and his cover would be blown. He began to doubt if Rothchild really was in on the plan, but it was his father running the show not him and if that's what his father had told him to say, then so be it. But it was all rather strange and try as he may, none of it made sense. He had to say something in defence of himself, as he knew that the plan was to have Rothchild shopped and not himself. He was now on the defensive.

"So, why didn't I close the drawer back up again instead of leaving it open ?"

"Don't patronise me, boy ! You had to get in here to speak to Charles before I got back and you knew that every single spare moment would be wisely spent in trying to convince Moore that those memory sticks were mine."

Moore told Rothchild to get out of his office and that he had less than forty-eight hours to return all the money he had stolen from the consortium. Rothchild began once again to protest his innocence, but it was in vain. Moore interrupted him saying that the police, fraud squad and Inland

Revenue would all be informed of his dealings, so he'd better quickly retrieve all of what he'd stolen. Saying no more, Rothchild left the office with an enraged face and badly bruised pride.

John sighed with relief, thinking that Rothchild really had gone over the top in his defence. He'd come too close for comfort in nearly convincing Moore that the memory sticks had indeed been planted by him. But as he thought on, he was the one left standing in Moore's office and he was the one that Moore believed. So when all factors were taken into account, Rothchild probably knew just how close to the edge he could go without falling over it. As he reflected, he knew that Rothchild would know Moore and the rest of the Board members better than he did. So once again, who was he to question his father's plan and the way it was being executed.

As this drama was taking place, another was unfolding three thousand miles away at the JFK airport. It was bedlam. Due to bad weather many flights had been delayed, this was exacerbated by planes having to have their wings de-iced. The passengers on flights back to Europe were piling up all over the airport.

Fairfax was in the VIP lounge after his domestic flight from Boston. He was accompanied by three Boston executives. He was still tired as he'd only dozed rather than getting in some quality sleep. Many factors had stood in the way of him getting some proper rest, least of all the fact that Jack Deer had seemingly been spotted in New York and he had had to let London know. But he couldn't be sure that the news had been relayed to all the members of the Board. He couldn't and didn't trust either Warlton or Peterbough...had they informed the others? Considering that the working week was over, he suspected that Warlton, being as lazy as he was, wouldn't have bothered to do anything and was probably waiting until Monday.....and that was if he remembered. Especially considering that Warlton had made it clear to him that he thought he was wrong about the sighting.

A hundred and one things were going through his mind and he was physically and mentally exhausted. It was suggested by one of his travelling companions that he stretched his legs and took a walk around the airport. He was reminded that he was going to be stuck on a flight for seven hours, even if he was flying first class..... as he always did. He strode around at a leisurely pace with one of the executives when he stopped to look at magazines in a rack outside one of the stores. Just as he picked up a 'Business World' magazine, Jack Deer appeared from around the corner. Fairfax didn't see him as he was mindlessly flicking through the pages, but Jack saw him.

Jack's heart began to beat faster. He just couldn't believe his eyes. In an instant and without even thinking he quickly turned on his heels and walked back in the opposite direction. He turned left and walked into a perfume shop to peer through the window and watch the movements of Fairfax and company. He watched them walk back in the direction of the VIP lounge. He just couldn't believe it. Fairfax in the company of office staff in the airport. He must obviously be flying back to the UK. Jack had no alternative but to go to reception and change his flight ticket. If he got on the same plane as Fairfax he might just be recognised by either him, or one of the entourage of office staff that he had with him. His plan would then surely be scuppered.

At the BA reception desk, Jack was able to change his flight to one that was going to fly later that day. One step ahead of the game and as cautious as ever, Jack kept to economy class, the same as what he'd flown out on.

For security reasons, due to increased terrorist attacks, the aviation authorities followed a new boarding procedure whereby business class passengers had to embark at the front of planes and economy at the back. How this helped with security no-one could fathom but it was the ruling of the aviation authorities, and so that was the way it was. But Jack turned this to his advantage. If consortium staff were on the same flight, they would be business class, so the chances of bumping into one another were, at best, remote. The loud speaker sounded,

"Will all passengers for flight BA 0178 to London, please Board at gate six."

Neither Fairfax nor any of the executives knew that they had narrowly missed an encounter with Jack Deer. Jack, meanwhile, was calming himself in a cafe with a cup of tea. He had only three hours to wait before he, too, would be boarding a flight back to London. Jack smiled to himself. For as careful as he was, that one near-miss encounter could have ruined everything. He praised himself quietly in his mind telling himself he was a *'jammy bastard'* and that the gods must be watching over him.

Laura meanwhile, was with Cavendish, who was now in a semi-conscious state. He'd been helped out of the back of the taxi by his butler but fell to the floor which woke him up. The cab driver hadn't even bothered to get out of his seat. He just sat there, watching everything with indifference. The butler was embarrassed for Laura, more than he was for Cavendish. Of late, this was more of a routine than anything. The butler offered her something to drink, a cup of tea or coffee. She'd been stuck in that cab with an obese, ignorant and ill-mannered pig and a moaning cab driver for company. A cab driver who moaned every five minutes repeating himself that should Cavendish be sick in his cab then, 'she' would have to pay to get it cleaned. Laura couldn't bear the thought of going into the house, in case Cavendish came round, nor could she stand the thought of getting back into the taxi with a driver whose only concern was his precious, bloody car. It was the lesser of two evils she had to decide. She presumed Cavendish would be taken to bed so as he could 'pass-out' and that she wouldn't have to humour a drunkard if she did decided to go into the house…going into the house would be giving herself a break if nothing else. Then after a cup of coffee she could be on her way. She decided to stay. The driver muttered under his breath for her to please herself. She hadn't been so pleased to see the back of anyone in a long long time.

As the car sped off down the driveway, grinding the grey-coloured gravel beneath it's wheels as it did so, Laura shivered as the cold winter wind cut though her like a knife. A maid came out to help carry Cavendish into the house. Laura was asked by her to come inside whilst she made something hot for her to drink and made some arrangements to get her home.

Laura sensed that she was another Mrs. Briggs. She was about the same age and had the same hospitable warmth about her and a smile that would have made the coldest heart melt. Saying that she didn't really have much choice, Laura followed her into the house. It was no ordinary house. This was Harlton Hall, the stately home of the Cavendish family.

Laura was shown to the dining room, but asked if she could sit with the housekeeper in the kitchen instead and have her coffee with her in there. She felt better, knowing that once Cavendish lay on a nice, soft bed he would be out for the count and she wouldn't be pestered by him. The maid just smiled at her and nodded her head, then walked through the hallway into a small corridor which led to the kitchen at the rear of the house. It was fitted out with all the latest equipment that you might expect of the modern age, which blended in remarkably well with the old fashioned eighteenth-century style of the house's architecture and decor. Paintings, which Laura had noticed adorning the lobby and stairways, looked as though they could have been even older but she only had a chance to glance at them. Even the kitchen itself had an early 1900's Delft rack running around it with plates and Toby jugs decorating it. It was so homely and cosy that Laura just had to comment on it. She was surprised when the maid told her that she had designed all the layout herself. Saying that she wanted it so that it was neither stuck in the past, nor was it clinically sterile….. as were so many of the modern-day domestic fashions. Laura was impressed and the charisma of the maid, made her warm to her even more. She asked what her name was.

"Stella…and you are ?"

"Laura Deer."

Her heart missed a beat. She had said it without thinking. The maid made a joke about it as she began to pour water from the kettle into a teapot saying,

"Milk and sugar my *'Deer'* Laura."

Laura didn't laugh or even crack a smile. She prayed she'd forget it. For however remote it seemed, she might just keep it at the forefront of her mind. She might then innocently mention it to Cavendish and doubt would be cast, causing awkward questions to be raised as to what her real name and identity were. Again, flash thoughts of letting her father down began to go through her mind. The maid poured her some coffee from the percolator, thinking to herself that she'd better watch this one, she's a bit touchy. If only she knew !

Laura finished her coffee and thanked Stella for her hospitality and consideration in taking it upon herself to have Cavendish's driver take her back to the office.

John was busy working on the rest of his presentation, ready for Barron on Monday. He was ecstatic at the fact that he was now in the complete confidence of Moore, and

believed that before the week was through, the rest of the
Board. Fairfax was already in the air returning to the UK
and Jack was just about to take off.

Day Ten - Saturday

Both Jack and Fairfax had arrived back in London and were now rested after a good night's sleep. The first thing on the agenda for Fairfax was for him to see and speak to Moore about the sighting of Jack Deer and what, if anything, Warlton had done about it.

The alarm went off in Fairfax's bedroom. Through tired eyes he could see that it was 7 a.m. He reached out and turned off the bleeper, convincing himself that he'd just have another hour. After all, it was the weekend and although time was of the essence, he knew that if he didn't allow himself one proper lie-in or day of rest, then he would be just too knackered for the remainder of the take-over. It would be another two and half hours before he would emerge from his pit.

Jack, meanwhile, was up at six-thirty. He'd showered, eaten breakfast and left the motel he'd stayed in that night rather than going home. He was in a hire car that he'd picked up at Heathrow. He had very important business that day. Much hung on his meeting with a key figure that day. If the plan was going to fail at anytime, it was today. He could only hope and pray that everything would go without a hitch. Only in the next few hours would he know whether or not he stood a chance of holding onto his empire. If it went wrong, he would definitely lose everything. As he sat at the wheel, he couldn't help but pray everything went according to the way he and his confidant on the inside had planned it.

John was still in his bed but had decided that he was going to go into the office that day, so as to clock up kudos points with Moore and the rest of the clan. Laura was to spend the day shopping in London. Other members of the Board would either be in the Marlborough, the Pelican or at home with their families.

Jack's car pulled up outside the gates to Brindel House. A call was made on the corroded intercom. It was half hanging out of it's wall fixing, and as a voice sounded from it, it was barely discernable amongst all the crackling coming from it. Jack could only think that his voice must have sounded the same to the person on the other end.

"Yes. Who is it ?"

Jack told them that he had a parcel which was recorded delivery and some registered post. The faceless voice on the other end of the wire was silent.

"Hello....Hello...can you hear me ?"

"Yes....Yes....O.K. Opening the gates now."

Jack smirked as he thought to himself that for all the money that had been spent on the security system, they didn't even have any closed circuit television cameras. He could be, and indeed had just proved, that he was able to pass himself off as anyone. The huge, wrought iron gates opened inward to let Jack in. As he drove up the drive he could see that the gates were closing behind him. He pulled up at the steps of the house, he could see the frown on the face of the maid who was there to meet him. He knew all of the staff who worked at the house but he didn't recognise her. She was new and she didn't know him either. He stepped out of the car carrying a small briefcase stuffed with papers.

"Who are you ? You're not a delivery man."

"No, I'm not, and you don't get any points for that one. Now where is he ?"

"This is private property. Get off it before I call the police."

Jack totally ignored her and walked into the open doorway of the house. He walked through the hallway and into the kitchen area. He had been to the house many times and knew his way around. When he could see that the person he wanted to speak to wasn't there, he asked where he was. Still the maid shouted at him to get off the property, otherwise the police would be called. Jack said no more but made his way upstairs. The maid, in her haste ran for the telephone and dialled for the police.

Jack had knowingly walked straight to one of the many bedrooms and flung open the doors. As they burst open, a man who was looking out of the window to see if he recognised the visitor's car, swung around. He was startled, but then shocked at seeing who it was that stood before him.

"Jack !"

"Don't you 'Jack' me, you slimy, slithering, little bastard, Rothchild."

The maid had run up the stairs and breathing heavily was now standing behind Jack. She started apologising to Rothchild, saying that she couldn't stop him, but reassured him by telling him that the police had already been called and that they were on their way. Rothchild just stood gormlessly in front of Jack. Jack, without turning around, but continuously staring at Rothchild, told her that he didn't think that 'Simon' thought calling the police was a good idea. Rothchild now totally flustered told the maid to ring them up again and tell them she had made a mistake. When she started to ask questions, Rothchild shouted at her,

"JUST DO IT, WOMAN !"

Frowning, in unbelievable dismay, she looked to Jack who remained facing Rothchild. She cowered and walked quickly back downstairs to the telephone.

Rothchild was speechless. Jack told him to put on his gown and go to the study. As Jack passed the maid at the bottom of the stairs, he told her to make them both some tea. She looked to Rothchild who was only a couple of steps behind him. He nodded his head to her as a signal that she should do as he said. Jack walked into the study and without turning around, told Rothchild to close the doors behind him. Then he was told to sit down at the desk as a folder from under Jack's arm was placed in front of him.

"Right, you thieving little bastard, here's the deal."

Rothchild sat there, hanging onto Jack's every word as he told him all he knew. Jack told him how he knew that he had been stealing from him and for how long. How Rothchild had opened different bank accounts in different countries where the money had been stashed. How he knew, that to save being discovered, he had entered into a correspondence with the banks through letters that were not sent through his secretary but posted by himself and how all replies, went to a P.O. BOX. Rothchild sat in awe of Jack. He thought that no-one would ever have known about the scam, let alone catch him at it. With all the evidence and proof that Jack kept bringing out of his folder he couldn't, nor was he going to deny anything and make an ass of himself. What topped it all, was when Jack started to be sarcastic, asking him whether his name really was Simon Rothchild or was it Roger Wakefield or Nigel Reeves or Claus Hermitt or Pierre Louis. Jack proceeded to read off a list of other names as Rothchild sat staring at the paperwork. When Jack had finished, he could see that Rothchild was starting to pull a smirking grin. Rothchild's mind was racing at a hundred miles an hour. He had covered everything so well, he truly believed that Jack wouldn't be able to prove a thing.

"It won't stand up in court. It will be my word against yours, and by the time..."

He stopped in mid-flow as Jack pulled out an A4 envelope from the briefcase and threw it down in front of Rothchild. Jack stared and smiled at him. Rothchild unnerved, snatched the envelope and looked at its contents. There were full on graphic photographs of him with young boys and prostitutes, partaking in orgies in his favourite haunt The Pelican. There was also a CD in the package. As he stared at it, Jack told him it was all on film, in crystal clear quality.

Rothchild turned as white as a sheet. Jack feared that he might faint on him. The maid knocked twice quickly on the

door and not waiting for an answer, entered the room
carrying a tray with a pot of tea and a few slices of toast
for Rothchild. Jack leant over to Rothchild and calmly placed
the photos back in the folder out of sight. No-one said
anything, apart from the maid who asked Rothchild if he was
alright. He couldn't answer her. His throat had seized up.
Jack answered her question for him.

"Oh, don't you worry about our Simon here. He'll be just
fine.......by the time I've finished with him. "

The maid simply squinted her eyes at Jack and saying no
more left the room, closing the doors behind her. Jack sighed
and walked over to the silver tea tray placed in front of
Rothchild, and once again made another sarcastic comment.

"I don't know, you just can't get the staff these days, can
you Simon ?"

Rothchild just sat there motionless, when he was told to
eat some toast and drink his tea. Still, he didn't move. Then
Jack shouted at him to snap him out of his mortified trance.
He jumped with the noise and looked to Jack, asking what
he was going to do. Jack told him once again to eat.
Rothchild clumsily bit into a slice of toast and chewed on it.
Jack was glad to see that he'd at least eaten something. He
didn't want him passing out on him.

"You know that you're looking at between ten and fifteen
years for this don't you ? And then there are the
embezzlement charges."

Rothchild pulled the cup away from his mouth and almost
dropped it onto its saucer. He felt weak and turned white
again. Fearing that he was going to pass out, Jack told him
to eat some more. He didn't move. Jack walked over to him
and physically pushed a piece of toast into his mouth. As
Rothchild pulled away, Jack slapped him hard across his face.
Rothchild's head jerked away from the strike and in an
instant he came to his senses. He quickly stood up from his
seat and was just about to retaliate when his eyes met Jack's.

They were burning through him like a blow torch. He stopped dead in his tracks. Jack didn't have to say anything but he did. For his own self-gratification he was going to let Rothchild know, without any ambiguity whatsoever, who was boss.

"Just try it!"

Rothchild sat down as Jack bent down to speak to him.

"I'm younger than you are. Stronger than you are. And I'm quicker, faster and better at this sort of thing than you could ever be, so I advise that you sit there, don't move and listen. You will do exactly what I tell you. Otherwise I'll rip your bastard head off and shit down your throat. Do you understand?"

Saying nothing, Rothchild just nodded his head. Jack then walked back to his chair. Looking at his folder, he continued calmly,

"Right, here's what's going to happen."

Jack then looked to Rothchild who was staring at him his mouth agape and a long weal mark left on his face where he had just been slapped. Jack stood upright, pointing his finger at Rothchild saying,

"The first thing that's going to happen is you're going to stop looking at me like that."

Rothchild looked away immediately.

"The next thing that you are going to do, is to listen and then carry out exactly what I tell you to do. That is, of course, unless you want to spend the next ten years behind bars."

Rothchild looked again to Jack and spoke for the first time.

"You mean, if I help you, you won't press charges and have me prosecuted."

Jack loved it. This crawling, slithering slug was at his mercy. Fearing that he might have to do time, Rothchild was ready and willing to do anything, even help Jack prevent the takeover. Jack was revelling. It was payback time, and boy, was he going to make Rothchild pay. He was now about to humiliate him, knowing full well he couldn't answer him back by simply patronising him half to death.

"My dear Simon, I'm a businessman. Nothing in this world is free now, is it? You scratch my back and I'll scratch yours. You help me get back what's rightfully mine and you don't go to prison for ten years. Simple."

"OK, so what's the plan, what exactly do you want me to do?"

Jack smiled at a rather ill-looking Rothchild. Then he began to tell him of the next stage of his plan and how it was he was to be a part of it.

Fairfax had just finished breakfast when he called Moore at his home. He told him that he had received and passed on his faxes to the dealers in Boston. He then spoke about the satellite equipment and how he had been there when it was being installed. Moore congratulated and commended him on his good work and all that he'd done, complimenting him by saying that he really was an indispensable asset to the company. Fairfax thanked him for the compliment but was more concerned about what he was going to do about another pressing problem at hand.

"Thank you, Charles, but what are we going to do about our unforeseen problem."

"Unforeseen problem! What unforeseen problem?"

There was a pause when Fairfax realised he must have already sorted it. He chuckled softly.

"Oh, already taken care of it have you?"

"Taken care of what Joseph? You're not making sense."

Again there was another long pause. It was Fairfax who broke the silence.

"You mean you don't know? He never told you?"

"Know what? Who is.... 'He'... exactly? Joseph you're still not making sense."

"That fat, lazy, bastard! I knew it was a mistake to tell him."

"Joseph, calm down, what's the matter? You're not making any sense."

"Did Warlton speak to you at all?"

"No, he didn't, why?"

"Oh, my God, I don't believe this. Charles, don't say anymore or speak to anyone about what I've just said. I'll be round your house in about forty minutes."

Saying no more, Fairfax slammed the phone down and calmly made his way upstairs to get his briefcase. Moore pulled the phone away from his ear and looked puzzled as he put the handset back in its holder. Something was evidently wrong...very wrong. Fairfax never got anxious and he never acted on impulse.

Fairfax called to his maid to have his driver get the car ready.

Once ready, he gave the instruction to his driver to put his foot down and get him to Oakwood Manor as quickly as possible. Saying nothing, the driver closed the door and hopped into his front seat.

They were at the Manor in thirty minutes flat. It felt like thirty seconds. Fairfax thought long and hard.

Waiting in the lounge was Moore. Calm, cool, unflustered and seemingly unconcerned. He raised his eyebrows when he saw Fairfax. Trainers, jeans, open-necked shirt. He couldn't believe the way in which he'd turned up and presented himself.

"My dear Joseph, what do you look like?"

"Never mind that. Has Warlton spoken to you about Jack Deer?"

Moore decided not to try and calm him as he knew that one, he would be wasting his time, and two, that it was best to let Fairfax get out what he wanted to say as quickly as he could.

"No."

"Has he spoken to you at all in the last twenty-four hours ?"

"No."

"I can't believe it ! I just don't believe it ! I won't believe it !"

"Can't believe, don't believe, won't believe what exactly ?"

Fairfax told him all about what Rainer had seen and how he had immediately put Warlton in the picture, how, although he explicitly expressed the dire need for him to inform the others and arrange a meeting to do so, he obviously hadn't done anything. Moore sat impassively without saying a word. Fairfax also told how he had doubted that he would say anything, even if he remembered, but then as a safeguard, had telephoned Peterbough only to be told he was down at the Pelican, again. Still Moore sat listening.

Fairfax went on to say that none of it made sense, how he could only think of a couple of reasonable and logical explanations as to why Moore knew nothing.

Moore wanted to be sure that he understood the situation. He went over everything with Fairfax,.....twice. Once he felt confident that nothing had been missed out, he let him continue with what he knew were going to be accusations.

"So, the only reasonable explanation that I can come up with is ...he's in with Deer."

This was what Moore was waiting for but had to hear him say it.

"Discrediting me under the guise of me 'over-doing it' and working too hard. Not calling a meeting would have meant that he would have had a chance to tell him that we were onto him. They would then have had time to come up with a different scheme."

"Listen to yourself man. Do you realise what you're saying ? This is a very serious accusation you're coming out with here, Joseph. It's ugly, I don't believe it, and what's more, to be honest with you dear boy, I believe or rather know you to be quite wrong."

Fairfax couldn't believe that he wasn't on his side. He tried again to explain why he'd come to this conclusion. But Moore interrupted,

"You're right, Deer is up to something, just as you tried to warn us he would be in the magnificent speech you gave. And you're right, he must have had someone on the inside."

Fairfax remained seated, tentatively looking at Moore as he stood up and leant on the fireside mantelpiece.

"It was a very clever plan, I must admit and one which was being executed for a very long time."

Fairfax sat gazing at Moore, as he went on to tell him all that had happened. Narrowing his eyes and looking to the floor Moore started to shake his head.

"So, who was he using to drain money away?....None other than Rothchild. It was he who was the spy within. A new starter John Hammond exposed him to me. He discovered a programme that Rothchild had developed to skim off millions, and the best of it is he's been doing it for years. Right under our very noses....Incredible !...."

Fairfax's head snapped back, to look up at Moore. Continuing to shake his head, he whispered over and over,

"John Hammond....John Hammond....No, don't remember him."

Moore waited for Fairfax to think and say his piece.

"I'm sorry Charles, but until I see Warlton and ask him why he never bothered doing anything, then I refuse to believe he's not in some way involved. Because if you think about it, if anyone ever helped Warlton out with whatever he was supposed to do, it was Rothchild. I don't believe for one minute that Rothchild is, or was in on the scheme alone. I still think that Warlton must have something to do with it. The fact that Rothchild is in on it, doesn't make sense to me anyway. Jack Deer had little or no love for any of the Board members, least of all Rothchild. You know that as well as I do. He said to me on numerous occasions, how he had one of those smarmy faces that once he started hitting, he wouldn't be able to stop. It just doesn't sound right to me Charles, it doesn't sound right at all. It just does not make any sense. I suggest that we call an emergency meeting tomorrow and find out exactly what's going on, with us all being present. For as much as even I don't like Rothchild, I'm sorry but I cannot believe he's in this with Jack Deer."

"Joseph, I'll agree to call a meeting, but you must promise me one thing."

"Name it."

"That you won't just come out with unsubstantiated claims that Warlton is on the scheme, or that this fellow John Hammond is wrong about Rothchild."

"I promise …….. but that's something else that's niggling me."

"What is ?"

"I had the final review of the list of names of all the new executives before passing them over to Warlton, but I don't remember seeing anyone by the name of John Hammond on it."

"Joseph, you're good, probably the best on the Board, but it's impossible, even for you to remember everything. This John Hammond fellow went through the whole thing with me, slowly and methodically explaining everything. Then, he even took the liberty of demonstrating how it all worked by ringing up the accounts department to prove his findings. No. We've got the right man there alright, of that I promise you."

"OK, but I still think that we need to call that meeting and all turn up tomorrow in the office, even if it is a Sunday."

"As you wish, I shall see to it later. Would you care for a drink ?"

"No thanks, I'm going to head off back home now and prepare for tomorrow."

Fairfax left the house with even more on his mind than when he had arrived.

Moore, meanwhile, gave a call to all the relevant parties telling them that it was imperative that they attend a meeting at 9 O'clock sharp the next morning. He didn't elaborate on the matter, he just told them the time and place and that they were expected to turn up. All, with the exception of Rothchild, were told to be there and all gave their word that they would be there 'on the dot.'

Chapter Nine

Day Eleven - Sunday

It was a quiet and tranquil Sunday morning, as all the boardroom members rose from their beds, unconcerned about the meeting that they were due to attend that day. Even though, when weekend meetings were called, they were only ever to deal with issues of the utmost gravity. As with all meetings, minutes would record the course of action to be taken, who was to take that action, and when the matter should be resolved. Truth of the matter was, that almost immediately after the meeting, whomever was actioned, always invariably put the onus on their personal assistant, who in turn, delegated the work to their respective subordinates. It was a downward spiral every time, starting at the top and working its way down to the lowest levels of the hierarchical structure of the office. It's set-up and organisation was, in essence, no different from any other major firm throughout the world. So, with such an efficient team below those at the top, there never really was any need to panic or have any cause for concern, because they knew all problems would be sorted, and if not, then they would always have someone below them to lay the blame on. But as with all the people that Jack had in his workforce, no problem had ever arisen that couldn't be sorted. No matter how big or difficult, it was always resolved. Teamwork was Jack's engine. And under Jack's regime it was well-oiled and well-fuelled.

The Board members were where they were quite simply because of their position, title and influence. They knew and so did Jack. Therefore, why should they worry? For them, life really was a bowl of cherries.

They had all, except Rothchild, arrived at the office and the meeting was about to commence with them all in their respective seats. It was 8.55 a.m. None of them looked worried or concerned about what the meeting could be about. They each sat making pathetic small talk. Almost all of them grumpily expressing their desire that whatever had to be sorted, was done so without taking up too much of their very precious time. Moore, as always, had been the first to arrive. He'd spoken with Fairfax on what was to be said, and how it was to be said, ensuring the delivery was cautious, but affirmative in breaking the news that there was a spy in their midst, and that Jack Deer had been spotted in the New York Offices.

Moore addressed everyone, telling them that they had been called into the office to urgently sort out a matter of utmost importance.

Peterbough, in yet another of his hopelessly vain attempts to be the leader of the pack, let himself down once again by interrupting,

"We'd gathered that Charles, so what's so important that it couldn't have waited until tomorrow ?"

Moore just looked at him blankly and so did the others. Peterbough sat there uncomfortable and embarrassed, once again wanting to be seen to be the man amongst the men. He had failed, dismally. Although all had been asking the same question of each other, none of them came to his aid in backing him up. Peterbough, to save face, apologised. Moore continued.

"Gentlemen, as I was saying, we have a matter of the most dire importance that I must bring to your attention. So urgent is this issue that I had no alternative but to call you all here this morning. I will pass you over to Joseph to explain."

As Moore sat down, all the eyes of the room now switched to Fairfax who stood up to speak, coughing to clear his throat. Warlton looked around the room and asked where Rothchild was. Both Moore and Fairfax looked at him. There was silence as Warlton raised his eyebrows and nodded his head forward gesticulating with opening palms that he was waiting for an answer. Fairfax said that Rothchild was attending to a serious family matter, but that he would be contacting himself and Charles later that day. Warlton just nodded his head. Fairfax began to tell everyone the news about the week's events. He told them all about his visit to the States, the arms dealers, the delivery and successful installation of all the satellite equipment. They were impassive. None of them thought for a moment that this was the reason why they had been called to the office at such an early hour on a Sunday morning, and how right they were.

"Now gentlemen, let me explain the real reason why you've all been asked here this morning."

"Come on then, out with it, Joseph" said Warlton in a contemptuous manner. Fairfax leant forward to speak to Warlton.

"Oh, I'll come out with it alright."

Moore looked at Fairfax as he quickly shook his head as a clear indication for him not to say anything out of turn. Indeed, it was what they had both talked about earlier, before anyone else had arrived. Fairfax, seeing this discreet signal, pulled back from his leaning stance to recompose himself and collect his thoughts before resuming.

"Gentlemen, I warned you at our first meeting over a week and a half ago about Jack Deer, of how he would and could, if given the chance, ruin our bid to takeover the consortium."

Warlton shook his head and groaned as he lobbed his pen on the table, as he obviously knew what Joseph was to say next. In yet again another contemptuous manner he began to dismiss what Fairfax was about to say.

"Oh, really, Joseph. I must say that....."

Moore butted in, not waiting or wanting to hear what it was that he had to say. As calm and unflustered as ever, he spoke firmly to Warlton and put him in his place.

"Shut-up, Warlton and let's hear what Joseph has to say and all of what he has to say. You and you especially should listen. It's because of you we are all here."

He looked to Fairfax and this time gave him an appraising nod to carry on, he couldn't help but smile. The tables had been reversed from the last confrontation he'd had with Warlton in the presence of Moore. This time, instead of being seen to support Warlton, he was on Fairfax's side and was letting everyone know it, there and then. Everyone knew that Moore fully supported Fairfax all the way. Fairfax looked to Warlton scornfully.

"As Charles has just said, it's because of you that we are all here."

All eyes were now fixed on Warlton, surprised that he was the cause of the meeting and at how Moore had, for the first time, put him in his place. Fairfax continued,

"Jack Deer was and still is in all senses of the word, a man to watch. Gentlemen, my warning to you was neither fickle nor was it one to be taken lightly. Jack Deer has been spotted in New York and has been in our offices over there. He is clearly working on some sort of scheme to regain what it is he stands to lose. I put it to you, gentlemen, that if he's got friends in America, he's got friends everywhere."

Fairfax paused and made eye contact with everyone but Moore. The silence was deafening, the atmosphere tense.

"Gentlemen, we have a traitor amongst us."

Everyone sat back in their seats as the atmosphere sank heavily, with the sinister accusation and inference that there was a Judas amongst them. This was the part of the delivery that Moore had warned Fairfax about. Moore had assured Fairfax and indeed just proved his allegiance to him, but that was only if he was successful in not estranging the rest of the boardroom members or alienating them from each other.

"Now, I'm not saying that there is one in this room before any of you start to think that, but I must warn you that there are people at the very top, or people close to the top that we must assume are in some way advising him of our every move. Otherwise, why would he be in America? Obviously he's trying to muster support. We suspect who he may have contacted, a chap called Killen but we cannot be sure, so we're keeping a close watch on him. However, that's on the other side of the pond. He probably has someone on this side telling him of our latest moves, so I warn you, once again gentlemen, that we must keep on our toes. We must keep things very much to ourselves. We must not even trust our personal assistants with any information, no matter how seemingly insignificant or worthless it is. The less we trust the people around us, the less likely we are to let anything slip which might help Deer to sabotage us."

Yet again, Fairfax had proved himself to be, quite simply, the best in the art of diplomacy. He had informed them all of what they should know, warned them all that Jack was making moves, but most of all, Warlton wasn't accused nor was it insinuated that he might be collaborating with Deer.

Barron then asked the question, what did he now expect them to do about the situation, apart from being very careful. Joseph replied by telling them that they should more than ever, be wary of the older executives as they might have been tipped off that they were all going to have their contracts terminated, regardless of how well they performed, so giving them a motive to side with Deer. Also, that they should watch the new executives, as they were in essence an unknown quantity and therefore should be treated with caution. The last thing that they were all told was that the minute they felt things weren't right, it was to be shared with either Moore or himself. Fairfax was finished, and sat down. They all still looked at him blankly and without questions. Warlton started again.

"How can you be so sure it was Deer, I mean......."

Moore interrupted and raised his voice thanking everyone for turning up. Then he looked to Warlton and asked if he could stay behind as both he and Joseph wished to speak to him. Almost in a childish, sulking mood he agreed, with a quick 'OK' coming from his tightly-puckered lips. The entourage all started to sift out of the office. As they did so, Cavendish was at the back, when he stopped in his tracks. Turning round, he asked if he could speak to either Moore or Fairfax. Fairfax nodded to him saying 'yes' but could he please wait in his office, whilst he and Charles had a word with Henry. He nodded and left the office. As the door closed behind him, Fairfax's questioning, or rather interrogating of Warlton began.

"The minute I heard the news about Jack Deer, I told you and asked you to inform the others. So why didn't you ?"

"What are you trying to say exactly, Joseph ?"

"I'm the one asking the questions here, not you, so kindly answer them."

"I didn't tell anyone, because I thought that you had been overdoing it and had quite simply made a mistake."

"But I told you that it was Rainer who had seen him, not me, so how could I have made a mistake ?"

"Oh, I don't know, it all just seemed so wrong. I thought that we'd seen the last of that uncouth working-class scum and so didn't want to set off any false alarms. I mean, how can Rainer be so sure it was him ? It all sounded just too incredible for me to believe."

Moore spoke and once again backed up Fairfax.

"Well, we can only suggest that from now on, if you're told anything or hear of anything, that you tell us immediately rather than taking it upon yourself to just dismiss it, because you personally can't accept it. Right ?"

"Right."

As Warlton left the office, he was followed closely behind by Moore and Fairfax. They both said that they would speak with him when he was at the Singapore office, then wished him a safe journey. Warlton just grunted in acknowledgement without turning to face them. They both then walked into Fairfax's office where Cavendish was waiting.

"So, what did you want to see me about, Arthur ?"

"Its probably nothing, but you did say no matter how trivial it was, that you wanted to know everything that could possibly be construed as part of Deer's scheme."

"Yes, we did. Why do you know something ?"

"As I say, its probably nothing but I spoke to the maid on the way out of the house this morning and....."

"Yes and what ?"

"Well, she said to me that the girl I had taken home with me the other day, you know the new personal assistant I have ?"

"Yes. Go on."

"Well, she told me that in one of her conversations with her she introduced herself as Laura Deer."

"What ?"

"Yes, it does sound rather corny, but I thought I'd let you know."

"Thanks, Arthur, I shall investigate the matter first thing in the morning. You did the right thing telling us."

Cavendish just nodded his head and walked out of the office. As soon as the doors closed, Fairfax asked Moore what he thought. He told him that they had to be very careful not to upset the applecart and that he had his doubts about Warlton. Then Moore asked Fairfax what he thought.

"Well, it seems to me that Warlton may have been working with Rothchild. And if what Cavendish has just said is anything to go by and Laura Deer is working for him, then Warlton is definitely another spy amongst us. After all, it was he who was supposed to sanction and check all of the new people that were to start with us."

"Well, we'll see tomorrow then, won't we ?"

"Yes, we will indeed."

As this was happening, Jack had been spending some quality time with Sammy at her parent's house. She had been so pleased to see him, throwing her arms around him, hugging him and holding onto him tightly. They talked and walked together through the country village, happy just to be together. Neither of them brought up the subject of the consortium. Neither of them wanted to upset the other with such talk and both were relieved that it hadn't reared its ugly head. For Sammy, just to be in the company of Jack, with no worries, was the best remedy for her condition. She'd had a nice break with her mother and father, away from it all. She told Jack that she was disappointed that neither John nor Laura had been able to visit, but because both of them had telephoned every day to see how she was, she didn't really mind. Jack told her nothing about all that had happened.

Day Twelve -Monday

Monday morning began the same as any other, with all the office staff trudging into work. They moved around the office like termites in their mound, busy scuffling from desk to desk, shuffling pieces of paper. All were enslaved to the need and want of PC's, phones, mobiles and e-mail.

They had each prepared their work, ready for presenting to the Board. All were ever hopeful that this was going to be the making of them. If only they knew.

Fairfax was in his office, preparing his work for the day when Moore came in to see him. He stopped what he was doing to talk about the week's agenda and how everything was to take place according to their plan. One subject that came to the surface was what Cavendish had told them. Fairfax couldn't bring himself to believe that it was the same Laura Deer that was Jack's daughter. But if it was true, how had she got into the company? As he talked this over with Moore, he told him not to worry as that very morning, in only a couple of hours time they would find out what was going on.

Fairfax fixing himself a drink asked Moore if he would like to join him, but he declined. As he raised the glass to his lips he gazed out of the one-way mirror of his office. His eyes were fixated. He was mesmerized.

"I don't believe it !"

Moore turned to look at Fairfax, staring out of the window. Moore got up to see what he was looking at, but all he could see was office staff scurrying around.

"I just don't bloody believe it !"

"Believe what Joseph ? What's the matter ?"

Not bothering to answer Moore or explain, Joseph walked straight over to his phone, and hastily dialled for security, ordering them to get up to his office immediately. Moore just stood there looking at him, frowning, not being able to make head nor tail of what had obviously upset Fairfax. He walked over to the window himself to see if he could see what was wrong but to him there was nothing out of the ordinary, just a bunch of office staff doing their jobs. As he thought this, he was joined by Joseph who stood by his side and was now also looking through the dark-tinted glass window.

"What is it, Joseph ?"

"I just cannot believe it !"

"Believe WHAT ? You're not making any sense."

Joseph's breathing rate had increased. Shaking his head, he continued to talk nonsensically. Moore frustrated, asked again what it was that had excited him but all he got from Joseph was him singing Jack Deer's praises.

"I knew that Jack was one clever bastard but my God, even I never thought that in my wildest dreams he would have been able to have pulled this one off."

Moore, shaking his head as he looked at Fairfax, before once again looking out of the window, sighed, expressing his wish that he would tell him what the hell was the cause of his palpitations.

"Oh, you'll see what they're about, just as soon as Security come through that door."

They stood there whilst Moore's eyes scanned the whole office indiscriminately looking for something, he didn't know what, whilst Fairfax's were fixed and were most discriminating. He now stood motionless as he regained his composure. Two security guards could be seen at the end of the office. It was now that Fairfax decided to tell Moore the cause for alarm.

"Do you see that red head over there, talking to those clerks ?"

"Yes. What of her ?"

"That….is Jack Deer's daughter."

"What ?"

Fairfax didn't answer him, but like a surprise hurricane burst open his office doors and walked purposely and deliberately in the direction of Laura. She almost turned white and felt quite sick when she saw who it was marching towards her. She was in so much shock that she just stood silent and motionless as though someone had cast a fairytale spell on her and turned her to stone. Her mouth was open and had dried up in an instant. When Fairfax was only a few feet away from her he stopped in his tracks and pointed at her. His face was blood red with anger.

"Get this woman out of this office, off this floor and out of this building....NOW."

The security guards stopped in their tracks to listen to their instructions and without any hesitation or murmur, obediently did as Fairfax demanded. The office had turned into a library at a morgue. You could have heard a pin drop. The only noise that could be heard was the sound of the guards escorting Laura down the corridor to the lift. All of the faces in the office had a mixture of shock and horror upon them. Obviously, none of them had any idea why such a scene had just taken place, but all were glad that it hadn't been any of them. Moore hadn't moved from Fairfax's office door which was still open. As Fairfax demanded to see what work she had had access to from Helen Auldrich, who had been standing only yards away from the incident, Moore made his way into Warlton's office. He wasn't in, as per usual. Moore looked at his watch, it was 9.20 a.m. Shaking his head and sighing heavily he muttered to himself,

"I thought as much."

He then went to Cavendish's office. Again, he uncharacteristically barged in and told one of the office clerks in the most impolite manner to get out and shut the door. Walking over to a startled Cavendish, an interrogation began.

Did he know who the girl was who had been assigned to work under his personal assistant?

What had she had access to?

What did he know of her?

Had he disclosed anything he shouldn't have?

Did he suspect that she may now have knowledge of their intentions over the next week?

All of these questions were asked, one after the other, in quick succession, with Cavendish only answering directly with one word answers where he could, not being able to get a word in edgeways. Although he did try numerous times to ask what all the questions were about, he never got any answers himself. The door burst open again. It was Fairfax. He started to ask all of same questions that Moore had been asking only seconds before. Moore interrupted him and said that it was OK he'd asked all the questions. But Fairfax continued,

"Did you know who that woman was?"

"I assume the woman you're talking about is the one assigned to work with my personal assistant, Helen. And the answer to your question is 'No' I don't know who she is, but I can only assume that she must be Laura Deer?"

"What the hell!.....so you did know?"

Moore, the ever-ready calming mediator, stepped in.

"Joseph, please, please. It was Arthur who warned us that it could be her, remember?"

Joseph shook his head as he put his hand up to his forehead and immediately apologised.

"Yes, yes I'm sorry. I got a bit carried away, I'm sorry, Arthur, I wasn't thinking straight. It was just such a shock to see her in the office. I panicked I know, but to see her here, supposedly working for us, when she's obviously working for her father, it was just too much even for me to take in. I'm sorry Arthur, I just got carried away I didn't mean to shout or swear at you, please accept my apologies."

Cavendish, still in a state of shock himself just nodded his head in acknowledgement and said nothing. It was abundantly clear he wasn't used to such verbally violent attacks and least expected one from either of the two men who stood in front of him.

Fairfax then asked if he could see Moore in his office. Moore nodded. He then told Cavendish that he would be in to see him later and would explain everything.

When they got into his office, Fairfax started to give Moore a run down on all that he thought had happened.

"I've not had a lot of time to think Charles, but I don't like what I've just seen, nor do I think, that to wait until this time next week before the consortium's divisions are sold off, is a good idea. I think that we should act now. It will mean that whatever Jack Deer knows, if anything, will not be able to be used against us, because he simply won't have time. If we act immediately, today in fact, then he will not have the time to execute whatever plan he may have, which from what we have both just seen, he evidently does. If he was able to slip in his daughter of all people to work for one of our very own boardroom members under our very noses, he must have more friends on the inside than we dare imagine. Therefore, I urge that you act today. Call for the meeting to take place in the respective countries in two days time and send the necessary people to attend. The satellite equipment is all ready and the quicker we act, the more likely we are to pull it all off."

"OK, Joseph, we'll do just that. I'll have my secretary arrange airline tickets for them all to fly off either this afternoon or tonight. Anything else ?"

"Yes, there is as a matter of fact."

"What ?"

"On Saturday, you told me of a new starter that had exposed Rothchild and how he'd been stealing money from the company, did you not ?"

"Yes, I did. John Hammond and he was right, he proved it to me. What of it ?"

"Well, do you remember me telling you that I didn't remember seeing his name on the list that Warlton was supposed to have checked ?"

"Yes."

"Well, I got to thinking last night. It seems a little bit suspicious to me that he would have stumbled on those memory sticks by accident. It's just too coincidental for my liking. In fact, I would like to see this person and ask him a few questions of my own about that little incident we had earlier."

"What are you saying Joseph? Are you making the accusation that Warlton is in some way involved with Rothchild?"

"I only wish I knew, but until I see either of them I can't be sure. Neither of us is an Einstein, but we're not fools either. But it doesn't take a genius to realise that something is amiss. We're not to let ourselves be the clowns in a circus ring with Jack Deer as the ring master."

"Warlton should be in now, let's go and have a word with him."

They got up from their chairs and made their way to the door when Fairfax stopped dead in his tracks. Moore turning to face him before opening the door stopped and then quickly looked out of the smoked glass window into the open-plan office. He looked back at Joseph who stood there frowning and shaking his head from side-to-side with a look of unabated disbelief upon his face.

"What's wrong Joseph? What's the matter?...... Joseph what is it?"

Moore looked to the office staff, but as before he couldn't see anything untoward. Joseph was like a pillar of stone.

"Joseph, if it's anything similar to what happened before, I don't want you to cause a scene, nor do I want to find out what it is the way I did before. So what's the matter?"

"That John Hammond, he's not that bloke over there with the blond hair talking on the telephone, is he?"

"Yes, it is. Why?"

In utter disbelief and sheer dismay at lightning striking twice Joseph proclaimed,

"I know you're not going to believe this, but that is Jack Deer's son."

"Jesus Christ, you've got to be kidding me?"

Fairfax said nothing, nor did he move from the spot, it was as if he were glued. Moore was the same. Neither of them could believe what they saw. Moore told Fairfax to ring security. It was done without hesitation. Moore, still staring out of the window, was joined by Fairfax. They waited in silence. The security guards arrived and John, just as his sister, was escorted off the premises. As John disappeared down the corridor, Moore led the way in to Warlton's office followed closely behind by Fairfax. Warlton had arrived. Unlike Cavendish's questioning, his interrogation was going to be a little more discreet, subtle and restrained. Moore began by asking him everything about the man who was supposed to work for Barron. Every time Warlton gave an answer, it was with splendid ignorance. He quite clearly didn't have a clue about who he was, had never checked up on him, nor any of the other junior executives. He had never even bothered having them checked against their photographs which were all contained in the folder which Warlton had been asked to produce. He was responsible for investigating each and everyone of the new recruits, but had done nothing. Moore looked at Fairfax, flicked his head toward the door, indicating that he'd like a word with him in private. As they walked to the door, Moore told Warlton he'd be in later to speak to him. They entered Joseph's office. Both now had food for thought. Jack Deer's sighting in New York, Laura Deer and then her brother found working in the offices. Rothchild, who'd supposedly been caught stealing, by what they now knew to be, a fictitious, John Hammond. Also that he may now have been falsely accused of being part of a sabotage plan, and Warlton, who was supposed to have vetted all new people that were to be hired into the consortium office to organise the take-over bid, hadn't sussed them, or had he? Nothing was clear anymore. Everything was grey. Nothing appeared black and white, as it so clearly had before. It was Moore who spoke first.

"You're right Joseph, we've got to act now. Jack Deer is on our tail and just as you warned us all, he's going to destroy our plans if we don't act quickly. I shall make the necessary arrangements, right this minute, to have the Board members flown to their respective divisions for a meeting in forty eight hours."

Moore, who hadn't even bothered sitting down, started to make his way to the door when Fairfax called him back and asked him to take a seat.

"Not so quick Charles, I've just thought on."

Moore, grimaced, turned to face him. He didn't like what he'd just heard, considering that one minute Fairfax was calling for immediate action and then wanting to sit down and talk rationally before anything was done. But he obliged and sat in the chair opposite. He waited to hear what he had to say, wearing a perplexed and puzzled expression, Fairfax aired his thoughts aloud.

"Listening to Warlton, I wanted so much to believe that he was in on the scam with Rothchild, but I no longer believe this to be the case."

He started to walk around the room. Moore was perplexed at Fairfax's complete turnaround in thinking. He sat and listened.

"Let's face it, Warlton really is one lazy bastard. He makes a sloth look like the roadrunner. I mean, let's be honest, when have you ever seen him do any work? Not....*when did you last see him do any work*, but..... *when have you **ever** seen him do any work*? I'll tell you when....never! He is the definition of sloth. So I think he really is being genuine when he says that he knew nothing of John or Laura Deer. Because never.......never in a million years, would that fat bastard ever have thought to have run a check on any of the new juniors. Work to him is the ultimate four letter word. No! I believe that he's telling the truth and that even Jack Deer himself wouldn't sink so low as to use or trust him in any plan of his to regain control of the consortium."

"We can't afford to take the risk. I say we get rid of him."

"No, think about it! Jack, as we all know, only ever had the useless bastard with him in the position he holds, because of who he is and the connections he has, with his title and ties with the aristocracy. We must take a note from his book and keep Warlton on our side. That way, we'll be able to use him, just as Jack has."

"But can we afford to risk it?"

"Everything we're doing is a risk but I don't want to burn any bridges, behaving like a charlatan on a witch hunt. The more I think about it, the less I believe that he's in with Deer."

"So what do you suggest then?"

"I believe it's better to have him on our side than Jack's. If we were to get rid of him now, by getting the others to vote him off the Board, he could quite easily side with Deer and ruin everything. If he did go, he'd be taking away a tremendous amount of clients and custom with him. No, he's definitely not with Deer. He's just been lazy, once too often. Only this time it's caught up with him. Besides, when you think of all the times that Warlton has vindictively slagged off Jack Deer, calling him working-class scum and the like and knowing that it was never said light-heartedly or in jest, he'd never side with Jack and vice versa. Warlton meant every single word that came out of his cesspool mouth. He despised Jack for being in the position he was and that he was underneath him. The only reason he stayed here, was due to the deal and contract he was on. No, Warlton was never, nor would he ever be, on Jack's side. Never."

"So, Rothchild worked alone did he? To be honest I thought that your first notion of both Warlton and he working together was the most feasible one of all. They're never out of each others pockets."

"Exactly! Which is why I know you're not going to believe what I'm going to say next."

"What?"

"I don't believe that Rothchild is in on it either."

"What? You really have changed your tune. You were ecstatic when you heard the news about him. More than that, I'd say that you were euphoric. Bloody Hell, Joseph! You really have done a U-turn in your thinking. I'd love to hear why you and you of all people, don't think it could be Rothchild. Especially since everyone knows you hate his guts."

"You're right. I loathe the swine, but think about what you've just said and think about what happened the other day in your office, when you were told by....'John Hammond', that he'd been stealing from the company. Rothchild and Warlton are always in each other's pockets, so if Rothchild was the Judas amongst us, does it not stand to reason that his greatest ally would have been Warlton. By my reckoning, there's no way that any plan, no matter how clever, that's been devised by Jack could be carried out by only one person on the inside. Indeed, proof of this has to be what we've both just seen this morning. Not only did we find his daughter under our noses, but not two minutes later we find that his son is here as well."

"But that still doesn't explain why Rothchild couldn't be in on some sort of scheme, by himself or with someone else perhaps. After all, it's impossible to ignore the fact that the memory sticks found with the programme on them were Rothchild's and he had been stealing from us. Even accounts backed up the hardcore evidence of the demo given by Jack's son. Then to prove everything, we went back over the records, even before we'd devised our little overthrowing scheme. The way I see it, Jack just wanted some way of having Rothchild thrown out before we took over. And as far as I'm concerned, Rothchild really is as guilty as sin."

"I don't doubt for one minute that the memory sticks were his and that 'yes' he's not only been stealing from Deer but had no intentions of stopping once we'd taken over. That I want to believe anyway, but Jack hates Rothchild almost as much as I do. I do not believe he would stoop so low as to risk trusting someone like Rothchild.

I put it to you that either the memory sticks were planted by John Deer or that if they weren't,......yes, he has been stealing from the company, but that in no way would he be in with Jack Deer in helping to reinstate him as the consortium president. I'm sorry, Charles, but I just can't see it at all. I would suggest that Rothchild be invited back onto the Board for three very good reasons."

"My God, Joseph, you really do move quickly I'm having trouble not just in keeping up, but in understanding why you, and you of all people, want him back with us. These had better be three damned good reasons."

"OK. Firstly, I believe that Jack Deer set the whole thing up so we would be told of the memory sticks, exposing Rothchild for the thieving and greedy swine he is. He must have known all about Rothchild and what he was up to for some time. He then has his son...his son of all people....get into the offices, working under our very noses to expose him. This part of his scheme went according to plan because it would and did have the effect of us banishing Rothchild from the Board. In doing so, it either gave him one less person to fight against, or cast doubt amongst ourselves, so as not to really trust one another. And what's more, if he has got someone else working on the inside for him, which I most certainly believe he has, then wouldn't this throw us off the scent? Wouldn't we assume that the person helping Deer was exposed and had been dealt with, lulling us into a false sense of security and making us lower our guard?"

Everything that Fairfax said made perfect sense and couldn't be faulted. Moore was in awe of Fairfax, as the wheels of his mind turned in perfect unison, expressing his thoughts in a precise and comprehensive way. He continued, as Moore sat there, nodding his head in the acceptance of all that Fairfax was telling him.

"Secondly, if you don't invite him back in, we'll never stand any chance of recouping any of the money he's stolen over the years. Remember that when the figures are announced, we have to say that a mistake was made and that we'd made more than at first calculated? If we have him back in with us, we'll be able to add some substance and credibility to our claims, because we'll be able to 'strong-arm' Rothchild to give back all the money he's stolen,...threats of prosecution for embezzlement and the like. Let's face it, with the international connections that we and the company have, where on earth could he run to and hide? He may be able to run, but not forever."

Fairfax paused for a moment, to let Moore take everything in. Moore was in total agreement up to this point. He said nothing and neither did Fairfax.

The third and last reason was still yet to be aired. Moore looked to Fairfax, as he stood staring wide-eyed at him. Finally, the silence was broken.

"Am I making sense? Does everything I've said so far gel? Do you understand what I'm trying to say?"

"Yes....Everything. Everything makes perfect sense and is not far-fetched. So, what is the third reason for letting him back with us?"

"Think about it, it's the last thing Jack Deer would expect."

Moore cracked a sly grin. Fairfax was taken aback. He thought he was actually going to smile. Moore was about to do something else that was again just so out of character. He swore. It sent a signal to Fairfax that he was coming through loud and clear.

"Hell, Joseph, you're right, you're absolutely right! That's the last thing he would expect us to do. Jesus, we've done exactly what he thought we would do. We've kicked

Rothchild out, suspecting he must have been in it with Deer. Then, when we find out he couldn't have sided with him because it was his son that shopped him, we start doubting Warlton, believing Warlton to be the one who's helping him. And if we'd convinced ourselves that that's the case, then we'd have got rid of him, too. We'd have put back the meeting about dissecting the consortium which would have meant that Deer would have more time on his hands to dream up more scams for us to turn against one another. Jesus, what a truly clever bastard he is."

Fairfax stood impassively, looking at Moore who rapidly returned to his normal collected self. He regained his composure and nodded his head at Fairfax. With a knowing look he told him that he was a very smart and perceptive man, expressing his admiration, that in only a short period of time, he'd been able to suss out the thinking behind Jack's little scam. Fairfax, now smiling at Moore, repaid the compliment by telling him that he was a very shrewd and 'slim customer'.

They knew what had to be done. Moore would make arrangements for the flight tickets for the Board members and ask Rothchild back in to the company. This last point however was a cause of concern for Fairfax. He said that he should be the one to ask Rothchild back. Moore couldn't believe what he was hearing. Of all the people who would have been glad to see the back of Rothchild, it was Fairfax, and yet here he was, asking that it should be he to beckon him back. Moore was aghast,

"You ask Rothchild back?"

"Yes, me. If you ask him, he'll probably say yes but won't give us half the money back that he's stolen. Whereas, if I ask and explain that we know everything but guarantee him we'll not press charges, he'll know we mean business. After all, he likes me just as much I like him. We need each other like we need a hole in the head."

"Very well, if that's the way you want to play it."

Moore paused.

"Yes. Thinking about it, if you ask him it'll have a lot more credibility than if I asked him and with the way that Rothchild thinks, he'll have it in his mind that you'll be beholden to him because it's he that's done you the favour. Yes, you're right. You ask him, Joseph. You ask him back."

They once again nodded to each other and left the office.

Moore instructed his secretary to purchase airline tickets for the Board members, including Rothchild. Then he told her to inform them all that a meeting was to be held in the boardroom in the next quarter of an hour and that it was imperative that they all attend.

Fairfax had made his way out of the building and into his chauffeur-driven car. He was going to be the one that was to beckon back Rothchild into the fold.

It was time for the meeting and as they all entered into the boardroom, Moore was sitting at the head of the table. Cavendish asked when did he want to speak to him, Moore told him that it didn't matter now and that all would be explained in the next few minutes. Warlton asked if the same applied to him. It did. They all took their seats, the only two boardroom seats not being filled were Rothchild's and Fairfax's. Moore spoke for only a few minutes telling them that Jack Deer was making moves on them, that the two people who had been dismissed that morning were Jack's son and daughter and that in the present light of things, tickets had been purchased for them all to travel either that afternoon or later on in the evening to whichever country their respective divisions were in. He explained that because of the present situation, they were bringing forward the overseas meeting, especially now that all the satellite equipment was ready. Moore explained that time was, more than ever, of the essence and that they had to move now and quickly. They were all in agreement and left to go and see their personal assistants to confirm their flight details. After pottering around, leaving brief messages with their secretaries, they one by one, left the office. Some made straight for the airport to check in, as calls had already been made to their wives to have bags packed for them and sent onto the airport. Those on later flights had time to go home and pack themselves. Warlton was one of them.

He had landed himself in the position, 'Head of European Operations', as this division could, more than any other, look after itself, without any real decisions ever having to be made. Not surprisingly, Warlton was happy to have this department as his sphere of concern and it was happy to have him. He never had to do anything except sit back and let the thing run itself, and they were happy to have him as their figurehead. Like it or not, Warlton, quite simply, was one of the most influential people on the Board. When decisions had been made by the managers of the different departments and authorising signatures were needed, pieces of paper were just shoved under Warlton's nose for him to sign. They got all the work done with the minimal amount of fuss for which he received all the credit.

Warlton arrived home. He got out of the car and walked up to the imposing castle-like doors of his house. He was surprised no-one was there to greet him as he rang the bell. A few seconds passed before the door was answered. Warlton's face almost hit the floor when it was. He stood in shock and he sighed, as he quietly uttered,

"Jack"

Jack had a wry smile as he invited Warlton in.

"Come in, we've got a lot to talk about."

Chapter Ten

Day Thirteen - Tuesday

Jack returned home, just after midnight. He was greeted at the door by John and Laura. Laura's mascara had been running, she had a lump in her throat and John's eyes were watering. Jack's immediate concern was to comfort Laura. They made their way into the lounge. John just couldn't find the words to let his father know that they'd been rumbled. Jack put them both out of their misery by telling them he knew everything that had happened. John asked how.

"My man on the inside. Don't worry, you were supposed to be rumbled, it was engineered that way. "

John did a double-take and Laura stopped sniffling,

"What did you say ?"

"I said you were supposed to be rumbled, found out, dismissed."

John and Laura stared at Jack. Jack began to smile.

"Everything is going according to plan, don't worry about a thing, it couldn't be going better."

John had an indignant look on his face. He snapped,

"What do you mean ? We were supposed to be rumbled, everything is going according to plan, things couldn't be better ?"

"Just that."

Laura had stopped crying,

"But we were so upset we'd let you down. It was Fairfax he…"

"Yes, I know who it was and how it all happened."

John just couldn't contain himself any longer.

"You bastard. We've been sitting here fretting, worrying ourselves sick, thinking that we'd let you down and all the time you'd planned for us to be dismissed all along."

"Yes, that's right"

"Well, why the hell didn't you tell us. We're all supposed to be on the same side......or don't you trust us either?"

"Think about it guys. If you'd known you'd be waiting for it. You wouldn't be behaving the same. You might have given the game away."

Laura sat shaking her head.

"No, we wouldn't dad, and you know we wouldn't."

"Laura love, believe me, I know what I'm doing."

She quickly stood up and made her way out of the room. She started crying again.

"Yeah, exactly, 'YOU' know what you're doing. 'YOU', can't even trust your own kids. You used us."

Jack felt awful. He tried desperately to reason with John but stopped in mid-flow, as John, too, made his way to his bed. Jack, once again, was in more ways than one, left on his own.

Days before, Killen had flown to Buenos Aires, to meet up with Adam Younger. He'd handed him the envelope Jack had given him. He then boarded a plane the same day and flew back to New York and then onto Houston.

Cavendish had just arrived at Buenos Aires airport and was greeted by Adam Younger. Adam drove him straight to the offices, much to his dismay as he wanted to go to his hotel room for drinks...more drinks!

He was shown into the boardroom which was eerily empty. Adam pulled out one of the leather clad chairs from under the boardroom table for him to sit in. In front of him was a silver letter opener, a large bottle of mineral water and a crystal drinking glass. Once seated, Adam walked over to his briefcase which he'd left in the corner of the room. He reached into it and pulled out an envelope and handed it to Cavendish. Cavendish started to ask what it was, but Adam ignored him, as he made his way out of the room, the heavy and highly polished oak doors closed silently behind him. Cavendish just looked at the envelope. He was about to open it when the window blinds started to close and the room lights dimmed. Then a 'state of the art' satellite camscreen started to lower at the top of the table. Cavendish's eyes were transfixed as he sat silently. A deep and slow-speaking electronically disguised voice came from the screen.

"Open the envelope."

Cavendish sat motionless. The voice repeated,

"Open the envelope."

Cavendish fumbled with it in his hands. A spot lamp in the ceiling above his head, lit up.

He opened the envelope and pulled out its contents. His stomach churned. He felt wheezy.

"Take a drink."

Cavendish just sat there, staring at the contents in his hand.

This time it wasn't disguised,

"Take a drink."

Cavendish looked up to the screen in total disbelief and said curiously,

"Jack !"

The screen came alive. It was indeed Jack Deer. Cavendish felt sick. He could feel the blood draining from his face.

"Good this new technology, don't you think ?..I installed most of it, you know ?..Sorry, where was I ? Oh yes....you've got a dark and nasty past, haven't you ?"

Cavendish stared at the screen, speechless.

"What's the matter ? Cat got your tongue ?"

Cavendish looked at the papers in his hand. It was the realization of his worst nightmare. He was staring at his birth certificate.

"What are you going to do ?"

"Well, you and I both know what would happen if I expose the fact that you're the bastard son, don't we ?"

"You wouldn't. You couldn't, I'd be ruined. I'd be penniless. Oh, God, no.... you wouldn't."

"What's it like to be on the receiving end, Cavendish ? Not nice is it ? Your face is a picture. All the hard work has been worth it, just to see you squirm, you little maggot."

"Please, Jack, not this, I'll be ruined. I'll do anything."

"Anything ?"

"Yes, anything, just don't shame me or my family, please, anything but that."

"How can you care about such things in this day and age. You're an illegitimate child, so what ?....you've been an utter bastard all your life anyway.....Oh, that's right, silly me. If it's discovered who and what you really are, the law, or should I say Barron will rape you for every penny....correct me when I go wrong..."

"Ok, Ok, you've made your point. What do you want me to do ?"

Jack leant forward to speak closer into the screen, his angry face bearing down on Cavendish.

"That's more like it, you little shit, now listen carefully because this is what you're going to do...."

Meanwhile, Barron had arrived in Houston. He was greeted by Killen. Killen drove him to the offices, and just like Cavendish he was shown into an empty boardroom, seated and presented with an envelope. Shutters on the windows closed, the lights dimmed and the camscreen lowered from the ceiling at the top of the table.

Barron opened his envelope. It was all there. Pictures of his ex-wife, Lady Jane, whom he'd beaten up, the police statements and the charge of G.B.H. against him. If this got out he stood to lose everything, his title and his 'respectability'. Just like Cavendish he began to squirm and was ready to sell his soul.

As before, Jack proceeded to tell him how things were going to be.

Day Fourteen - Wednesday

It was time for the Board meeting. Both Fairfax and Moore were full of themselves. Everyone was strategically placed to sway Board votes in favour of Moore's take-over and inevitable dismemberment of the consortium. Barron in Houston and Cavendish ready in South America. Rothchild was on the European Board in Geneva. He'd flown there straight after his slapping from Jack, and Warlton was in Singapore.

Warlton had been presented with many papers upon his arrival, little did he know what they were. But that didn't matter because he never read what he signed anyway. He'd signed away his shares and stockholding in the consortium over to Jack Deer, all 7% of it. Jack already owned 12%, so his grand total stood at 19%. But he needed 51% to take control. Both Moore and Fairfax held 8% each, with the rest on the open market with the shareholders. But worse than that, they could sway the city's vote in their favour.

Now was the day of reckoning. With everyone in their respective in-country offices, the worldwide conference call could now be made via the camscreens.

Sitting in the London head office were Moore and Fairfax. As contact was made with all the respective offices, the faces of the other Board members appeared equi-spaced on the screen, Barron, Cavendish, Rothchild, Peterbough and Warlton.

The profit and performance announcements could now be made to the financial markets and media around the world.

Jack walked into the room. Moore was taken by surprise, Fairfax said nothing. Jack was a little nervous and apprehensive. His heart was beating a little faster than usual with his breathing deep and rapid. But no-one would ever have know....Jack was as cool as ice. He was confident, he had conviction, he knew where he was going, but most of all he was the one that had been wronged and injustice had been brought against him. He was going to fight back and fight back hard. In his mind it wasn't the fact that he wasn't going down without a fight.....he just simply wasn't going down....end of story. He'd done his homework and now this was his exam.

He sat at the table and pulled out a remote control device from his top pocket. He said that they should get down to business and with the press of a button on the remote control, a full-size picture of Cavendish took up the screen.

"So, Cavendish what shareholding do you have."

There was a slight delay on the satellite link.

"I have a 7% stake"

"So tell us, what way do you vote with it ?"

Again there was a pause,

"I've already signed my shares over to Jack Deer."

Jack looked to Moore,

"So that's 26%."

Jack said thank you to Cavendish and that that would be all. His nerves had left him he was confident, strong and full of fighting spirit. He pressed another button on the remote control and Rothchild's face took up all the screen. He went through the same questions. He announced that he was signing over his 8% stake over to Jack.

"So, that's 34%"

It was Peterbough's turn. He too signed his 8% share over to Jack. Jack's total share was now 42%. Then it was Barron's turn. His 8% share was signed over to Jack.

Jack looked confidently at Moore who was scathing. He sat upright composed himself, and pointed a finger at Jack saying,

"That's not good enough. That's only 50%. I can still call a stalemate and call a vote of no confidence and bring the share price to rock bottom."

Jack laughed,

"50% where do you get that from ?"

The two men stared at one another. Jack was smiling, Moore was frowning. Jack pointed the remote control at the screen and pressed a button which brought up the face of Rothchild.

"Rothchild, as we all know, has had his fingers in the till for years, haven't you ?"

Everyone looked to the screens in their offices. Rothchild's face filled them. They were all interlinked. His confession was about to be heard and seen 'worldwide'. An embarrassed Rothchild was looking rather sheepish. Jack repeated himself with a raised voice,

"Haven't you Rothchild ?"

"Yes"

Moore was desperate to know who had been helping Jack. He was ready to point the finger at anyone.

"You bastard Rothchild, so it was you that was helping him"

"No, I didn't"

Jack explained,

"Rothchild…No, no, no, he only helped me when faced with ten years prison for embezzlement….and things…..didn't you, Simon ?"

No-one spoke. Again Jack repeated himself with a raised voice,

"Didn't you Rothchild ?"

Rothchild answered with a snappy 'Yes'. Jack looked to Moore and continued,

"So, what do you do with that amount of money ? Well, I don't know what you would have done with it, but I invested it in MY company. Not all, just enough to buy 1%"

Moore was stunned. He knew what this meant. He sat in utter disbelief,

"You mean this was all a set-up, it was all an act ?"

"Yes."

There was a horrible pause. Fairfax began to explain,

"Act...hhmmm now there's a word. Do you remember the little chat we had a couple of weeks ago, after all that drama in the boardroom when Jack was told he was about to lose everything?"

Moore frowned at Fairfax but said nothing.

"Remember? We talked about our acting days at Cambridge."

"Yes, so what of it?"

"Cast your mind back to Jack vowing he was going to make us all, *'regret the day that we ever met him'* and how he was going to make us all, *'crawl on our bellies'* and how he singled me out, calling me 'Judas.' Well, Jack's words and delivery were all coached by yours truly. You must admit, he convinced you all that even I was part of your scheme."

"WHAT?"

"He was quite dramatic, don't you think? quite 'in your face', so to speak."

Moore was taken totally by surprise.

Fairfax proceeded to spell it all out from the very beginning, letting Moore know everything.

"For years I could see this day coming even if Jack couldn't. I knew it was inevitable that you lot would conspire against him. So I made it my business to find out all your little or 'not' so little secrets. Barron, Cavendish, Peterbough, Rothchild all of you. I made up a little dossier on each of you including one on myself and Jack kept them as his 'ace up the sleeve' should he ever need them.....like now!"

"As far as pulling off our little plan, Jack really was a hard act to follow. I had to pull out all the stops to convince you that I was part of your plan. That speech I gave, just as Jack left the office, well, I had you eating out of the palm of my hand. The best part was when I shouted,

"Shut up, you fool," at one of the junior executives."

"Was he part of your plan too?"

"No. The executive's outburst was just perfect timing as I could then play on it, milk the situation and ad-lib to convince you all that I was indeed with you. Let's face it, you all had your doubts and dare I say it, Charles, you doubted me more than anyone. But when I fell out with Warlton calling him a 'very ignorant man' …..Well, it was all unrehearsed, but by God, did it add spice to the plan. But that wasn't the clincher though. It was when I let you convince me that I must join you and your cronies, as it was the best chance I had of getting into the arms market, making my father proud of me."

Moore looked at Joseph with a piercing stare. He was perplexed.

"The plan nearly failed on a number of occasions. Jack and I had to keep changing it to suit the circumstances and the latest developments. In fact, I very nearly blew it on the first day. I was about to make a connection to Jack after he'd left the offices when you walked in Charles. God help me, I had the presence of mind to end the call and wait till you'd left my office. Then there was the call from Bradley Rainer telling me he'd spotted Jack in the New York offices. We…Jack and I…quickly turned that to our advantage. I simply told Warlton who I knew wouldn't do anything about it. And to make doubly sure I also made a point of trying to contact Peterbough. He is so predictable. I knew he wouldn't have got the message until it was too late and on top of that, it bought us valuable time to change our plan once again. Another close call was when I was at JFK airport and Jack was 'wandering around'."

Joseph looked at Jack, raised his eyebrows and shook his head smiling.

"Could you imagine if those executives had recognised you……, how the hell would I have talked my way out of that one ? Then, there was the mistake Laura made in introducing herself as 'Laura Deer' to Cavendish's maid. How you never made anything of that Charles, I'll never know. However the pièce de résistance was John Hammond and Laura Briskel. We arranged to get them into the building to work undercover, but their joining, just like the other junior executives was too late in the day to do anything….let's face it, you were going to fire every last one of them anyway, weren't you Charles ?…. But, that's not the reason they were there. It was so that I could spot them, dismiss them and bring forward this meeting. The fact that I was able to interrogate Warlton and Rothchild was just an added bonus. Plus it took away any lingering suspicion from myself."

Moore had quite regained his composure. He really was shocked. He tried to appeal to Joseph's family tradition,

"But Joseph, those arms deals. They will be worth tens of millions. Your father, think of him. Joseph, it's still not too late. You vowed to make him proud, you still can. Join me, we can still work something out."

Joseph looked at Moore indifferently.

"I made peace with my father years ago thanks to Jack. Jack has always been dead against the arms industry and the misery it brings. The ugliness of war, the ending of young lives and the making of widows. In a meeting between the three of us years ago, my father confessed that having seen war at first hand Jack was right to avoid the arms market. My father was more proud of me for standing on my own two feet and making my own path in life, rather than opting for the soft and cushy number of following in his footsteps, holding onto his coat tails just because of who he was. That, he said, was the coward's way. Anyway, the arms deals are only any good if the takeover goes ahead. But it's not. Instead, it is you Charles, you and your cronies, who will be out in the cold with nowhere to go."

Moore was seething. He wanted to rip Fairfax's face off. He couldn't contain himself anymore. He jumped up from his seat, his arms outstretched, ready to put his hands around Joseph's neck, screaming as he did so,

"I'll kill you, you bastard, I'll kill you."

Just as he was within an arm's length of Joseph, he suddenly grabbed his chest and fell to the floor. No-one moved. Joseph looked to Jack who was looking at Moore indifferently as he lay motionless.

"Jealousy is the only killer here." Jack said quietly. An ambulance was called and Moore was taken away to hospital.

Jack and Joseph embraced each other. The hug was hard and well-meant. Jack told Joseph he was a true friend and that he could trust him with his life. Joseph didn't say a word but nodded in acknowledgement. Both men made their way out of the office. Jack just wanted to be with Sammy. Tel was waiting in the car park, but Jack made his way to the helipad on the top of the building. After about five minutes a helicopter landed and Jack was on his way to his mother and father-in-law's to be with Sammy.

Meanwhile, Joseph made his way to the cemetery to pay his respects to his father and say thanks.

Jack met up with Sammy and went with her to an out-of-the-way exclusive country hotel. John and Laura had been asked to make their way to the hotel too.

They were all together in the hotel's penthouse suite.

Jack explained to John and Laura why things had had to be the way they were, and that although they may have felt used, it had never meant to be that way. The plan was never designed to hurt anyone, and that without them he would never have been able to pull it off. However, Jack didn't have to say anything because John and Laura had had time to think and concluded that their father had no choice, and had to do what he did. Knowing the life he'd had, what he'd achieved, what he stood to lose and how he had kept from losing it all, only made them admire and appreciate him. Neither had ever truly done this before, as everything had always been handed to them, they'd never had to fight for anything.

18 Months later

Those that had helped Jack such as Killen and Younger were now in top positions of their respective areas of the world. John and Laura had gone back to work for Jack, only this time as the controlling in-country managers. Joseph remained ever loyal to Jack, as his right-hand man. As for the Board members…

Peterbough's lust was caught up with him when he was discovered having sex with an underage girl in the back of his car after the clean-up of the Pelican.

Warlton, 'the sloth' just disappeared into oblivion and was never heard of in the city again.

Barron's anger got the better of him when he lost it with a young man in a pub after he'd brushed passed him and accidentally spilt beer down his suit. Barron, already drunk, had swung for him, but still had the beer glass in his hand. The young man lost an eye and was left with a horrible scar on his face running from his eye socket to his lips. Barron was facing at minimum of eight years in prison.

Cavendish's gluttonous appetite for drink let him down badly when was exposed by delving reporters after they preyed on his addiction. Once drunk everyone was his friend and confidant to whom he slurred out his secrets…..all of them. He woke one morning to discover that he shared his secrets with the rest of the nation courtesy of the tabloids. His assets had been frozen under the new inheritance laws and Barron laid claim to his fortune. Cavendish knew Barron would win. He was depressed and got so drunk one night he collapsed onto his bed face up. He choked and died on his own vomit.

Rothchild's greed needed to be satisfied. He had moved onto a multi-national oil company. Within six months, he was under investigation and after nine, he was up on embezzlement and corruption charges, all due to deals he'd shadily set-up in Russia and the Middle East.

Moore's envy did indeed kill him. He never recovered from his stroke. Only hours after his admission to hospital his condition had deteriorated rapidly. Within an hour he was on the operating table, and shortly afterwards he was pronounced dead.

One day during the summer

It was a hot summer's day and Joseph was at the Deer's house. He sat with Jack, Sammy, John and Laura in the pavilion, enjoying a cup of tea. The view of the countryside and man-made boating lake was breathtaking. Mary approached with a rather excited look upon her face and the post in her hand.

"Mr. Deer, Mr. Deer."

"Yes, what is it?"

"It's a special letter, it's a special 'official' letter, by special courier no less."

Everyone just smiled at Mary's excitement. Mary handed Jack the letter. It was 'official' alright. It was made from fine embossed paper, slightly off-white in colour, the front of which bore a regal-looking crest. Jack opened the letter and read it. All was quiet in pleasant anticipation. Joseph enquired,

"Is it what I think it is?"

Jack just looked at him and smiled. Sammy, John and Laura looked at Joseph. He too, was smiling, knowingly.

"Tell us, tell us," Sammy said excitedly, gazing at Jack.

Joseph asked Jack if he was going to tell them.

"No, you tell them."

Joseph looked at them all and smiled.

"You're now in the presence of 'Sir Jack Deer'... congratulations Jack."

Sammy let out a delighted scream and threw her arms around Jack. Both John and Laura had grins like Cheshire cats and Mary was just so happy, she could have burst. Joseph stood up and shook hands with him, each giving the other a knowing nod. John and Laura joined in, hugging Jack. All was well and all was well-deserved. More than his knighthood, Jack had something that money couldn't buy and prestige couldn't bring. The love of his family the friendship of a true friend and his pride.